PRAISE FOR

"Brian McAuley keeps you guessing the whole gory, satisfying way through this one. Come to this retreat for the blood. Stay for the healing."

—Stephen Graham Jones, *New York Times* bestselling author of *I Was a Teenage Slasher*

"I found my bliss in *Breathe In, Bleed Out*'s bloodshed, and you can too. Brian McAuley will forever be my slasher sage, my guru of all things gruesome, my purveyor of tantric panic, my phobic yogi. He brings such a joie de vivre to his holistic homicides, you can practically feel the back spatter splatter off the page."

—Clay McLeod Chapman, author of *Wake Up and Open Your Eyes*

"I absolutely inhaled this holistic horror hack-'em-up. Brian McAuley knows how to twist the knife and have us scream for more. This is sharp, witty, compulsive slasher storytelling at its finest. Check in and bliss out."

—Josh Winning, author of *Heads Will Roll*

"It's no stretch to say Brian McAuley is our crown prince of slasher literature. But hold on to your sit bones because with the cutting and sardonic *Breathe In, Bleed Out*, he's become an artisanal asana assassin. These ain't the hot springs you're about to dip into; it's a bloodbath."

—Nat Cassidy, author of *When the Wolf Comes Home*

"*Breathe In, Bleed Out* is a breath of fresh air for the slasher genre—classic kills combined with a cheeky new age spiritual journey makes McAuley's newest entry a blast from start to finish. This novel goes straight for the chakra with a bloody blade, and you'll be putting together the pieces of this whodunit slay-fest until the last page. Great stuff."

—Philip Fracassi, author of *Boys in the Valley*

"*Breathe In, Bleed Out* is a propulsive, nasty little new age nightmare that turns the desert inside out so we can read the bloody entrails. You'll never feel the same way about heading out to Joshua Tree for the weekend."

—Liz Kerin, author of *Night's Edge*

BREATHE IN, BLEED OUT

A NOVEL

BRIAN McAULEY

Poisoned Pen
PRESS

Copyright © 2025 by Brian McAuley
Cover and internal design © 2025 by Sourcebooks
Cover design by Caitlin Sacks
Cover images © CSA Images/Getty Images, Katrina Brown/
Shutterstock, Dan Thornberg/Shutterstock

Sourcebooks, Poisoned Pen Press, and the colophon are
registered trademarks of Sourcebooks.

All rights reserved. No part of this book may be reproduced in any form or by any electronic or mechanical means including information storage and retrieval systems—except in the case of brief quotations embodied in critical articles or reviews—without permission in writing from its publisher, Sourcebooks.

No part of this book may be used or reproduced in any manner for the purpose of training artificial intelligence technologies or systems.

The characters and events portrayed in this book are fictitious or are used fictitiously. Any similarity to real persons, living or dead, is purely coincidental and not intended by the author.

All brand names and product names used in this book are trademarks, registered trademarks, or trade names of their respective holders. Sourcebooks is not associated with any product or vendor in this book.

Published by Poisoned Pen Press, an imprint of Sourcebooks
1935 Brookdale RD, Naperville, IL 60563-2773
(630) 961-3900
sourcebooks.com

Cataloging-in-Publication Data is on file with the Library of Congress.

Printed and bound in Canada.
MBP 10 9 8 7 6 5 4 3 2 1

*For those who found release
and those still seeking it*

1

DRAGGING A BODY THROUGH SIX INCHES OF SNOW IS EVEN harder than I expected.

The snowshoes strapped to my waterproof hiking boots are designed to help, but I'm too exhausted to walk straight. Every ten steps, the clunky plastic edge of one shoe catches on the edge of the other, sending me face-first into white powder.

When it happens yet again, I scream into the icy ground, melting it into slush with my dragon breath. Then I stand up, dust myself off, and press onward.

How many miles have I trekked already? It's hard to say with the visibility getting worse by the minute. My shoulder aches from the rope slung over it, the other end tied tightly around Ben's ankles. I used a figure-eight knot, just like he taught me, so it's not coming loose anytime soon.

Still, every now and then I steal a glance back at him just to make sure he's still there. Motionless on his back, arms slung above his head like a pair of useless rudders in the snow. His eyes are wide open, staring into the clouds above. Ben doesn't blink.

He never will again.

I can't bear to look directly at his chest, but even out of the corner of my vision, the goopy half-frozen blood from several puncture wounds pops like a splash of paint on the modern art canvas of his puffy green parka.

Stop looking back. Just keep moving forward.

I refocus on the path ahead. The imprints from our trek up the mountain are fading fast under new snowfall, and I can't afford to lose them completely. Those prints are my only lifeline out of this endless tundra, back to civilization.

Left foot. Right foot. Left foot. Right foot.

At this point, I'm not even thinking about saving my own life. I just have to get Ben out of here. The time for weeping over his dead body is over. I can grieve my lost love later, but not now. The only thing that matters is getting Ben off this mountain, out of these woods. Once I get him back to his family, I'm sure I can explain everything. Ben deserves a proper funeral. A nice man like that has so many people to mourn him, especially when they die at the tender age of twenty-six.

I certainly can't just leave his body out here in the wilderness, even if Ben might've preferred that option. He thinks—no, *thought*—that graveyards were a sentimental waste of precious natural space that should be filled with life instead. Ben cared more about wild animals than he did most humans.

That's why we came out here to begin with, so he could take photos of the animals, the trees, all that untamed nature. After everything he's taught me about the Northern California wilderness, I know his carcass wouldn't last long after nightfall. The hungry wolves and cute little badgers will creep out of the shadows to feed. Whatever's left in the morning, the birds and the bugs will polish off. By the time someone finds his body, there will be nothing left but a shredded winter coat wrapped around gnawed bones.

I have to stop thinking of him like that, like he's nothing more than a sack of meat. But it does help to keep my emotions at bay so I can focus on the task at hand. Dragging him through the snow like I'm on some deranged reality competition show.

Left foot. Right foot. Left foot. Right foot.

The blistering cold stings my face while an impossible warmth radiates under my down jacket. Ben picked it out for me at REI last week. These rugged trips were child's play to him, but he wanted to make sure I was prepared. Winter backpack camping is no joke. I was ready to pack it in after our first night, but Ben promised that our destination would be worth the long trek up the mountain.

None of it seems worth it now as the birds caw overhead.

Are they circling? Waiting for me to drop dead too, so they can start their feast?

The large wingspan tells me they're condors, an endangered species that Ben had been documenting for some time. I want to exterminate them all now as I scream up at the winged demons. The birds take the hint and keep flapping onward. As the sharp cries fade in their wake, the air clears for me to hear something else now.

A primal roar.

Maybe a bear coming to finish me off?

I squint through the trees at the glint of metal flashing through slats of bark.

No, it wasn't a beast I heard.

It was an engine.

The echoing din of a distant car hones into focus, not too far ahead.

The road. I finally made it.

"Help!" My voice is hoarse from hours of clenched silence. I drop the rope and wave both hands, but I'm too far into the trees for anyone to see.

Reaching down to grab the rope again, I start running, bracing for the dead weight, but it never comes as I stumble, catching myself this time. The rope came loose after all.

I turn back to Ben, but he's not there anymore. Only the imprint where his body had lain, like a limp-winged snow angel.

"It's okay, Hannah." A whisper in my ear.

I turn back to find Ben standing between me and the road. His big blue eyes have already gone cloudy gray. Snowflakes stick to unblinking lashes.

"It's okay," Dead Ben says again as I stumble backward and collapse into the snow.

I shake awake, body thrashing in white powder.

No, not snow. Just white sheets flailing in front of my eyes as Ben keeps saying, "It's okay, Hannah. It's okay."

He's shirtless beside me in the bed, blue eyes burning bright, even in the darkness. Ben wraps his arms around me, those lanky skeletal limbs I've always found strange comfort in. Soaking in his warmth, I catch my breath and settle back into reality.

"It was just another bad dream," Ben assures me as hot tears stream across my cheeks.

"Oh God, it was so real." I choke on the words in our humid apartment, throat stinging from the memory of cold.

"Well, it wasn't." He kisses my wet cheek. "Mm. Salty."

The joy of safety flushes back into my body as I smile, putting a hand on his freshly shaven cheek. Ben's the only man I've ever known who actually shaves every morning. He says stubble makes his skin feel itchy.

"You want to tell me about it?" he asks. "Your dream?"

"Nightmare," I correct him. "It was a nightmare. And we were in the wilderness."

"Sounds about right."

"It was snowing."

"I hope we were wearing snowshoes," he replies.

"You insisted on it."

"Smart move, Dream Ben."

"Not smart enough. You died."

"Ouch."

"And I was trying to bring you home."

"That's very kind of you." He squeezes me tighter in his arms. "But you should've left me for the wolves."

"That's exactly what Dream Hannah thought!"

"I trained her well. Anyway, we're out of the woods now. We're home."

I look around at our cramped bedroom to ground myself further. All the framed photographs on the wall of nature and animals that

Ben's taken over the years. The houseplants sitting in every corner, hanging from every window.

Our West LA one-bedroom isn't much, but we've made it a cozy home, assembling all the pieces together. From Goodwill trips to Rose Bowl Flea Markets, never a brand-new item. Always secondhand.

"Okay." I quietly accept his assurances.

"One question," he says. "Did you do it?"

"Do what?"

"Kill me." He grins.

"Shut up." I shove him in the chest.

A whistling wind ripples through the room, and I shiver. My eyes dart to the window, only to find it closed.

"Did you?" Ben asks again. The smile melts from his face, overtaken by a tragic frown.

My throat seizes. When I finally force out a "Ben..." my breath is visible in the room. Snow falls gently on the comforter. I look up to the ceiling, now a blanket of cloudy gray skies.

My eyes fall back down to Ben, his face charred black with frostbite. Chapped lips crack with blood as they part to release an agonized scream.

Scrambling backward, I land on the hardwood floor knee-first, then crawl back against the wall until I can see the top of the bed.

The empty bed.

My head tilts up to the cheap popcorn ceiling that's returned above. The walls are all bare, peppered with holes where the nails had been driven in. The photographs have long been stowed away, and the monstera plant in the corner is dried brown, dead.

I know for sure now that the nightmares are over—that this is my reality. I'm home. But there's no comfort in this truth as my knee throbs with pain.

Ben really is dead, and I really did try to drag his body out of the snow a year ago. But at a certain point, I gave up. I dropped that rope and let him go to save myself. To get to that road where I collapsed, riddled with frostbite and racked with hypothermia. Where that truck driver found my half-dead body and rushed me to the hospital.

By the time the search party went out into the storm to look for Ben's body, it was too late. They didn't find a thing. No evidence to corroborate my story of what happened out there, of how he died. But then, nobody blamed me; nobody even questioned me. Even Ben's parents, who were devastated to bury an empty box.

Now I live alone in our hollow apartment. Almost like he was never really here at all.

I reach for the mid-century bedside table (fifty dollars at the Melrose Trading Post, thanks to Ben's ruthless haggling) and pull out the bottle of Xanax. Only a few pills left, rattling in the bottle. I pop one and swallow it dry. Good thing I have an appointment with Dr. Grady after work to get another refill.

Unfortunately, that means I'll have to tell my psychiatrist that the nightmares are only getting worse. Little Russian nesting dolls filled with memories. A dark one encased in a joyful one encased in an awful one.

The clock reads 2:46 a.m. I have to be at work in three hours, and my alarm will go off in two.

I could try to go back to bed now, but I know sleep won't come. He won't let me rest.

2

"YOU REALLY FIT THE HOT NURSE STEREOTYPE."

The man's leg is already broken, but I think he might do better with a broken jaw.

"I'm not a nurse," I explain for the thousandth time to the thousandth male patient. "I'm a medical intern." Plunging the IV needle into his arm, I watch him hide a wince.

The chatty ones always wince.

"Even better." He smirks. "I've got a few interns back at my Houston office."

Those poor college students, just trying to get the résumé credit without enduring too much harassment from this salt-and-pepper snake. In their honor, I lift his leg a little too high, eliciting a squeal that he can't hide, even if he does try his best to turn into a "Hoowee!" whistle.

"So, Mr. Fox." I check the clipboard. "I see you were riding an electric scooter when you swerved into traffic and got hit by a...Smart car?"

He blushes. "Those little fuckers are dense."

"Right. So, what brings you to Los Angeles?"

"I'm a venture capitalist, in town to hear pitches from young developers. Everybody's looking to create the next big app."

Working at a hospital near Silicon Beach, I've encountered my fair share of tech bros looking to *Shark Tank* their way to the top.

"Heard any good pitches?" I'm not actually interested in his answer, but exhaustion from my sleepless night has set in, and I need any stimulation I can get just to stay conscious.

"So far, twelve different dating apps, ten new delivery apps, and six dog-walking apps. It's all been done."

"Maybe someone should make an app that beeps really loud when you veer out of the bike lane."

"Smart *and* funny!"

"Who says I'm smart?"

"They don't usually let dummies be doctors," he says, southern twang rising to the surface.

This is true. I've worked my ass off to get here, all because I wanted to help people and heal the world, one patient at a time. I was prepared for the grueling education, all the blood and the death, if it meant being of true service and saving lives.

How dumb was I, thinking I could ever be anyone's savior?

"You know," Mr. Fox trots on, "with those bright green eyes and red hair, you could be a model."

Original.

Ben always referred to me as "striking." Not "beautiful" or "hot" or "sexy" like all those tech bros at the bars would. *Striking*. Only a photographer could see another human through that lens, as if gazing upon something otherworldly and ethereal. I haven't been seen that way since, certainly not by Mr. Fox now as his clumsy eyes roll over my body.

I hug the clipboard against my chest. "I didn't go through eight years of medical schooling just to get my picture taken."

"Well, I'm sure someone would be happy to pay your debts."

It's not the first time I've been hit on by a patient. It's not even the first time someone has offered to be my financial benefactor. Several of my classmates in med school had a sugar daddy or mama, and I don't judge anybody for getting by however they can in this stupidly expensive city. But I'd rather die than accept one gifted cent from the smug bastard in front of me.

"You're gonna be off your feet for a while," I say.

"Fine by me. I prefer to be on my back anyway," he responds with painful predictability, putting his hands behind his head. "Listen. When I get out of here, I want to take you to dinner. You like sushi? We'll go to Nobu."

"Oh, I love sushi." I set the levels on his morphine drip. "But I don't date patients."

"Why's that?"

"Because I'm taken." The latex glove snaps off my hand, and I flash the glittering engagement ring. It never had a chance to fulfill its final purpose, but it works damn well as a shield against unwanted advances in Ben's wake.

"The good ones always are."

My phone dings with a notification, and I pull it out on instinct, even though I'm not supposed to have my phone on the floor. It's rare for me to get messages these days, so when I see the name *Tess* flash across the screen, my heart leaps a little.

"That the old ball and chain now?" Mr. Fox asks.

I ignore the question and walk away with a "Rest up" over my shoulder.

The *Alarm Will Sound* warning gives me no pause as I push through the door and duck into the empty stairwell. That sign's been false advertising for months, making this the only place where I can catch my breath alone. The other interns are nice enough, but they're always trying to drag me to happy hour and be social. Be friends.

I don't want friends. I struggle enough with the ones I already have.

Friends like Tess, who text things like:

> Happy Birthday, Banana! You never responded about dinner tonight and I'm not letting you off the hook this easily. Get back to me. Or else.

The message is punctuated with a skull emoji. Classic Tess, the emo girl turned Wicca woman. I can't help cracking a smile, which quickly flows into a wave of guilt for intentionally ignoring my friend's text last week.

And the week before that.

And the month before that.

Ever since Ben's death, I've gradually retreated from my entire friend group. Especially Tess. I don't want to feel seen, and my best friend can always see straight through me. I certainly don't want to celebrate my birthday because that marks another anniversary. It was, after all, the reason that Ben dragged me out to the mountain that day for our special trip. That and the other reason.

The surprise.

I twist the engagement ring on my finger now, the ruby shining in the dark of the stairwell. My birthstone. Ben knew me well, but not as well as Tess does.

Sorry, just seeing these messages! I text back. Got stuck with a night shift. Maybe another time!

The exclamation points just scream sincerity, right?

I hate lying to my best friend, but I'm not in the mood to celebrate anything yet.

A sudden chill flows up the stairwell from the darkness below. I reach into my pocket for a loose pill, my last one, and pop it without thinking.

Wait, how was that my last one? How many have I taken today?

The lack of sleep is really taking a toll. I run a hand through my hair and take a deep breath before heading back out onto the floor to make my rounds.

Mr. Fox is snoring like a pig when I get back to his bedside to switch out his morphine bag. As I set the fresh drip, a patient starts screaming across the hall.

All I can see through the curtain is flailing limbs until I drift closer to peek within.

Ben is thrashing in the bed, fresh blood gushing from his chest as he cries out for me.

"Hannah! HANNAH, PLEASE!"

I stumble backward with a cry, then rush forward to yank the curtain open. "Ben!"

But it isn't Ben at all. It's an old man, not thrashing or bleeding. Just sleeping soundly as a nurse scribbles in his chart.

"You okay, Hannah?" She clearly knows me, but I can't even remember her name as I try to ground myself.

"Sorry, I…" My vision goes woozy as I rub my eyes and float back across the hall to Mr. Fox.

Shit. Too much Xanax. That's not good. I need to—

Beep-Beep-Beep.

The high-pitched sound could just be in my head, but no.

It's coming from Mr. Fox's monitor. My eyes lock on the IV drip, and I see that it's already empty.

Shit, shit, shit. I fucked up the flow rate.

"Code blue!" I scream and grab for the call button.

Lights flash as the panicked hospital cacophony swells. Everything becomes a blur of light and sound as I slap Mr. Fox's face. "Wake up, wake up, wake up…"

"What the hell happened?" My attending physician, Dr. Mohai, looms over my shoulder, eyes wide behind horn-rimmed glasses.

"Morphine," I manage to mutter as I slink away from the patient, backing into the corner. "I gave him too much."

"Jesus, Hannah."

I take a step toward the bed, suddenly compelled to fix my mistake. "I just need to—"

"You need to get out of my way." Mohai pushes past me to the patient's side. "You've done enough. Go to my office and wait for me."

Mr. Fox's eyelids aren't moving as Mohai starts chest compressions. My mouth goes totally dry as hospital staff flood in around me.

I killed him.

The words course through my mind, spinning like a record on repeat.

I killed him. I killed him. I killed him...

My brain is swimming in the fish tank behind Dr. Mohai's desk while I wait. A single angelfish flutters in circles around a rock cave and a few fake plants. These plastic toys are meant to make the habitat feel real, but does that really trick the fish? It has to know it's trapped in a false reality, right?

"He's going to live," Mohai says, storming in behind me and taking a seat at the desk. He runs a hand through his wavy black hair, broad shoulders now blocking my view of the little spinning angel in its liquid cage.

"Thank God." I exhale with relief. "I'm really sorry, Dr. Mohai. I don't know what happened."

"I do." He takes off his glasses and stares directly into my eyes with his knowing gaze. "You were high, Hannah. Still are."

No sense arguing at this point. I clearly took too many Xanax without realizing it. Overdosed myself and then overdosed a patient. I'm ashamed of what a danger I've become to myself and others, but I can't let my supervisor see that.

"It was an accident. I mean, I wasn't intentionally high." It sounded like a good defense in my head, but when the words leave my lips, I wish I'd just stayed quiet.

"Look." Mohai sighs. People only sigh in real life for dramatic effect, so I'm dreading the drama to come. "It's not that I don't blame you, because I do. But the truth is, I blame myself more." He softens, switching gears from stern principal to disappointed father figure. Which is way worse.

"When I found out what happened to your fiancé, I should've made the decision right then. You're in no shape to be working."

"Please." I don't want to beg, but I will if I have to. "Work is the only thing that's keeping me going."

"And you were good at it when you first got here. I felt so lucky to have you." The kind words only make me feel worse. Mohai and I had developed such a great rapport. In the early days, I would stay late after work to pick his brain. He'd offer hours of his free time just to help me until his angry wife called from home asking where he was. Our teacher's-pet mentorship also made the other interns more than a little jealous, but all that special treatment is gone now. "You're a good doctor, but you almost killed someone today. Of course, *he* doesn't know that, on account of being high out of his mind. But we'll be lucky if he doesn't sue the hospital for malpractice."

I imagine that would be a boon for a venture capitalist like Mr. Fox. There's a lot of money to milk from the medical industrial complex. But that isn't a very compassionate thought about the man I almost killed.

"I'm putting you on leave." Mohai punctuates the blow with a definitive: "Indefinitely."

It's probably just the Xanax making me all rubbery inside, but I can feel tears welling up in my eyelids. Please let them help my case and not hurt it. "Just give me another chance."

"That's exactly what I'm doing." Mohai comes around the desk and puts a hand on my shoulder. "I can clean up this one mess, but if you slip again, there's no fixing it. Everything you've worked for will be gone, and I won't let you do that to yourself. Go home, Hannah."

I want to tell him that everything already is gone, especially at home, but I keep my mouth shut. Better save the sob story for my psychiatrist.

3

"DO YOU WANT TO TELL ME WHAT HAPPENED AT WORK TODAY, Hannah?"

With his side-parted chestnut hair and freckled cheeks, Dr. James Grady gives major goober vibes. That's exactly what made me choose his *Psychology Today* profile a year ago when I was looking for a psychiatrist to treat my anxiety and insomnia. The boyish doctor seemed like an easy mark to get what I wanted: not therapy, but drugs. In reality, he's gotten me to open up more than I planned to in these weekly meetings. That's why I have to be extra careful with my words today.

"I was overtired, and I made a mistake. I just didn't sleep well last night because I ran out of my medicine." If I tell my psychiatrist that I was high on the job, he'll never refill my prescription, and after today's events, all I want is a benzo escape. Every cell is vibrating for the little pill that will quiet everything and wrap me in a warm blanket of darkness.

"The pills were never meant to be a permanent solution,

Hannah." Grady's pen taps absently on his pad. "Besides, you're blowing through your refills faster than you should be."

He's stubborn, good at his job. Not what I want from him right now.

"Well, I can think of another permanent solution," I say, "but I don't think people in your profession encourage it."

Grady leans forward, eyes wide with earnest concern. "Are you talking about suicide?"

"I'm joking." But he's already jotting something down in his little notebook. Whoops.

"That's not something to joke about. Have you thought about taking your own life recently?"

"Never," I lie, unable to meet his gaze.

Instead, my eyes graze the clean, modern office I've grown extremely familiar with over the last year. Everything is so orderly, with no signs of Grady's personal life. Each month, I expect maybe some new photograph will land on the wall or I'll catch him with half a sandwich from lunch on his desk. But the man is careful with boundaries. A blank slate.

The clock ticks on the wall behind him, and I must be staring at it because Grady says, "Still got thirty-four minutes. Why don't you tell me what was happening at work *before* the accident?"

The image of bloody Ben thrashing behind the hospital curtain flashes behind my eyes, but I shrug it off.

"I got hit on," I offer instead, slumping deeper into the couch.

"And how did that feel?"

"It felt...invasive. Like worms crawling underneath my skin."

Sometimes I think I play up my morbid side just for him. Am I testing my psychiatrist, trying to make him squirm? If so, it's not working.

"Do you think Ben would want you to be happy?" Okay, now he's pushing *my* boundaries. "To find someone who could make you happy?" Grady always brings it back to Ben, but every time his name enters the room, I shudder, fearing he'll follow with it. Summoned like Bloody Mary.

"I don't think Ben wants anything anymore." I hope my blunt reply will shut down this line of questioning.

"Well, what do you think *would* make you happy?" Grady's eyes dig into mine, but it feels gentle, not wormy.

"If I knew what would make me happy, then I'd just be happy, wouldn't I?"

"I happen to believe that happiness is an inside job. What do you think about that?"

"I think I saw that written on a piece of driftwood at HomeGoods." Maybe his line of inquiry works better with other LA patients. Lots of people come to this city to find happiness, usually in all the wrong places, and having a therapist point out their toxic pursuits must be a real revelation for some. But I'm not ignorant of my bad habits. I embrace them.

"All I'm suggesting is that you investigate your own desires, your own joy," Grady clarifies. "What made you happy in the past, before Ben?"

I flip back through my memory, hopscotching past every image of Ben, straight back to my college days. "My friend Tess and I used to stay up in our dorm watching *Grey's Anatomy* and drinking Diet Peach Snapple spiked with peach schnapps."

"Sounds peachy." Grady loves his dad jokes.

"It was. We had a lot of fun together." I leave out the part where we took pictures of each other's bare feet to sell to CoEdToes.com, funding expensive brunches on the Upper West Side.

"You haven't mentioned Tess in a while."

"Guess she's just on my mind because she texted me today."

"Because it's your birthday," he notes. My face must be doing a surprised thing because he adds: "Date of birth is a pretty common piece of information on a medical record."

"Right."

"So, are you going to see Tess tonight?"

"No. I blew her off."

"Why do you think that is?"

"Because I don't really feel like birthdays are worth celebrating."

"Ben did."

"Why do you keep bringing him up?"

"Because that's why you're here, Hannah. You lost your fiancé—"

"I hate that word. *Fiancé*. Makes me think of people who call croissants *cwah-sahns*."

Grady ignores the diversion, pressing onward. "You lost your fiancé in a tragic accident that left you with survivor's guilt."

A tragic accident. That's what everyone calls it.

Of course, Grady doesn't know the full story. Nobody does.

That's between me and Ben—a story he took straight to his grave.

"But I think you've come a long way since we started working together," Grady says.

"Then why am I still having the nightmares?" *That's* why I'm really here, the thing that needs fixing. In physiology, it's so simple. *This bone is broken, but we can fuse it. This skin is torn, but we can stitch it.* Why can't the psychological stuff be just as simple? *This memory is killing you, but we can remove it.*

"We've talked about this," Grady says. "When someone suffers the kind of loss that you did, sometimes your subconscious tries to do the healing work when your guard is down, while you're sleeping. It's just processing feelings and images in its own creative way."

"But it's not just in my dreams anymore, Grady. I saw him at the hospital, and it felt so real, like he's…"

Haunting me.

Those are the words I want to use, but I don't believe in ghosts. I've seen enough dead bodies to know that when we die, there's nothing after that. We don't float around in the shadows and fuck with the living. We decompose into rotting flesh. Atomic matter that was once packed tightly goes loose again, drifting off into meaningless dust. Science has no use for a soul.

"Hannah." Grady adjusts in his seat again. "If these nightmares are escalating into waking hallucinations, interfering with your daily life, then we really need to consider a more serious treatment plan."

"I know the difference between dreams and real life." The assertion feels false on my tongue.

"We all like to believe that, but emotional pain is an adaptable beast, and grief hallucinations are more common than you might think. Maybe it's time we addressed your root trauma head-on."

God, I hate the T-word. It's become such a catch-all buzzword that it's lost all real meaning. To me, *trauma* means open wounds and endless blood. My friend Luna, on the other hand, is a certified trauma-informed yoga teacher. Why anyone needs a certification to learn that you shouldn't touch people who don't want to be touched is beyond me.

Head-on trauma healing with my psychiatrist sounds like a new kind of nightmare, but I find a kinder phrasing. "I'm not sure I'm ready for that, Grady."

"If not now, when? You've been isolating yourself from loved ones, leaning on medication, busying yourself with work. I'd say today's slip-up proved that your life, as it stands, is not sustainable."

"I hear you." I mean, ouch, I really do. "But at least I can't busy myself with work anymore." My cutesy shrug is met with a professional blink.

"Which is why now is the perfect time for you to commit to intensive treatment. I help supervise a residential program in Malibu that I think you could really benefit from. We can detox you from the medication, get your mind clear."

"You really think I'm that far gone?" The thought of going from practicing medical resident to recovering psychiatric resident is nauseating, no matter how Grady spins it.

"I think you're in need of a cocoon. A brief rest to reset, and then you can break out and spread your wings."

"Come on." I can't help but laugh. "A butterfly metaphor? You can do better than that, Grady."

I've never made my doctor blush before.

"Okay," he says, "how about a phoenix rising from the ashes?"

"Still a cliché, but way darker. I like it. What about the medication?" I can feel the itch already, been feeling it since I walked through the door. "I mean, I can't just quit cold turkey, right?"

Grady considers me for a moment before caving and scribbling out a prescription. "I'll give you one last refill." Score. "Along with some light homework." Woof.

"I did my homework through years of medical school. Please don't give me more."

"It's not that kind of homework."

I'm bracing myself for one of the cheesy psychological gimmicks that Luna would go gaga for. Like a gratitude journal or a daily affirmation or—

"I call it a self-date."

"Dr. Grady, did you just prescribe me masturbation? Because I assure you—"

"That's not exactly what I meant." He clears his throat, utterly scandalized. "I mean take yourself out on the town, do something that brings you joy. Reconnect with Hannah to remember just how special she is. How deserving she is of happiness."

I've got way too many red flags to ever want to date me. But I say, "I will, I promise."

Part of that med school homework was Psych 101. I know how to tell a psychiatrist exactly what they need to hear to get what I want. I almost feel bad playing Grady for the meds as he comes around the desk in white New Balance shoes that pair well with all his dad jokes.

"Happy Birthday, Hannah." He smiles, handing me the prescription.

"Thanks." I tuck the slip into my back pocket.

It's the best present I could ask for on my second-worst birthday ever.

4

SODIUM METABISULFITE.

I'm standing in the frozen-food aisle of Walgreens, reading the ingredients on an iced-over burrito package while the pharmacist fills my prescription.

Maltodextrin.

In all my years of medical schooling, I've never come across some of the chemical compounds they put in food like this. But I don't care. I toss the burrito into my basket and pair it with a bag of Tapatío-flavored Doritos. This qualifies as a dignified meal by my current standards. It isn't that I can't afford healthier alternatives; it's just that I don't want them. I crave the food coma that only trans fats can provide.

When I was with Ben, it was all about the macronutrients, which is why I'd lovingly call him the Protein Packer. He wasn't beefy by any means, more lean and muscular. It was almost robotic, the way he looked at food as fuel for his outdoor activities. We never cooked together because he always meal-prepped for the week. Lots of organic chicken breasts and rice; no processed foods allowed. I used to hide string cheese in the vegetable crisper and take secret bites when he wasn't looking.

Actually, a Polly-O appetizer sounds pretty good tonight. I pluck a rubbery stick from the metal bar, then grab a second one for good measure.

"Hannah Reynolds?" the pharmacist calls from behind the counter. "You know the drill with these?"

"I know it's a bad idea to practice medicine on them."

The pharmacist glares over his spectacles. "It's also a bad idea to drink alcohol with them." He eyes the magnum of Barefoot red wine in my basket.

"It's for a friend's birthday." I spill my goods on the counter. The candy rack below calls to me as I remember Grady's words: *Do something that brings you joy.*

I grab an Almond Joy and toss it in with the rest of my feast.

There. Joy.

Once I've paid the bill for my gourmet meal and meds, I hurry back to the apartment.

It's not *my* apartment because it had always been *our* apartment, so now it's just *the* apartment. The place is way too expensive for one person, but I'm not spending my disposable income on anything else these days, so it's just been easier to stay put.

As I climb the exterior stairs of the building, I'm already thinking about pairing my benzo–wine–sodium bomb with a true crime docu-binge to really hammer home this substance-induced coma.

Let the "self-date" begin.

I crack into the pills before reaching the top of the stairs, popping one. Just as I swallow, a hand slams down on my shoulder.

The bag falls to the ground, shattering the wine bottle within.

My fingers clench into a fist, and I spin to face—"Tess."

"In the flesh." Tess's hair is buzzed even shorter than the last time I saw her. The sheer number of rings and bracelets that she's accumulated explains why her hand felt so damn heavy on my shoulder. "Didn't mean to spook you."

"I wasn't expecting company." It isn't meant to sound mean, but it does.

"They let you off early?" She bends down to help clean up the mess.

"Well, it was a slow night and..." A red puddle leaks out of the bag as Tess lifts it and eyeballs me sideways. "No. I lied."

"I know." She peers inside the plastic at the burrito and chips. "Oh, absolutely fucking not. Let's go. I'm taking you out for dinner."

"Tess, I appreciate it, but I'm really beat, and I just want to—"

"Eat shit food and stew in misery?" Tess looks over the balcony edge and drops the bag into the dumpster below. "Too bad. You owe me. Liar."

———

I can't remember the last time I went to the Venice Boardwalk. Tess and I used to spend full days at the beach before heading to our favorite poke shop to watch the sunset. Of course she would drag me here for a birthday dinner.

We get our usual spicy tuna bowls and sit on a bench facing the ocean. It's too dark to see, but the sound of crashing waves makes it worthwhile.

"I've missed you," Tess says.

I focus on using my chopsticks to separate my seaweed salad. "I know. I've missed you, too."

"Have you? Don't bullshit me."

"Yes, T. I really have." I didn't actually realize it until I said it. Deep down, I've been wanting to reach out and spend time with my best friend, but my social anxiety has taken a crippling turn. As much as I despise small talk with patients, it's easier than real talk with friends.

"Good," Tess says. "Because I'm extremely missable."

"I can't believe you showed up at my doorstep. Stalker."

"I had an important birthday gift to deliver." Tess hands me a folded piece of paper. Not regular paper, but some kind of aged brown parchment.

"What is this, a new art project?"

"It's an invitation."

I unfold the parchment and read the handwritten calligraphy. "Dear Ms. Sampson. After reviewing your letter of intent, I am delighted to extend an invitation to you and your friends on the requested weekend. We look forward to welcoming you at Avidya Healing Retreat."

"This place is super exclusive," Tess explains. "No website or Instagram page. It's just word of mouth. This sculptor from my gallery told me about it. I actually had to write a letter to the retreat leader to get us booked for your birthday weekend."

The signature at the bottom of the invitation reads "Guru Pax?" My eyes roll so hard I'm afraid they're going to plop down into my poke bowl. There are few things more gross than the G-word in LA wellness culture, where self-appointed experts prey upon the insecure and the vulnerable.

"I know, I know," Tess says, reading my mind. "But this place sounds super legit, and it's right outside of Joshua Tree. Totally tech-free, stress-free. We're gonna have an amazing time."

"Who's we?"

"Jared, Luna, Miles... Remember them? Our friends?" Tess gives me a little shoulder nudge.

"What about Kelsey?"

"We broke up." Tess shrugs it off.

"Oh, Tess. I'm so sorry."

"It's fine. You know me. On to the next one."

Tess wears her serial-relationship status like a badge of honor, but I know she's really seeking the stability of long-term commitment. Still, I can't help feeling guilty for not being there for her through this most recent heartache. Especially since Tess was there for me after Ben's death. Or at least, she tried to be. I rejected her at every turn, retreating further into my shell. And yet here she is, coming back for even more of exactly the same.

"Look, I appreciate the gesture." I fold the parchment. "But you know this spiritual stuff isn't my thing."

To say that I'm unspiritual would be a gross understatement. My parents forced me to go to church every Sunday as a kid, even though they weren't religious themselves. It was just a performative gesture to keep up WASPy appearances. I was barely out of grade school when I realized that religion is just another way that humans desperately try to control the chaos of reality. But in the end, there are no rewards for good behavior. Nothing matters. Why more people don't take comfort in that truth is something I'll never understand.

"So, fuck the spiritual stuff," Tess offers, bracelets jangling on her wrists. "Focus on the hot springs and sauna, the yoga and sound baths, the nature hikes and stargazing. A chance to decompress outside of this stressful city."

She has a point. Even though the ocean and beach are right here, Venice isn't the magical seaside town many people imagine. The increasingly high cost of living has driven folks out of their homes and into tent encampments along the boardwalk. I've done some volunteer medical work in the community, but it always feels like putting a Band-Aid on an arterial wound. Society is failing us all, and I often daydream about leaving it behind. Tess just painted a pretty nice image of what that could look like, at least temporarily, and this little vacation sounds way nicer than a mental health facility.

A cold breeze rolls off the ocean, reminding me that I don't deserve a vacation.

"I'm sorry, T. I'm just not ready yet." I hand the invitation back to her, and she deflates like someone just pulled the plug on one of those inflatable waving tube men.

"Will you at least sleep on it?" she asks with her last puff of air-hope.

"I'll sleep on it." But I can't even promise the sleep part will happen.

"That's the strongest commitment I'm gonna get out of you, isn't it?"

"I must be your type," I quip back.

Tess gives me a shove, causing a laugh to jump from my throat. It's a strange sensation, the first true laugh I've had in months. What a depressing realization.

"Come on." Tess links her arm in mine, pulling me from the bench. "I'll walk you home. Can't be too careful out here."

"I can handle myself." I parlay the arm link into a farewell hug.

"Fine." She whispers in my ear, "But if you ghost me again, I will hunt your ass down."

"I believe it. Stalker."

I push her away with dramatic flair, and she spins off into the night, throwing a "Later, Banana" over her shoulder.

The long walk home leaves me alone with my thoughts. Maybe spending time with friends is exactly what I need. It would be nice to see Miles again. I take out my phone and click my way to his Instagram page. Scrolling through pictures of him behind turntables all over the world, it looks like DJ Miles2Go has built quite the career for himself. The scruffy beard doesn't look half-bad on him, either. Hot women appear by his side in a few photos, but none of them consistently enough to mean they're a girlfriend.

Wait, why do I care anyway?

I close Instagram and google *Avidya* next. Tess was right; there's no trace of a retreat with that name, but the search does pull up the Sanskrit meaning of the word.

Ignorance. Lack of self-knowledge, in particular, is the root cause of human suffering.

What a cozy namesake for a retreat.

Do I lack self-knowledge? Back in college, I had such a strong sense of self. I was confident, social. Ready to take on the whole world. Then I met Ben. It's not that I changed completely for him; it's just that my priorities shifted a bit. It wasn't codependence, but when you start to share your life with someone, you become part of them and vice versa. When that part of you gets ripped out, you're left with this gaping hole.

Nothing hammers that home more clearly than the apartment I'm now opening the door to.

Looking around at the familiar, hollow space, it suddenly dawns on me that without work, I will have no reprieve from this place and the endless nightmares that come with it.

I'll never turn into a butterfly here, because it's not a cocoon. It's a prison.

Peaking anxiety inspires me to reach for the pills in my pocket and pop one without a thought. But the thought comes after, along with the shame.

Am I really going to stay locked in this shitty cycle of pills and depression? This stagnant state of perpetual victimhood?

I toss the pills on the bed and pull out my phone. Grady gave me his number when we first started working together, in case of emergencies. Is this really an emergency, though? It feels like it, and feelings aren't facts, but fuck it, I'm already pulling up his contact info. Google synced it with that *Psychology Today* profile photo, so I press my thumb against his goofy-ass smile and listen to the ring.

"This is Dr. James Grady," he answers, voice strangely distant.

"Grady. Hi, it's Hannah."

"Hannah, hold on one second. My AirPods are having trouble connecting. Stupid things." His technological deficiencies only add to the goober vibes and immediately help to calm my nerves. "There we go." His voice comes through loud and clear now. "Is everything okay?"

"I think you're right. I need a reset. If I stay here in this apartment, I'm going to lose my mind."

I stare at the hole in the wall where one of Ben's frames once hung. Was that photo of the fox or the eagle? The images are fading.

"That's great, Hannah," Grady replies. "I really think this break from work might be a blessing in disguise."

I've always hated that expression. Blessings are bullshit, and disguises are trickery. Why would I want bullshit wrapped in trickery?

"I can email you some information about the residential program now. As soon as you have a chance to—"

"Actually," I gently interrupt, "I was thinking about a different kind of getaway. Tess just invited me to this…healing retreat?"

I'm embarrassed by the phrase as my psychiatrist repeats it back to me. "Healing retreat, huh? Which one?"

"It's called Avidya, out near Joshua Tree. I guess it's really remote and exclusive."

"Hm. Never heard of it, and I know more than a few. You have to be careful with those places. Some of them can be pretty scammy."

"Yeah, that's what I thought, too. I just... I think it might be good for me to spend a weekend away with friends, get back to normal, ya know?" I have him on speakerphone as I flip through Instagram photos from the good old days. "Have fun again?"

"Are you suggesting that my mental health recovery program might not be *fun*?"

My smile is so big, it's probably audible on the other end. "I'm sure it's a blast, Grady."

"Either way, I think you may be right. A little vacation could be good for you. Help ease the transition. And when you get back, we'll settle you into a more supportive treatment plan. Deal?"

"Deal." But receiving my psychiatrist's approval doesn't give me the immediate relief I'd hoped for. "It's going to be a pretty intense re-socialization with my old friends, though. Are you sure I'm not jumping into the deep end too fast?"

"Sometimes exposure therapy is exactly what the body needs to shake things up."

My hand is trembling on the phone. "What if I'm so shaken up that I can't be unshaken?"

"You're a human being, Hannah. Not a martini."

I laugh out loud this time. "Damn, Grady. That was actually a good one."

"Sorry. You caught me in the unprofessional off-hours."

"No, it's nice." I let a little warmth creep into my heart before the anxiety sneaks back in. Grady must sense it through the phone because he says: "I've worked with a lot of patients, Hannah. None as strong as you. I know it feels like you've hit bottom, but it's not the end."

"Time to rise from the ashes, right?"

"That's right. I'm glad we settled on a metaphor that works for everyone."

"Me too."

"In the meantime, I'm here if you need me, so call whenever. Day or night."

"Does insurance cover that? Because now that my payroll is on pause, I'm not sure I can afford the copay for—"

"The calls are free, and we'll work out a sliding scale when you get back. I'm not abandoning you now, okay?"

"Okay." Relief blossoms in my chest. All this time I thought I was using him for the drugs, but I've been taking for granted how much he's helped me stay sane. I say it as sincerely as I can: "Thank you, Grady."

"Take care, Hannah."

I hang up and take a deep breath. As supportive as Grady is, I really don't want to commit to a residential program. My real hope, however hopeless, is that this retreat will fix everything, and then I won't need so much help when I get back.

I'll return from the desert with my head on straight, my ducks in a row, my shit unstuck.

Self-doubt is already creeping in, so I text Tess before fear gets the best of me.

Fuck it. I'm in.

Opening the closet to retrieve my suitcase, I realize that the last time I went on a real trip was with Ben. When I left his body out there in the wilderness.

But he came back in his own way, didn't he?

This time, I'm coming back without him.

5

ABBOT KINNEY BOULEVARD IS THE HOLLOW HEART OF VENICE Beach culture that I usually try to steer clear of. A strip of hip brunch spots, juice bars, and boutique clothing shops where everything is overpriced and everyone just wants to be seen. It's also the location of FLO (Free Loving Oneness), the yoga studio where Luna works and the designated meeting spot for our Joshua Tree departure.

I'm sitting in my car across the street, watching Tess wait outside.

It's not too late to bail. I'd told her that I was able to "move some things around at the hospital and make it work," but I could still claim there was an emergency. I mean, hospital emergencies are *real* emergencies.

My hand grips the steering wheel a little tighter, and the morning light sparkles through my red engagement ring.

No more running. It's time to exorcise my demons.

I take a deep breath, grab my bag from the trunk, and approach the studio entrance.

"Banana!" Tess rushes up for a hug. "Honestly, I can't believe you showed. I totally thought you were gonna bail at the last minute."

"The thought never crossed my mind."

Tess squints knowingly. "So, how long were you sitting in your car staring at me?"

"About ten minutes, yeah. But I'm here now!"

The yoga studio door opens and a gaggle of Lycra-clad women file out. Luna is right behind her students, a shepherd with a sheer white shawl draped around her shoulders.

"Namaste, everyone." Luna flashes her bleached teeth and bows, letting her bleached hair hang down below her probably-bleached asshole.

"And drink lots of water!" she calls after the class before turning to see me. "Hannah! Is it really you?" She flutters over, cloth wings flowing beneath her open arms as she wraps them around me.

"Hi, Luna." I give a gentle hug back, afraid I'll snap her frail frame like a twig. It breaks my heart to see her starve herself in the name of patriarchal beauty standards. Social media is plagued with influencers passing off disordered eating as a "health-conscious lifestyle," but the medical community is just as guilty of harmful disinformation, pushing bullshit metrics like the BMI that have nothing to do with actual health.

Luna puts her bony hand on my chest. "How is your heart?"

"Still there, I think." I retreat from her unwanted touch, wondering what the hell happened to all that trauma-informed training.

I've never felt especially close to the cheerleader-turned-sorority-sister-turned-yoga-teacher. The constant identity swapping (like changing her name from Lauren to Luna as soon as our friend group moved to Los Angeles) always felt a bit unstable. A chameleon who takes on the colors of whatever crowd she slithers her way into, Luna's true nature is still catty as ever beneath that adaptable skin. Lauren was a hazing ringleader in college who landed one pledge in the hospital with alcohol poisoning, but *Luna* doesn't drink that "poison" anymore out of respect for the temple that is her body.

She frowns at me now, or at least tries to, but the premature Botox makes it hard. "I miss seeing your beautiful face in my vinyasa class."

I only ever went once, but Luna's approach was less of an unwinding and more of a boot camp, so I never went back.

"I just don't think I'm really built for it," I say.

She leans in, the stink of sage wafting from her skin. "You want to know the best way to build a yoga body?"

"I'm gonna go ahead and guess the answer is yoga."

"The answer is yoga." Luna smiles smugly.

"Where's Jared?" Tess asks, gratefully interrupting.

"Running late, as usual," Luna responds. "He had CrossFit this morning, and the guys always grab beers after their workout."

"So he's drinking before picking us up for a road trip?" I ask. "That's comforting."

My eyes drift back to my car across the street. It's still not too late to bail.

Tess steps directly in my line of vision, hands on hips. "Whatcha thinkin' 'bout?"

"Oh, I was just thinking about...sandwiches." I point to the restaurant behind my car. "Food for the road." *Great cover*, I think.

It doesn't matter anyway, because the sound of skateboard wheels scraping sidewalk makes Tess look past me with a slight smile. "Can I offer you a man sandwich instead?"

She puts her hands on my shoulders and spins me around.

Miles rolls up on his longboard, a backpack slung over his shoulder. His dark curls bob as he kicks the board up and catches it with one hand.

"What's happening, friends?" He does a visible double take at the sight of me, which I have to admit feels good. "Hannah. Oh man, it's been like, forever."

"Forever and then some," I say, and immediately wonder what the hell I just said.

His beard actually looks better in person than it does on Instagram. Damn it, a grown man in a Baja hoodie should not be so attractive.

Miles starts in for a hug but stops and extends a hand for a shake instead.

"Sorry," he says. "That was supremely awkward. I'm just trying to be conscious of consensual touching. It's something we're encouraging at all of my shows to make sure everyone has a safe, fun time."

"I respect that." I can only imagine how many Molly-fueled gropings happen at EDM shows. The music alone is an assault to my senses. Add thousands of sweaty bodies to the mix and that's a big nope for me.

Out of the corner of my eye, I catch Luna and Tess exchanging grins, and I want to slap them both.

Okay, yes, Miles and I have a history. But it's more like an almost-history. There was this *one* night in college when we came back to the dorm from the bar, drunk and chatting on the hallway floor. I was dealing with relationship stuff with my high school boyfriend, Keith. Miles was a good listener. I put my hand on his, just to thank him, but then I just...didn't retract it. Suddenly, we were holding hands, talking until morning, no longer about shithead Keith but about our hopes and dreams and futures. It was one of those moments that teetered on the endless precipice of almost turning into a thing. But Miles walked away before anything happened. He respected that I was still in a relationship, even if my boyfriend had just requested a temporary break to "find himself."

I ended up getting back together with Keith, which was a total clown move in retrospect, as my entire college experience was dampened by the half-assed long-distance relationship. Miles and I stayed close friends, albeit friends with intense sexual tension. After graduation, I learned that Keith had been "finding himself" in the beds of other women throughout college while I stayed true.

I met Ben not long after that. A safe bet, or so he seemed.

"So how have you been?" Miles asks.

"Good, you know. All things considered." I don't consider sharing the things that I'm considering in this moment. "I see your DJ career's really taking off. You were just in Bali?"

"Yeah, that's right. I didn't think you were following me."

Shit. That's true. I've been stalking, but not officially following him on Instagram, which is even weirder.

"Oh, I just...browse every now and—"

HONK-HONK.

A black Range Rover skids to a stop at the curb beside us. The window rolls down and Jared leans out, his high-and-tight haircut glimmering with fresh pomade. "What's up, dick licks?"

The buff Silicon Beach bro was in a fraternity in college, and somehow all of those guys filtered into digital ad sales. Probably because the job is mostly just taking clients out on the town and getting them drunk on the company's dime.

"Throw your shit in the trunk and let's ride," he says.

Luna hops into the passenger seat and kisses Jared with audible tongue. They may have changed into shiny new LA shells, but they're still the same sloppy college couple at heart. Kind of endearing in its own way.

Miles is putting my suitcase in the trunk while I'm distracted by Tess, who's stepped away for a phone call.

"I'm not the crazy one, Kelsey," she says. "You are. I told you it's over, so please respect my boundaries and lose my fucking number." Tess hangs up and exhales.

"Hey," I say. "Everything okay?"

"Yeah, all good. Just Kelsey being an embarrassing cliché of a clingy ex. Trying to wedge her way into our weekend plans like a total—" Tess's phone rings again, and she shudders, turning it off. "I am so ready to turn my phone off for the whole weekend."

Tess hops into the back seat, leaving me and Miles to figure out who's riding in the center.

"I'll take middle," Miles offers. "It's no big deal."

"No, you're too long." What is wrong with my brain? "I mean, your legs, you're long-legged..."

"Right." He grins. "*Tall*, I think, is the word."

"Yes. You're a tall boy," I mutter, jumping into the middle as Miles climbs in behind me.

"Did somebody say tallboy?" Jared leans over the seat with a sixteen-ounce can of PBR. "Long time no see, Han Job." A nickname he gave me in college, for no other reason than *Sex stuff funny!* to his caveman mind.

"Jared." I take the offered beer just so I can tuck it in the back seat cup holder, far from the driver. "How goes the ad game?"

"Oh, I'm crushing it. Just helped Coke rebrand with a new canned kombucha. Calling it Coke-bucha."

"Clever boy."

"Clever enough to pay for this new rig. Speaking of which, everybody listen up to the rules of the Rove. No food or drink." He steals my tallboy back, cracking it open and placing it in his own cup holder. "No smoking"—Luna passes him her vape and he takes a puff, exhaling out the window—"unless you're sharing with the driver. And no grab-ass in the back seat."

He throws a wink back at Miles, who rolls his eyes.

"Tess, you got the address?"

"Uh, yeah. The invitation just says, 'Take Dead Man's Due Road to the end of the line.'"

"That's not ominous at all," I say while Luna pulls up the Waze directions.

"DJ Miles2Go," Jared calls out. "The Bluetooth is at your command."

"Okay, I've been curating this playlist based on the projected travel time. We're going to ease into some chill vibes with this new track from—"

"Jesus, Miles, we want a set list, not a TED Talk."

Miles sighs and presses *Play*. The beat kicks in as the car rolls back onto Abbot Kinney, toward the 10, taking us east.

Away from Los Angeles and into the weekend that I hope will fix everything. Fix *me*.

6

LOS ANGELES TRAFFIC IS A CLICHÉ COMPLAINT FOR A reason, and the energy of our takeoff is quickly slowed as we creep bumper to bumper along the 10. Jared is doing his best to keep us all pumped, which means he's doing his worst.

"Everyone psyched for the big party weekend or what?" he asks.

"Avidya is not a party," Luna reminds him. "It's a retreat."

"Retreat, party, spiritual orgy. Whatever you want to call it, it's gonna be lit."

"I just hope it's legit." Luna chews at her fingernail. "I went to this winter solstice gathering outside of Big Bear last winter. Turns out it was run by some crazy evangelicals who were just luring 'heathens' to purify their souls. As soon as I saw that big old church, I hightailed it back to LA."

Grady mentioned how scammy these retreats can be, so it doesn't surprise me to hear about Luna's experience. Altruism is a farce. There's always some ulterior motive just below the surface.

"Well," Jared says, "if this place is as exclusive as it sounds, I'm gonna pitch this Guru Pax guy as a potential client." Speaking of ulterior motives. "They've got zero online presence, which is cool and all, but you still need people to find you."

"I think that's the idea, to keep it from getting too touristy," Tess says. "Like that Leo movie, *The Beach*."

Miles leans forward, his bare knee brushing mine. "Is that the one where he's on the island, investigating the mental hospital?"

"That's *Shutter Island*," I correct him. My brain lights up with the image of 1950s DiCaprio grasping at the ghost of his wife until she crumbles to ashes.

"Right, right," Jared says. "But it turns out *he's* the crazy one."

The grieving ones always are.

"Spoiler!" Luna slaps Jared.

"Guess what?" he says. "Romeo and Juliet? They die."

Everyone laughs, and I can't help joining in. They're idiots, but they're *my* idiots. Comfortable, familiar. I remember all the fun times we had in college, eating drunk pizza at 3 a.m. without a care in the world. They don't seem to have lost that lust for life, that sense of fun. Is this how most people still live in their late twenties? Did med school and a serious relationship, topped off with some capital T trauma, drain all the fun out of my precious youth?

An endless barrage of chain restaurants and housing developments glide past the window, glimpses of lives I'll never understand. A road sign promises "Other Desert Cities" on the horizon, and the suburban homogeneity soon cracks open, giving way to tall white windmills stretching for miles. I can't help thinking of Don Quixote and his useless quest as I stare up at the spinning blades.

Am I just as naive to think that I can conquer my demons with one weekend away from the city? I'm lost in thoughts of overwhelming self-doubt until Luna squeals:

"J-Tree, baby!"

I've never actually visited this bohemian mecca before, so I'm a little surprised at how underwhelming it is as we pull up to a little strip of shops. It really doesn't look all that different from where we just left. The Los Angeles takeover of Joshua Tree has been well underway for years with wealthy Angelenos snatching up second homes and turning the small community into their own desert getaway. The main drag of dusty road is now a mix of old-time eateries and quirky gift shops squished between pricey boutiques and alternative medicine practitioners.

As I step out of the car into hundred-degree heat, my shirt instantly sticks to my back.

Luna points a dainty finger. "There's a vintage store over here that I've been dying to check out."

I try not to groan at the sign for Ineffable. But the short walk has me sweating, so I'll have to stow my judgment if I want to taste the sweet air-conditioning that awaits us inside.

We catch the owner scrolling through Instagram behind the counter, a carbon copy of Luna with her blond hair and flowy dress. The sound of new customers makes her perk up.

"Welcome, weary travelers!" She rounds the counter to greet us with a smile.

"Oh my God," Luna says, "I've been following you for years, and I'm just obsessed with your aesthetic."

"Oh my God, you're too sweet!" Ms. Ineffable gives Luna a hug.

"Oh my God," Tess whispers to me, rolling her eyes and motioning to the white and wood minimalism around us. "Shit is bougie as fuck."

"Come on," I say. "I thought you loved this kind of stuff."

"There's a difference between a serious spiritual practice and this Disneyland New Age nonsense," Tess argues. She looks at a tag on a nearby shirt. "Two hundred dollars for an oversized doily? That's not spiritualism. That's capitalism."

"Speaking of," I say, "you never told me how much we owe you for the retreat." I'm a little concerned now that my income has halted, but I do have some savings to get me through this temporary leave. *Hopefully* temporary.

"Nothing," Tess replies. "They're still in the early phases of developing the experience, so it's kind of like a free trial."

"So, we're what? Spiritual guinea pigs?"

"We are grateful VIPs, Hannah. And from what I've heard, Avidya is the real deal."

"Okay, but what does that even mean?"

"It means we should be ready for a true spiritual awakening."

I squint at my crystal-bejeweled friend. "Just how far into Wicca have you gotten since we last hung out?"

"Oh, I've gone off the deep end, my dear." She gives me an Elvira smile, eyebrows raised.

Tess dressed the part long before she started acting it. Lots of black clothing and silver jewelry, reading tarot cards and casting harmless spells of intention. But after Ben died and I confessed that

I'd been having visions of him, she suggested we try to contact him directly with a séance. I said no fucking way, leading to the only real fight we've ever had. It was the main reason I pulled away from my best friend when I needed her the most.

I guess I kind of compartmentalized that memory too, but it's hard to forget now as Tess is dragging me to this—

My phone rings and *Mohai* lights up the screen. "Shit."

"Everything okay?" Tess asks.

"Yeah, I just... I need to take this." I step out of the air-conditioned store, back into the desert heat. My throat grasps for words as I raise the phone to my ear.

"Doctor Mohai."

"Hi, Hannah. I hope you're getting some rest."

"I am, thank you." My feet lead me off the main road down an empty side street. "But I'm pretty eager to get back to work."

"Well, that's why I'm calling. Mr. Fox is threatening to sue the hospital for malpractice after all. And he's specifically targeting you."

"*Targeting* me?" The word feels a bit extreme, even for a Texan.

"He's playing it coy for now, says he doesn't want the whole barrel to rot because of one bad apple."

"Lovely metaphor." I kick a loose rock down the dirt road. "So what exactly is this bad apple supposed to do?"

"Just lay low. He was making some ridiculous demands, wanting to know your home address so he could send the paperwork. I think the hospital's legal team's got him diverted for now, but we couldn't stop him from getting your full name. I just wanted to give you the heads-up in case he comes after you directly."

"Do you really think he'd do that?"

"My unofficial professional opinion? The guy is unhinged. I just want you to be aware, so you can take whatever precautions you need to."

"I appreciate that, Dr. Mohai." Sounds like I picked the right time to get the hell out of town. "And I promise you, I'm doing everything I can to get myself back on track."

"That's good to hear, Hannah. In the meantime, I've got your back, okay? You just take care of yourself."

"I will, thank you." I hang up and lean against a nearby chain-link fence to catch my breath, rattling the metal with my trembling grip. My whole career is coming crashing down around me over one little mistake.

Looking over the fence, I see a red wooden sign.

Chemehuevi Indian Burial Ground.

Benches have been placed in front of trees, encircled with small stones. It feels much more peaceful here than the sea of gray headstones in the cemetery where Ben was buried.

I still haven't visited his grave since the funeral. That day was more painful than my near-death escape from the wilderness. Surrounded by all his friends and loved ones. I was just about ready to crawl into an empty grave myself, pull the dirt over me and call it a life.

Pushing away from the fence now, I walk back up toward the main road. The crew is gathering outside of Ineffable, but I'm not ready to be social yet, so I quickly duck into the nearest storefront.

Bumping straight into a very tall man, I mumble a "sorry" and look up into his featureless face. Turns out I just apologized to a faceless mannequin, dressed up like an old nineteenth-century gold miner. A brown wide-brimmed hat looms over suspenders and knee-high boots. Clutched in his plastic hands is a very real pickaxe with a wooden handle and a black iron head.

"All genuine articles." An old man in Coke-bottle glasses peeks out from behind the mannequin.

"I didn't realize Joshua Tree was a gold-mining town."

"You bet it was. From the 1890s through the 1930s. Yessir, there's hundreds of abandoned mines out there." He peers out the window, surveying the land. "You staying in town?"

"Uh, no. We're headed to this retreat, north of the valley. On Dead Man's Due Road?"

"Mm." He smacks his gums. "You give my regards to Waylon Barlow."

"Who?"

The man points to an old photograph on the wall with a placard below.

Dead Man's Due Mine, 1892. The Barlow Gang.

A group of rough-looking men pose in front of the dark mine entrance. Their leader, front and center, wears the kind of cold stare that feels like it could break right through the glass.

"Looks like a friendly bunch," I say.

"They were ruthless bank robbers." The man blinks hard behind his glasses. "Disappeared into the desert to escape the law. Course, everybody knew exactly where the Barlow Gang had set up camp. Coppers were just too scared to confront 'em. Wasn't long before

Barlow realized the biggest vault of all was right beneath their feet. He led the charge, digging that mine, producing more gold than all the banks in the West could muster. But he just wouldn't stop. Made his men dig deeper, and deeper, and deeper into the darkness. Until one day, that darkness dug back."

"What exactly happened?"

"Now, that story's too grim for a nice lady such as yourself. But my grandpappy used to sing a rhyme. Just something the old-timers would say to keep kids from playing out in those dangerous mines. 'In the dark of Dead Man's Due, Waylon Barlow waits for you. He'll hack you up without a trace, pick your bones and steal your face.'"

"Wow." I shake off a shudder. "Thanks for sparing me the grim details. So, is there any truth to the legen—"

"Hey." Tess leans on my shoulder, startling me. "We're gonna hit the bar for one last drink before we head out to the retreat."

I twist to face her. "Sounds good." When I turn back to the old man, he's already settling back behind the counter. "Thanks for the history lesson."

He opens his local paper and blocks me out.

Tess loops her arm through mine, leading me out of the museum. "I'm sorry. Did you want me to invite your boyfriend to drink with us?"

"Hilarious. You should join Kelsey in Groundlings."

"If I ever date a comedian again, please put a pickaxe through my heart." She pats the mannequin's shoulder on our way out.

As we step outside, I swear I can feel eyes on my back. I throw a glance over my shoulder, expecting to see the old man watching through the open doorway.

But the blank-faced miner stares back, gripping that sharp iron T in his lifeless hands.

7

THE DUSTY DIVE BAR SMELLS LIKE STALE PISS AND FRESH PBR, which also smells like stale piss. I haven't been in a place like this since college. A few grizzled old-timers are glued to their stools as Jared unceremoniously squeezes between them to place his order with the bartender.

"Let me get four shots of Patrón, a seltzer for my lady, and I'll take a vodka Red Bull. Don't skimp on the vodka, but I still want a lot of Red Bull."

There's a scoff from down the bar where a uniformed Marine sits.

"Something funny?" Jared asks.

"Not from around here, are you?" the muscled Marine responds.

"What gave it away?" Jared eyes the guy's uniform. "Not as stylish as you?"

Luna tries to snuff out the agro-spark. "Babe? Can you pass me my seltzer?"

"Here." Jared turns, handing her the drink.

"I asked for a lime wedge."

"I thought you weren't doing that anymore because of the pesticides on the rind."

"But I can still squeeze the juice and not—" Luna's left eye twitches before she closes them both and takes a meditative breath. I can see her tight tummy ripple as she stuffs that rage deep down. "It's fine," she announces, sipping her seltzer through the tiny cocktail straw. "I have everything I need in this moment."

The Marine swigs his straight whiskey, muttering under his breath. "I'm sure you do, princess."

Jared clocks the guy's uniform name tag. "What exactly is your problem, Dennings?"

"My problem is you. 29 Palms is a military town for military families, and we're tired of the LA hipster invasion. Entitled brats driving up real estate with their overpriced coffee shops. Know your place."

"Oh, like the United States military knows its place?" Jared responds. "How many foreign countries have you and your buddies invaded with overpriced bases?"

I'm honestly floored by Jared's unexpected geopolitical perspective, and I'm thoroughly enjoying this dispute from the sidelines.

Dennings kicks his stool out and stands. He's shorter than I expected. "You better watch what you say next."

Miles grabs my hand and lifts it in the air. "I say we dance! Come on, guys."

He guides me away from the delicious drama toward the open

floor near the jukebox. Luna takes the cue and pulls Jared from the Marine's glare while Miles selects a tune.

"Cool," Tess says from the barstool where she sits alone. "I'll just chill here then?"

Luna puts a hand on Jared's cheek. "You need to relax."

"Whatever." The vein in his neck bulges. "Soldier boy can get fucked."

Dennings kills the last of his drink and throws one final glare in Jared's direction before pushing through the front door back into the daylight.

"I think we narrowly avoided a war," Miles says into my ear as we sway.

"Thanks to your slick diversion tactic," I respond.

"It wasn't a diversion tactic." He spins me on my feet. "It was a hidden agenda." Damn, he's way more suave than he was in college. "Anyway," he adds, "I've learned how to deal with Jared's antics over the years."

"As I remember it, you used to be quite the party bros together."

"Well, I like to think one of us has grown up a bit since then. I don't see him very much anymore, especially now that I'm traveling a lot for work."

"It's a pretty cool job you got there, DJ Miles2Go."

"I'm not saving lives, that's for sure."

"Neither am I. Just delaying the inevitable."

"There's the Hannah I know and love."

The L-word lingers between us as we dance in smiley silence. Not awkward, just comfortable. I forget myself, forget my life for a precious stretch of seconds until...

"Listen," Miles says. "I was really sorry to hear about Ben." The mention of his name sucks the air from my lungs as Miles keeps talking. "And I wish I could've come to the funeral, but I'd just booked my first stage at Burning Man and—"

"It's fine, really," I reassure him, even though I'm tired of reassuring people of just how fine it is, how fine I am, how not supremely fucked up my mind has become.

I'm so perfectly fine that I'm definitely not seeing Ben right now over Miles's shoulder. Standing in the corner in his blood-spattered winter coat. Watching me with icy dead eyes as I dance with another man.

Miles gives me another twirl, and my stomach twists in knots until my eyes land back in that corner. Ben is gone, the corner filled with nothing but shadows.

"I just want you to know," Miles says, "that I'm here for you. I mean, we all are. If you ever need—"

"I'm sorry." I cut him off, pull away. "I just…need to…"

My feet carry me into the bathroom, where I duck into a stall, close the door, and sit on top of the seat, catching my breath.

This is the escalation Grady warned me about. I'm seeing things that aren't there, not just in my dreams but in my waking life. I'm hallucinating.

I dig into my purse in search of my pills as the bathroom door creaks open.

Probably Tess coming to check on me. "I'm fine, Tess. Just needed to piss after the long drive."

The only response I hear is the icy crunch of footsteps against the tile floor. I look beneath the stall door and see snowshoes approaching my stall.

Ben's snowshoes.

Bang-bang-bang on the door, rattling its rusty hinges.

Not knowing what else to do, I try communicating. That's the most important thing in any relationship, right?

"Ben, I'm sorry. But please, please leave me alone."

Plop... Plop... Plop...

Blood drips on the tile between his snowshoes.

I close my eyes. "Leave me alone, leave me alone..."

Bang-Bang-Bang.

"Leave me the fuck alone!"

SHUNK!

The tip of an ice axe pierces through the flimsy stall door. My body shakes as the blade hacks over and over again until I can't take it anymore. I jump to my feet, twist the lock, and shoulder the door open, stumbling out on the other side.

The bathroom is empty. The door unmarred.

I should be relieved that the attack wasn't real, but isn't it worse if it's all in my head?

My fingers slip into my pocket for the Xanax. For the first time, it occurs to me that maybe the meds are only making things worse. If I'm going to fully commit to this holistic healing weekend, I need to cleanse my body entirely. I need to detox now.

I toss the pill bottle in the trash and push through the bathroom door back out onto the floor.

Miles is hovering right outside. "You okay?"

"Uh-huh." I swerve around him toward the bar, where Tess sits alone, scrolling on her phone.

"Come to give me your sloppy dance-floor seconds?" When she sees my face, her brow knits in concern. "Hey. You okay?"

"Will everyone please stop asking me that?" The shots Jared ordered are still sitting on the bar. "Are we doing these or what, Jared?"

"All right!" he shouts. "There she is!"

I lift my shot glass. "To burying the past."

"Okay." Jared shrugs. "Little dark, but I can dig it."

We clink glasses and down our drinks. The burn brings me to life with a fiery purpose. This weekend is going to change my life. I know it because I've decided it. I'm manifesting it.

Tess checks her phone. "We better get going if we want to make it there before dark."

We stumble back out into the sun to find Dennings still there, leaning against his Humvee with a lit cigarette.

"You all have a nice stay now." He exhales smoke.

"Jared," Luna whispers. "Do not respond."

Jared bites his tongue as he gets behind the wheel of the Range Rover. I walk toward the back door, but Dennings lurches into my path to open it for me.

"See," he says, putting a hand on my back as I climb into the car. "Chivalry's not dead."

"Touch me again and you will be." I slam the door in his face. Dennings doesn't hesitate to spit against the tinted window.

"Motherfucker!" Jared shouts.

"Just drive," Luna says, and the car peels out, kicking up dust.

"Was that really necessary, Hannah?"

"I'm sorry—was *I* the one who picked a fight with a Marine?" I probably shouldn't have added fuel to the fire, but that guy really pissed me off. I look over my shoulder to see if the Humvee is following us. Gratefully, it isn't.

"Turn right, turn right!" Luna shouts, holding up her phone map.

Jared swerves hard onto a dirt road. "Thanks for the heads-up."

I nearly fall into Miles's lap but catch myself and adjust upright.

"It didn't even look like a road," Luna says. "The directions Tess got aren't exactly helpful."

Jared drives faster into the desert, toward the mountains in the distance, while the town recedes into the dust behind us.

"Man," Miles says. "There is nothing out here."

The setting sun casts a purple glow over the landscape, and I can't help admitting: "It's beautiful."

The music cuts out. "That's it for the tunes," Miles says. "I just lost service."

"GPS is gone, too," Luna says.

"That's the point, folks," Tess reminds us. "We're going totally unplugged."

"Unplugged?" Jared says. "I thought this was gonna be like a resort spa situation."

"I may have left out a few details," Luna admits. Their love language is Lies of Omission.

"Well, then I'm gonna have fun while I still can," Jared says. "I haven't had a chance to test this puppy off-road yet. Hold on to your dicks!" He tugs the wheel, veering off the dirt road and tearing into untouched shrubbery.

"Jared!" Tess yells as the car bumps along. "This is protected land! You're fucking up the ecosystem!"

"Oh, relax, SJW. Nothing lives in the desert anyway." The rig throttles over a large hump, wheels slamming against the car's heavy frame. "These aftermarket shocks were totally worth it!"

My palms are pressed against the roof as a vivid memory floods back to me.

I'm half-alive in the passenger seat of my savior's truck in wintry Northern California.

"Stay with me." The driver who found me repeats it over and over again. "Stay with me..."

My body shakes with hypothermia as I stare ahead, the truck speeding and bumping along the mountain road.

"Hannah? Hannah?" Tess's voice brings me back into Jared's Range Rover, but my breath doesn't come with me.

I can't fucking breathe.

"Jared!" Miles screams. "Pull over, man!"

"Why?" Jared turns toward the back seat. "Shit, if she pukes on my leather—"

"Bunny!" Luna screams.

Jared swivels his head back through the windshield to see the rabbit scurrying in front of the car. He swerves, wheels rolling over the critter with a tiny *thump* until the car skids to a stop.

Miles gets out of the car, and I stumble out next, rushing off to catch my breath like I'm emerging from underwater. It's a familiar feeling, a panic attack that I barely dodged back at the bar. The bar where I dumped my Xanax, the only thing that helps curb this awful feeling.

What the hell was I thinking?

Time for Grady's grounding exercise.

Deep breaths. Five things I can see.

Car.

Dirt.

Dead bunny.

Dead bunny.

Dead fucking bunny.

This is *so* not working.

I pull my phone out of my pocket, thumbing my way to Grady's contact info. His smiling face looks up at me as my finger hovers over the *Call* button.

"Hey," Miles says over my shoulder, looking at Dr. Grady on my phone screen. "I don't think that call's gonna go through out here. But it's not too late to turn back if you need your doctor."

Yes, this was a mistake. I never should have come out here. I want to go home.

But home is nowhere.

My eyes fall from my phone back to the rabbit in the dirt. Twitching its little leg, hanging on by a bloody tendon.

"I'm gonna puke," Luna says.

I step closer to the squirming roadkill, watching the life slowly drain out of the animal until it's nothing but dead meat.

Just like Ben.

My nerves stop burning and my breath starts steadying.

Tess rubs my neck. "You okay, honey?"

"Yeah." I tuck my phone away. "I'm good."

"Hey, guys?" Jared says. "You seeing what I'm seeing?"

All heads swivel now toward the end of the road in the distance. A dotted line of orange flames, burning in the distance.

"I think that's it." Tess smiles wistfully. "That's Avidya."

"Well, let's get our asses over there before the sun goes down," Jared suggests as everyone climbs back into the Range Rover.

Miles stays by my side. "If you want to walk the rest of the way, I'm with you."

"I'm pretty sure we'd die of thirst," I say.

Miles shrugs. "There are worse ways to go than dying in a thirst trap."

"I don't think that phrase means what you think it means."

"Oh, I'm pretty sure it does." He holds the door for me as I climb back into the car to hide my blushing cheeks.

We roll onward, toward the flickering fire in the coming darkness.

8

TORCHES LINE EITHER SIDE OF THE LAST STRETCH OF ROAD that ends in a big natural stone archway. The Rover's headlights illuminate a man sitting cross-legged in the dirt beneath the arch. White linen jumpsuit, gray hair pulled back into a bun. His eyes are closed as the fire flickers off his face, which slowly turns up into a grin as we all get out of the car.

"You must be the next party," he says in a soft voice, opening his crystal blue eyes. "I am Pax. Welcome to Avidya."

He stands and bows. I'm immediately irked that Guru Pax is a white man, but some part of me expected that. Even if his skin looks like he peeled it off and stretched it out to bake in the sun before slipping back into the burned leather.

"Come." He waves. "Let me show you your new home."

Pax leads us into the adobe building beyond the arch. In the main hall, we're greeted by a large mirror with water trickling down its surface into a pool filled with crystals of all shapes and colors.

"Upon entering, I ask that you pause for self-reflection here,"

Pax says. "The water runs on a nonelectric pump. As I'm sure you're aware, this is an unplugged retreat. There is no technology or electricity of any kind. You won't find Wi-Fi or cell service here, so Kimi will collect your phones now."

He motions to a young woman with brown skin and black hair tied back in a braid. Kimi holds a burlap sack toward us. "They'll be returned at the end of your experience."

"Seriously?" Jared says.

Luna nudges him, and Jared sighs dramatically, tossing his phone in the sack.

I don't mind this part. Most of my recent nights have been spent mindlessly scrolling until my eyes throb, desperate to drown out my dark thoughts with cute animal videos. But it's time to leave those habits behind as I drop my phone in the bag. Even that symbolic act gives me a small feeling of catharsis, severing the digital umbilical cord.

Pax gives a grateful bow. "Kimi will also move your bags from your car to your lodgings, if you'll please entrust her with your keys."

Jared reluctantly places his key chain in Kimi's open palm. "I better not find one scratch."

I shake my head and turn to Kimi. "What he means to say is 'Thank you, Kimi.'" She seems utterly unbothered by Jared's assholery as she takes the keys and heads back outside.

"Come." Pax motions for us to follow him along the curved hallway. "Does anyone know what *avidya* means?"

Luna brightens like a star pupil about to answer the teacher, but I can't help beating her to the punch to say, "Ignorance."

"That's right." Pax smiles at me, his icy eyes somehow warm. "Very good."

"I knew that, too." Luna just can't help herself. "But good for you, Hannah!"

"The word is Sanskrit," Pax explains, "but there's a name for it in every culture, every language. The goal at Avidya is to transcend the human ignorance that divides us, to connect with the true, unifying essence behind all religions, behind all people."

The wall is decorated with ancient artifacts, stone tools and knives, even a pickaxe. "In order to break free and rise above, we must first remember our roots. Our ancestors created tools like these to survive, to support life in the wilderness. Until we turned them into weapons to hurt one another and reap death." Pax points to a tapestry on the wall. "It is time to get in touch with your primeval self."

The woven imagery features a violent transformation of a man into a wolf. Not quite as encouraging as the butterfly metaphor, and it makes the phoenix look tame in comparison.

"Our connection to the animal world is part of the human experience," Pax explains. "We are beasts at heart. This is why our retreat strips away modern comforts and distracting technologies. We must return to the marrow of our bones before we transcend our very bodies."

Staying on theme, the next wall is covered in dozens of animal skulls, from tiny mice to horned sheep and antlered deer. I do a quick scan in search of a human skull but gratefully find none.

"Part of this journey involves familiarizing ourselves with every bone, every joint, every muscle." Pax guides us into the next room. "To that end, I welcome you to our yoga studio."

The setting sun cuts through the open windows with an orange glow in the airy space. I'm more than a little out of practice on the yoga front, but I'm eager to get back into it.

"Oh, thank God." Luna rushes to the collection of props in the corner. "I'm not gonna lie—I was a little worried this place would be so stripped down that you wouldn't even have props." She gives a tug to the fabric ropes hanging from the ceiling. "You've even got aerial straps!"

"We want to be inclusive of all needs, so you'll find everything you could possibly require to support you here," Pax assures her. "I can tell by your figure that you're a true yogi."

Luna blushes. "I actually just completed my second two-hundred-hour training. I think it's important for teachers to always be learning themsel—"

"Hey, Paxman." Jared clamps a hand on the guru's shoulder. "You got a *real* gym here? Some of us need more than stretching."

"Yoga *is* more than stretching," Luna says through gritted teeth. I'm surprised those pearly whites haven't been ground down to their bloody roots with all the condescension she puts up with from her boyfriend.

Pax gives Jared a patient smile. "I'm afraid the nearest gymnasium is quite a bit farther than a stone's throw. But yoga teaches us that all the weight and resistance we need is already built into our bodies. And our focus here is more on strengthening the mind."

"Great," Jared replies. "A simple 'no' would've covered it."

Luna pulls him aside for a whispered argument, which I'm choosing to tune out as Pax leads us into the next room.

"Speaking of mental expansion," he says. "That is precisely the purpose of our meditation den."

The white domed room is filled with bowls and gongs and other instruments.

Pax's voice echoes in the expansive space. "This is where I'll be performing our sound baths and guided meditations, the first of which will take place tomorrow."

Miles walks the perimeter, grazing his fingers along the wind chimes as the crystal-clear sound reverberates. "Rad. I would love to record something in this space."

Pax reaches out to quiet the chimes. "Not every experience needs to be captured. It's important to remember that your first love was the sound itself, not a secondhand recording."

I already feel antsy just looking at the meditation cushions. There was a time when I was fully committed to meditating every day. Bought my own special cushion on Abbot Kinney, downloaded the Headspace app, and did the full one-week free trial. But it turned out that sitting still was not my strong suit, so I left the app to die and repurposed the cushion as an ottoman. This will be different, though. I can learn how to start a proper habit under the right conditions and take it home with me.

The geography of this place is already throwing me for a loop as we exit the dome back outside, where a pool is carved into the rocks.

"Here, we have our natural hot springs pool," Pax says. "The water bubbles up from the earth's core, bringing all sorts of potent minerals along with it. Your skin will age backward as it absorbs the healthy nutrients."

Tess dips her hand in the pool. "That's a big promise, Pax."

"I don't make promises," he replies. "Only observations."

"Oh, shit! Sauna?" Jared smacks his open palm against a large barrel structure with a small door. "Now this is more like it."

"Sweat lodge, yes. In some cultures, they're said to induce a profound experience of the soul leaving the body. The steam is funneled directly from the springs, so do mind the valve and the vent inside."

The heat rising off the pool is strong enough to make me feel dizzy as I wipe the sweat from my eyes.

Pax must notice this as he folds his hands together. "I can sense from your collective energy that you've had a long day. Kimi will guide you to your yurts for a brief respite while I prepare our first supper."

I didn't even realize that Kimi had already reappeared behind us. "This way," she says, guiding us toward a cluster of six cloth yurts. These are not upscale glamping tents. These are the real deal—animal skin perched on sticks and weighted with stones.

"What do you think?" Tess asks, snaking her arm around my shoulder.

"Honestly?"

"Always honestly."

"Guru Pax?" I whisper.

"A bit cringe, I know."

"A bit colonial," I say. "The way he's appropriating all these different cultures into his own spiritual mash-up?"

"It's called *religious syncretism*, and it's actually really progressive." Tess motions to Kimi up ahead. "I don't think an Indigenous woman would be here if the place wasn't legit."

I don't have time to argue before Kimi spins on her heels to face us, and I can't help wondering if she heard Tess's comment.

"Hannah." Kimi motions to the nearest yurt. "Welcome to your dwelling."

Kimi leads the rest of the group to their new homes while Tess stays back for a moment.

"Just do me a favor," she says. "Promise me you'll give it a real shot?"

"I promise I will be...here...now..." I give a guru bow, forcing a laugh out of Tess.

"Okay, *Rude* Dass. See you at dinner." Tess hurries to catch up with the others.

Peeling the animal skin flap back, I step into my yurt. Not much to speak of in here as I collapse on the mattress resting directly on the dirt floor. "Mattress" is maybe too generous a word for the linen sack filled with lumpy hay.

I hate to admit it, but I can't help agreeing with Jared. I was expecting a relaxing resort experience, but this feels more like camping. Even more rugged than the minimalist backpacking trips that Ben used to drag me on with his high-end inflatable pillows, memory foam mattress pads, and...

No. I will not think about him. This weekend is about leaving the past in the past and moving forward. I won't think about Ben or the shitshow I left at work with Dr. Mohai and Mr. Fox.

I'm going to make the most of my time here.

I will reconnect with my primeval self.

9

THE DINING ROOM ISN'T ACTUALLY A ROOM. IT'S A LOW CIR- cular table set out in the open, surrounded by a ring of torches. There are cushions all around it, and we take our seats on the floor.

Kimi places the large wooden bowls of food in the center as Pax explains, "All of our meals will be served community style. So much of the food we consume in the outside world is hardly food at all. It's chemical mutations cooked up in a laboratory. All the food here is raw and organic. This will cleanse all those unhealthy toxins out of your body."

I feel attacked for all the frozen dinners I've been ingesting of late. Every night, I tell myself that I'll start eating healthier the next day. Every day, I'm too exhausted to brave the Whole Foods parking lot and pay hundreds of dollars for ingredients to recipes that would take me three hours to prepare. I'm grateful for the shortcut now as I serve myself a heaping serving of leafy greens and brown grains.

"How do you keep the food fresh without a refrigerator?" Miles asks through his munches.

"Contrary to popular practice, refrigeration can actually drain vegetables of their flavor and nutrients. Kimi gathers our food once a week from a nearby farm. Any waste is returned to the soil for composting."

"You can farm out here in the desert?" I ask. It's hard to picture anything growing in the dusty wasteland we drove through to get here.

"There's more life out here in the desert than you can possibly imagine." Pax has a funny look in his eye, like he just told an inside joke that nobody else is inside of.

Jared pushes some sprouted quinoa around on his plate. "I assume dessert is gonna be, what, a bowl of berries?"

"I'm afraid we don't serve sugar here," Pax says. "Even small amounts can upset your metabolic processing and negatively impact your neural processing. We're trying to keep the pathways open."

Luna chirps up, desperate to earn guru points. "You mean open to the vibrational frequencies of the universe, like the law of attraction?"

"I mean open for the spirits." Pax says it like it's the most obvious answer in the world. I have a million questions, but apparently it's not the time. "Let us take our first meal in silence as the monks of Tibet do."

We eat like monks. It's awkward.

When the plates are all clear, Pax stands. "We have one final activity before sleep."

He guides us into an open clearing adjacent to the table, away from the torches and into the darkness.

"It's crazy dark out here," Tess says.

"You'll adjust back into your circadian rhythms in no time at all," Pax assures her. "When darkness falls, we rest. When the sun rises, so do we. There's no need for electric lights. But it just so happens that you've come on the weekend of a full moon. The Hunter's Moon."

As if he's summoning it with his words, the bright moon breaks through the clouds. The natural spotlight casts its ethereal glow down to earth, illuminating a spiraling pattern of rocks on the ground right in front of us.

Pax stands at the center of the spiral, opening his arms wide. "This is the labyrinth walk. It's designed as a practice in meditation, a journey into the labyrinth of your unconscious mind."

The carefully placed stones form a pattern, like one of those plastic children's toys with the little marble inside. You spin it and spin it until the marble finally knocks into the center. I always got frustrated with that thing and ended up throwing it across the room.

"I want you to walk through the winding path to the center of the maze while searching your heart for an intention," Pax says. "Something specific, something charged. By the end of your journey into the labyrinth, the spirits will offer you a solitary word. This will be your mantra for the weekend."

Kimi hands out pens and pieces of parchment while Pax keeps speaking.

"You'll write it down, then speak it out loud to me, to the universe." Pax holds a small ceramic bowl in his hands. "Then offer it to the spirits so that they might answer."

Jared lets out an audible scoff, which Pax latches on to. "Jared. Why don't you go first?"

Jared walks straight over the stones, ignoring the patterned maze and making a beeline straight to Pax at the center. He's clearly found his intention: to be an asshole. Jared scribbles three letters on his parchment and holds it up to Pax, who reads the word aloud.

"Fun."

"Yeah. I thought we were going to be drinking all weekend, having *fun*. But I'm starting to think that's not gonna happen."

"In our dissociated culture, we are encouraged to drink ourselves into oblivion. Perhaps it's time to investigate whether or not this path is truly serving you," Pax says. "Either way, the spirits will answer."

Jared crumples his paper and tosses it in the bowl. Pax is being a bit pompous, but he does have a point. Alcohol is a socially acceptable path to utter detachment that I've leaned on a whole lot in the last year. I don't think I have a problem, exactly, but I'm also grateful for the forced separation. More grateful than Jared, that's for sure.

Luna ignores her boyfriend's shit attitude and keeps the levels up on her sunny disposition as she asks: "Can I go next?"

Pax nods.

Luna slips out of her shoes, closes her eyes, and walks through the maze. She's clearly intent on blindly feeling her way through the maze, even though that was not the assignment. It takes forever until she finally arrives at Pax and opens her eyes to beam with pride.

She writes down a word and shows him the paper, waiting for her A+.

"Flexibility," she says. "I'm really looking to push myself on the mat and get into some new poses that I've never done before. Physically and mentally, of course."

"That's good, Luna," Pax responds. "But yoga is not a competition, with others or with ourselves. Rather than trying to stretch away from yourself, perhaps it's time you truly got grounded in the weight of your body. The spirits will answer."

Luna shrinks a little as she sulks out of the maze, and I have to admit I'm starting to like Pax's style.

Miles shrugs at me before walking the maze next. His word is *Inspiration*.

Pax squints at him. "You're a musician."

"Yeah, totally. How'd you know?"

"I saw the way your energy interacted with the sound bath space. If it's new soundscapes that you seek, you will find them here. The spirits will answer."

Tess walks next. *Connection*.

Pax nods. "Perhaps the most universal intention of all."

"I've been dealing with some…confusing relationship stuff lately," Tess explains. "So, I guess I'm just here to figure some of that out."

That phone call with Kelsey sounded stressful. I wonder if there's more going on with Tess and her clingy ex than she's let on.

"Attachments are sticky things," Pax says. "When we move from one to the next, we lose sight of our individual wholeness. The spirits will answer."

Tess cocks her head. "Are you slut-shaming me, Pax?"

"Oh, I pass no judgments on physical unions. It's emotional enmeshment that bogs us down in dukkha. Suffering. Which brings us to you, Hannah."

I cross my arms at the strangely pointed segue. "What's that supposed to mean?"

"All I meant was that you are the final one to walk the path," Pax clarifies.

I was so caught up watching everybody else that I didn't realize I was the only one left. Shaking out of my defensive posture, I make my way through the maze. My mind is racing with a million thoughts, but it's the response to those thoughts that rings true when I finally arrive at the center of the labyrinth.

Let go.

But that's two words, and the assignment was one, so I settle for: "Release."

Pax looks at the word on the paper and drops it into his bowl. His icepick eyes rise to meet mine.

"You're frozen, Hannah. Trapped in the ice, desperate to break free. But in order to find release, you must be still. You must feel everything your pain has to offer, let it warm your soul and melt your heart. You will grieve here. The spirits will answer."

My chest clenches and I'm fighting back tears because…I believe him. I don't know why, but I believe Pax is telling me the truth. But how did he know I was grieving?

Pax's fingers snap over the bowl, and the papers burst into flames.

"Whoa!" Jared says. "Okay, here we go! Avidya's on that Benihana shit!"

I step outside of the stone circle to join the group as Pax holds the flaming bowl out toward us.

"If you remain open to my practices and teachings, I promise that all of you will make contact with the spirits you need to guide you into the next stage of your journey. You were driven here by a fire within, some unresolved pain still burning bright. But in the end, we will quell your fears. We will extinguish that flame."

Pax snaps a finger over the bowl again, and the fire extinguishes in a puff of smoke.

"You will be free." He places the bowl on the ground in the center of the maze. "I'll see you all bright and early."

Pax walks off as Jared claps. "Bravo, Gob Bluth!" He turns to Luna. "Did this guy train at the Magic Castle or what?"

I sidle up to Tess, trying to play it cool. "Did you know that Pax was going to be so..."

"Theatrical?" Tess says. "Yeah, kinda."

"I mean, the smoke-and-mirrors show is one thing, but what's with all the spirit talk?"

"Word on the witchy street is that Pax is a kind of...medium."

"Like a Ouija board, 'talks to dead people' kind of medium?"

"It's not like in the movies, Hannah. Some people are just very sensitive to the spirit world. But to be honest, I don't really know what his deal is yet. That's what I'm curious to find out."

Tess has been building her own Instagram following as a "spiritual creative influencer," a combination of words that makes me cringe out of my skin. I suddenly wonder if this trip has more than a tinge of self-interest for her, especially since I know she's been dabbling in séances. If I believed in any of that nonsense, I might have some weird feelings right now. But all I've got is sheer exhaustion.

"The spirits are calling me to bed," I say. "Night, all."

I'm still thinking about Pax's strange words about grief when I step into my yurt, only to find Kimi pulling a hooded sweatshirt from my bag.

"What are you doing?" I ask.

"Unpacking your things."

"I can do that myself." I rip the sweatshirt from Kimi's hands, then instantly regret the bratty outburst. "I'm sorry, it's just… personal."

"I understand. My apologies." Kimi ducks back out of the yurt.

It's personal because it's Ben's sweatshirt. I didn't mean to bring it; I'd just packed so fast. Or did some part of me bring it on purpose? Either way, it's getting cold and I need it. But I shove it back in the bag and cover myself in layers of animal skin blankets instead.

With my eyes closed, the quiet of the desert is soothing, so different from the thrum of Los Angeles traffic. But can I really sleep without my pills? Grady told me to wean off them, not go cold turkey, so I'm probably in for one hell of a withdrawal.

That's when the silence is interrupted by a slow scratching sound. It's coming from the animal skin wall above my head. I refuse to open my eyes, but I can see it in my mind's eye. The shadow outside my yurt. Ben dragging his ice axe down the leather wall. Over and over. He doesn't want me to rest.

But I don't care what he wants. Because he's not really there.

I focus my intention and slip toward the deepest sleep I've had in months.

With the ghost scratching outside my yurt and Pax's spirit talk bouncing around inside my skull, a final waking thought floats up. A simple request of the universe.

No more dead people, please.

10

LANCE CORPORAL DENNINGS WAITS UNTIL DARK TO EXECUTE his mission.

By the time the bar closes, he's got enough whiskey and beer in him to put down a horse, but that's never stopped him from carrying out the sacred duty he's assigned himself.

He must cleanse his community of outsiders.

Even though he's been living on the base for four years, seven months, and twenty-eight days, Dennings still hasn't seen any real action. When he was recruited as a high schooler, playing *Call of Duty* after class instead of doing his homework, he couldn't wait to be a real-life soldier. His Xbox trigger finger was itching to mow down a flesh-and-blood enemy with a wide array of weaponry.

But Dennings has never been called to duty. Boot camp was a nightmare, and his fellow trainees treated him worse than his online campaign partners did. At least in the game, they could only assault him verbally through the headset. At Marine Corps boot camp, they beat his ass with tube socks filled with soap bars.

That all changed when he got placed at the advanced training base in Joshua Tree. Being a specialized Marine was the ultimate dream, just like the commercials he idolized as a young boy. *The Few! The Proud!* He couldn't wait to be molded into a true stealth warrior, silently emerging from the murky waters with a knife between his teeth like they did on his TV screen.

Afghanistan was still a war zone then, and Dennings was ready to bring some American justice overseas. He tried to be patient and wait his turn, but it was hard to watch when the troops started getting withdrawn from the country.

Now, he's in a perpetual state of not knowing when the next war might break out. The higher-ups promise it will come soon, that there's always some backward country in need of democracy and freedom, but Dennings is getting antsy. That's why he started looking around at how he could serve his country on the local front.

Some folks have clearly been taking all those military sacrifices for granted. Living high and mighty with no regard for the blood spilled to keep the USA on top. So Dennings endeavored to make some sacrifices of his own.

The plan was simple enough and had worked many times already.

Step 1: Post up in the saloon until some LA hipsters arrive. (It happens every damn weekend.)

Step 2: Tag their vehicle with a LoJack device.

Step 3: Track down said vehicle under cover of darkness.

Step 4: Use his trusty Ka-Bar knife to teach those assholes a lesson.

The local newspapers have already given him a name, and he actually likes it a lot.

The J-Tree Terror.

It has a nice ring to it. Like a mythical figure or a superhero.

For obvious reasons, the police suspect the culprit is someone from the local military base, but they haven't done much to investigate. They probably like what he's doing too much to stop him. Kind of like how the cops treat the Punisher. Let vigilante justice prevail! Dennings had gotten that iconic skull inked on his chest at the local tattoo parlor after reading one of those Marvel comics. He's only read the one, but it was enough to know that the Punisher is a one-man army who takes no prisoners: just like Dennings.

Only difference is that everybody knows the Punisher is Frank Castle. Nobody knows who the J-Tree Terror really is, and that's why they'll never catch him. Dennings is too smart for that. He thought once or twice about wearing a mask, or at least a basic balaclava, but masks are for pussies afraid of getting caught. He's confident in his training, his ninja-like ability to slip through the shadows undetected.

Usually, his mission would lead him to some remodeled motel or fancy Airbnb. Those are the *real* terrors. The people who buy homes and don't even live here, make no attempt to integrate into the community. They just throw LA money at a house and then rent it out to whoever will pay. Often groups of partying twentysomethings who are always leaving a mess in their wake and undertipping servers at the diner on their way out.

One time, a drunk driver T-boned a local woman, killing her

on the spot while the outsider son of a bitch lived. Where had the driver come from? Los fucking Angeles, and of course he hired his fancy legal counsel to snake his way out of the charges.

Dennings can't stand the way rich folks can just buy their way out of consequences. That's why he started keeping a catalog of every new Airbnb listing in the area, so he can stay on top of the creeping invasion of liberal cockroaches.

But tonight, as Dennings drives his Humvee under cover of night, he doesn't find himself heading toward any of the usual side roads where those Airbnbs often are. He's driving out into the black abyss of the desert.

He double-checks the satellite signal on his GPS, and sure enough, the LoJack is blipping straight ahead. But there isn't anything out here for miles that he knows of. Only thing this far out is the base, but that's all the way on the other side of the mountain.

The group from the bar today didn't seem like the backcountry camping type, that's for sure. It had taken every ounce of Dennings's energy not to pull out his knife back there when that soy boy stepped up to him or when that redheaded bitch threatened him.

But patience is a virtue he learned in basic training. Making too big a scene in public would only draw attention to his mission. He's proud of himself for handling it well, for waiting until dark to unleash hell.

In the near distance, he can see lights. No, not lights, but actual fire. Torches burning in the night. The LoJack signal is coming from right up there.

What the hell are these LA idiots up to, starting fires in the wilderness? Some kind of Burning Man orgy? He can't wait to get there and find out.

With nothing else around to mask the sound of his approach, he decides it's too risky to come rumbling up in the Humvee. So he pulls over and walks the last half-mile on foot. It doesn't take long before Dennings can see the vehicle that he recognizes, parked just before the large stone arch where the torches are burning.

It's the brand-new Range Rover that asshole in the bar drove away in.

With his target acquired, Dennings unsheathes his blade.

It's time for the Terror.

He creeps up behind the car, crouching at the trunk. Taking out his tactical light, he bites it between his front teeth and carves into the black paint.

S-E

He's gotten good at it over the years, scarring all those tourists' fancy cars. Giving them a souvenir they won't forget on their Beemers and Audis, Rovers and Teslas.

M-P

The kind of people who wouldn't know how to change a tire with a gun to their head, who drive cars that barely have engines anymore.

E-R

His hand cramps up and he drops the knife to shake out the pain. He'd strained his trigger finger in a recent training exercise but assured his CO that he could still grip his rifle and do what needed to be done. After all these years, he can't let himself get discharged before his first deployment. Trapped in one desert and dreaming of another one, Dennings can only pray to God that someday he'll see some action.

Something rustles in the brush behind him.

Probably just a rabbit.

The sound of fast footfalls should trigger his training: *Enemy combatant on your six!*

Instinct should kick in, and he should reach for his Ka-Bar in the dirt, but his reflexes are dulled by beer and whiskey. Instead, Dennings spins clumsily on his heels, just in time to feel the heavy blow against his ribcage.

He bites down hard on the flashlight, cracking teeth, and his body does one full spin before his back hits the dirt.

A deep ache pulses through his torso. He can't seem to move a muscle as a shadowy figure shifts at the edges of his vision. The figure settles into the dirt behind Dennings, propping his head up in their lap so he can see the source of the heavy blow that knocked him off his feet.

The iron point of an old pickaxe sticks out of his chest like a devil's horn. The other end is buried somewhere in Dennings's ribcage, making the wooden handle wag with every ragged breath. His lower lip scrapes against broken teeth as he gasps a "Fuck."

The enemy holds the Ka-Bar in front of Dennings's eyes, giving him a clear view of the black blade like a grim promise. That knife is his most prized possession, a special gift from a staff sergeant who saw promise in the new recruit. It came with one important command from his old-school mentor: "Never let your Ka-Bar out of your sight."

As fate would have it, Dennings never does lose sight of that knife. He spends his final agonizing moments watching in first-person-shooter POV as the blade carves his face off with surgical precision. The desert air hits cold against his exposed cheek muscles when the bloody flap of skin peels away in one perfect piece.

The enemy dangles the severed face in Dennings's dying eyeline like a victory flag, signaling that it's truly game over for the J-Tree Terror.

11

I'M SUMMONED BACK TO CONSCIOUSNESS BY THE SOUND of a horn. Not the car horns that often startle me awake in Los Angeles. This sounds more like the rallying bullhorn before a battle scene in *Game of Thrones*.

My whole body feels lighter as I roll off the mattress. I didn't have any night terrors last night, no dark dreams starring Ben. Just me, wrapped in a blanket of utter blackness and delicious silence.

Wandering out of the yurt, I survey the property by the light of day. It's stunningly beautiful here, every structure blending into its natural surroundings. The sun is just barely rising over the mountains, the morning air is crisp, and my mind feels present, focused.

I can't explain it, but something released in me last night. Maybe it was the Xanax detox or the raw meal before bed. Maybe being surrounded by old friends and spending one night in nature really is helping reground me. Whatever the cause, I know I'm exactly where I'm supposed to be.

I follow the sound to the dining table, where Pax stands blowing into a large animal horn.

"What's that?" I ask.

"It's a shofar. Made from a ram's horn and used in Jewish religious services. It's meant to remind us of the ram that Abraham offered as a sacrifice in place of his son Isaac."

"Are you summoning us to be sacrificed?"

Pax laughs. "On the contrary. The shofar is most commonly blown on Rosh Hashanah to scare away demons before the new year begins. Were you visited by any demons last night, Hannah?"

"Nope." I mean, yes, there might have been one scratching at my yurt wall. Or it might have just been some hungry desert critter. Either way: "I think they're learning not to mess with me."

"Very good." Pax is sizing me up like I just passed some unspoken test. "Please, sit. I'll go check on the others."

I take a seat at the table where Kimi is putting out food for breakfast. It's mostly raw granola and some more leafy greens, but I'm actually looking forward to the meal.

"Thank you, Kimi. This looks amazing."

Kimi meets my eyes for a moment before quickly looking away, giving no verbal response. I hate to admit it, even to myself, but there's something unsettling about her presence that I can't quite put my finger on. Maybe not unsettling so much as unsettled. Like there's something she wants to say but can't.

I try breaking the ice. "How long have you been working here?"

"Long enough," she says.

Before I can ask more, Tess wraps her arms around me from behind and plants a kiss on my cheek. "Morning."

"Morning," I say, watching Kimi slip away.

"How'd you sleep?" Tess slides onto the seat next to me.

"Really well, actually. You?"

"Like a rock."

Jared approaches with a dumb grin on his face and his arm around Luna's shoulder. "Well, we didn't sleep at all. Right, babe?"

Miles takes a seat on the other side of me. "Yeah, I know. My yurt is right next to yours. Thanks for the primal sound bath, you two."

"Hey, Pax said to get in touch with our animal side, right?" Jared howls like a wolf.

Pax pops up over his shoulder to howl back.

"Jesus!" Jared yelps.

"He's welcome here, too." Pax smiles. "But if we're choosing modern idols, I prefer the Buddha."

I can't help laughing. Pax is a weirdo, for sure, but there's something magnetic about the man seated at the head of the table. An ageless confidence.

"Damn." Tess squints at my joy. "You really are embracing the experience, huh?"

"I promised you I would." I shrug, and she gives a grateful smile back.

"So, Pax." Jared tosses a handful of granola in his mouth. "What exactly *is* your deal? Religiously, I mean?"

"I believe we have something to learn from every religion, every text, every culture. Our modern society is too quick to draw lines in the sand and say, 'You shall not pass!'"

Did the guru just do a Gandalf?

"I endeavor to erase those lines," he says, "to make all spirits one."

"Eraser, but drop the second *e*," Jared says.

"I'm sorry?" Pax replies.

"I like your brand, bro. You just need a little help taking it to the next level. First, you sell the app. It's called *Erasr*, e-r-a-s-r. Customers have to do their spiritual prep work, unlock enlightenment achievements. Think Duolingo for the soul. If they beat the course and pay the extra upgrade fees, they get invited to the retreat. What do you think?"

I'm actually impressed by how quickly Jared was able to commodify the spiritual experience.

"I think," Pax replies, ever patient, "that would be contrary to the spirit of my intentions."

Jared rolls his eyes as Tess squirms.

"Hey, Pax?" she asks. "Is there a restroom around here? I've been holding it since last night."

"Of course, my apologies." Pax points to a lone outhouse at the edge of the property. "There's no plumbing, but you may relieve yourself in the composting toilet."

"Great. I would love to not know how that works," Tess says before hurrying to the outhouse.

"After breakfast"—Pax motions to the food he hasn't touched—"I'll host our first guided meditation. It should prove rather illuminating as we open your chakras for the spirits to work through you."

"You keep talking about the spirits," I say, no longer capable of letting the S-word slide. "Exactly which spirits are you talking about?"

"Every religion has its own mythological figures, and I believe the same is true of every human soul. I cannot tell you exactly how the spirits will manifest through your individual consciousness. That's for you alone to discover."

This is not the answer I'm hoping for. I already know how my spirits are manifesting. It's exactly what I'm trying to escape on this retreat. But maybe Ben will finally leave me alone out here. Maybe my unconscious mind will finally release—

A scream ripples across the open land.

"Tess!" I jump to my feet and run toward the outhouse. Before my hand can reach the handle, the door bursts open in my face, nearly knocking me on my ass.

Tess leaps from the wooden box like a prematurely buried person escaping a coffin, straight into my arms.

"Run," she gasps into my ear.

Hisssss comes next. The rattlesnake slithers from the outhouse door, through the dirt, toward us.

"Snake!" I scream because what else do you do when you see a snake? I pull Tess back to the table, putting it between us and the scaly beast.

"Kimi," Pax says. "It seems we have another serpentine squatter."

Kimi hurries into the building while Pax crouches down toward the snake.

"Hello, friend." The snake seems to be looking directly into Pax's crystalline eyes. It stops advancing and curls itself up into a coil, head still raised. "I'm truly sorry that we've intruded upon your land. But you'll have to find a new home."

The snake's tail rattles, and its fangs slide out. With a pointed hiss, it slashes through the air toward Pax, ready to sink its teeth through his leathery skin. Before the bite can land, metal tongs clamp around the snake's neck from behind. Kimi squeezes firmly on the handle, then tosses the snake in a burlap sack as it wriggles within.

Jared points at the bag. "That better not be the same sack our phones are in."

"Thank you, Kimi," Pax says, unfazed by the attack. "Please find a safe place for it."

"Far the fuck away," Tess adds.

"Are you okay?" I rub her shoulders.

Tess nods, placing a hand on mine.

Jared puts on a compassionate tone. "That must have been really scary for you, Tess. Been a while since you've wrestled with a big snake, right?"

Nobody laughs, and I glare. "Really, Jared? With the homophobic humor?"

Miles backs me up with a "Not cool, man."

"Oh, come on." Jared throws his hands up. "It wasn't a gay joke. It was a dick joke."

Tess strikes back faster than the snake. "The only dick joke here is between your legs."

The whole group laughs at this, and Jared blushes. "Okay. Solid dunk." He pulls a silver flask from his pocket and tips some pungent tequila into his tea.

"Jared," Luna says. "Did you really sneak booze into the retreat?"

"I'm on a juice cleanse." Jared does his best Pax imitation. "This organic mescal was sustainably harvested from local agave plants."

Luna shakes her head. "If you ruin this weekend for me, I swear..."

I can see the anger starting to brim in Luna's body again. Her slender frame has no way of hiding it when she shakes with rage.

"Relax, babe," Jared responds.

"Do not tell me to relax. I will not have a repeat of the weekend you met my parents."

"First of all, your mom drinks more than I do..."

As the couple begins to bicker again, I refocus my attention on Tess. "You sure you're okay?"

"I'm just trying to remember exactly why I invited these people. Maybe I should've just made it you and me, ya know? A BFF escape." Tess leans her head on my shoulder.

"You invited all these people because you're a good friend. Besides, having ample opportunities to call Jared out on his bullshit makes me feel alive again."

"In that case, it's totally worth it." Tess smiles.

"I'm glad we're here."

"Yeah. Me too."

Ever since we met as bright-eyed teens, Tess and I have bemoaned the way society values romantic love over platonic love. But friendship always runs deeper, carves its roots into the core of your heart. A true friend never wavers, even as needy lovers come and go. Maybe I've lost sight of that, but I'm grateful to be nurturing my connection with Tess again after a long, lonely drought.

"Dear friends," Pax says to the group. "It's time to begin our journey inward. Please follow me into the sound bath."

12

"PLEASE," PAX SAYS. "LIE DOWN WITH YOUR CROWN CHAKRA pointing in toward the center of the circle."

He stands in the middle of the sound bath den with a collection of white bowls while we all lie down in a circle around him. I try with every fiber of my biological being not to reject the chakra talk. I'm not here as a medical doctor who knows there's no evidence that chakras are real. I'm here as a broken human who knows there's no fixing herself without letting go of her loudmouthed ego.

"Lot of circles in this retreat," Miles notes.

"The circle represents infinity, the cycle of life and death." Pax moves toward a big golden gong at the edge of the room. "Today, you will experience your first taste of the endlessness of time and space."

My loudmouthed ego can't help noting, "That's a pretty lofty prom—"

Booonnnggg. Pax hits the gong with a mallet, shutting me up real quick as the sonic energy reverberates in my chest. He glides back into the center of the circle and takes his seat among the sound bowls. "Relax your spine. Open your mind to receive the vibrations."

Kimi lights a bundle of dried leaves and walks the perimeter at our feet.

"Kimi is cleansing the air with sage," Pax explains, "clearing the path for the spirits to communicate."

I inhale the sickly-sweet smell. I've never been a smoker, but Ben used to enjoy his daily weed. He swore it calmed his nerves, but when he didn't have it, he'd get anxious and irritable. I thought about confronting his growing dependency on more than a few occasions, but I knew he'd just evade all accusations.

"Unclench your lungs," Pax commands.

I didn't even know I could clench my lungs until I consciously thought about unclenching them. Just like that, a spaciousness fills my chest.

"Now, breathe deep. In…and out. In…and out."

Easy enough. I breathe every day, so all I have to do is keep breathing, filling and emptying that new space.

The slowing of the breath is starting to make me feel a little light-headed, but I'm hoping that's all part of the process. A cough rattles up my throat, but I quickly regain my rhythm on the other side.

"This is all normal," Pax assures me. "Let us begin."

Pax drags a rubber mallet along the edge of a sound bowl, creating a soothing warbling sound. I'm picturing the vibrations dancing in circles around my skull, moving down my body.

"Ommm." He guides us in the collective breathing exercise. "Say it with me."

I hate the om stuff, but "Ommm," I go.

"Keep your eyes open," Pax says. "Your mind a blank slate."

The room is filling with gray clouds.

"Ommm."

I roll my head to the side, but I can't see my friends through the haze anymore. I can only hear their collective oms, *feel* them reverberating off my ribs.

"Ommm."

How long have we been in here? Minutes? Hours? I've totally lost track of time.

"Now, close your eyes," Pax says, and I do. "Sink into the abyss within. Let the darkness envelop you."

One day, that darkness dug back.

That's what the man at the museum said about Waylon Barlow in the mine.

I'm suddenly picturing myself traversing a dark mine shaft, hurtling faster and faster into its depths.

"Go even deeper inward." Pax's voice resonates along with the singing bowl. "We embark on this journey as a collective support for individual healing. We started together, but you must move forward alone."

I wish that I felt alone in the dark, but I can sense something else. Some*one* else in the mine shaft of my mind.

"I want you to go back to your most profound memory. The deepest wound."

My breaths are longer than I've ever felt. Each inhale a morning, each exhale a night. Every breath a full day, a revolution around the sun.

"Hannah." Pax's voice cuts through the dark. Is he whispering in my ear? "Your fiancé's death was not your fault. You could not save him. You can only save yourself."

The ringing of a new bell breaks the meditative experience with a sharp sound.

My eyes shoot open, my vision suddenly flooded with white light.

I squint until the view comes into focus, looking out at the snowy valley below. I'm standing at the top of a mountain.

Not just any mountain.

I'm not in the sound bath den anymore. I'm back in a memory, *the* memory, observing it all again from the inside.

"Beautiful, isn't it?" Ben's voice by my side.

I turn to face him with a smile. "It's breathtaking. Literally."

I'm still catching my breath from the long trek up the mountain as he tucks his ice axe in his bag and pulls out his camera to snap a photo. We take a seat on a big rock and unclip the sharp crampons from our boots. The snowshoes got us pretty far, but we had to trade them out when the icy incline got too extreme. We don't have peaks like these in Los Angeles, and the highest ones only overlook a city choking on its own smog. Nothing like the snow-dusted evergreens we're miles above now.

"I wanted to bring you here," Ben explains, "because this is the one place on earth that makes me believe that anything is possible. Even when my darkest thoughts dig in, when I'm racked with self-doubt, I can look out at this view and know that it's going to be okay."

There are tears in Ben's eyes as he swallows hard.

"*Are* you?" I ask. "Okay, I mean?"

"Yeah, no." He clears his throat. "Absolutely."

Something is off with his energy. "Hey. I know you. What's going on?"

"The truth is, for a long time, I don't think I *was* okay. I wasn't whole." Ben slides off the rock and gets down on one knee in front of me. My heart leaps into my throat as he pulls a small red jewelry box from his parka pocket. "Until I met you."

"Ben..."

"Hannah..." He opens the box, revealing the blood-red ruby ring. "Will you marry me?"

Tears catch in my eyes and instantly harden in the cold. I can't find the words to respond. Instead, I cough. Then I cough some more.

I try to move my hands, but I'm stuck, spasming atop the mountain.

"Hannah?" Ben asks.

Before I can respond, my body is yanked backward, as if pulled on a string. Away from Ben and that beautiful view, back through the dark mine shaft and out through the other side.

I land back on the floor in the sound bath den, my body still twitching and coughing.

"Hannah?" It's Tess calling my name now, sitting by my side.

"Tess..." My eyes refocus in the room.

Kimi is using a hand fan to push the smoke away until I can finally see everyone clearly, all knelt around me. I feel like Dorothy, returning to her Kansas bedroom.

"There you are." Pax smiles reassuringly. "Welcome back. Kimi? Some water?"

Kimi hands me a cup of water, and I gulp it down as I sit up. Looking around at the group, I notice that everyone has tears in their eyes.

Were they crying for me? Or themselves?

"Did anyone else..." I start.

"Yeah," Tess says. No one else has any words beyond that, but they all nod.

What just happened in this room?

"Pax." Luna turns to the man who just led us through the sound bath. "I've done yoga and meditation every day for years, and I've never had an experience like that. The things you said... How did you know?"

Pax holds Luna's hands in his. "The location of this retreat was not chosen by chance. This is a sacred place. The veil is thin here, far from the clamor of civilization, and the spirits are loud. They speak to me, but I am nothing more than a vessel for their healing messages."

He releases her hands and stands to face everyone. "By the end of this weekend, you will no longer need me as your middleman. You will transcend on your own. This is the power of our process here at Avidya."

Pax must have given each of us our own personalized prompt, but I had only heard my whispered guidance. Everyone looks shaken. Even Jared is rubbing his arms, withdrawn and emotional.

"I'm proud of you, all of you," Pax says. "We've only just scratched the surface of our ignorance. But we must take care not to destroy the structural integrity of our minds as we search for our deepest truth."

Pax helps me to my feet.

"A little afternoon yoga will help get the circulation going. But before then, I recommend you all take some time in the hot springs bath. Refresh your senses. After leaving your bodies for a spell, it's important to come back and reground in the sensory world. Lest we lose ourselves in the ether."

Pax walks away coolly, as if he hasn't just blown every mind in the room.

13

SOAKING IN THE HOT SPRINGS POOL AND LOOKING AROUND at all my wide-eyed friends, I'm reminded of that metaphor about boiling frogs. Toss a frog in boiling water, and it will leap right out. But if you put it in cold water and slowly raise the temperature? The little green guy will stay totally oblivious to the danger and just let itself be cooked to death. Why anyone would want to boil frogs is another question entirely, but here we are. Boiling.

"So," Miles finally says, breaking the silence and pulling me from my amphibious reverie. "That was intense."

I jump at the opportunity to unpack the experience. "What exactly happened to everyone else? What did Pax say to you?"

Miles scratches the back of his head. "He said that the poverty I endured in childhood does not define me. That I need not live in scarcity forever, and it's time to embrace abundance. Then I was back in a memory from when I was a kid. Like, really living through it again. Some classmates caught me dumpster diving after school and locked me in. I was trapped there in the dark overnight."

He shivers despite the warm water.

"Oh, Miles." I put a hand on his shoulder, even though I really want to give him a full-on hug. "I had no idea."

"It's not exactly something I talk about often. In fact, I hadn't thought about that particular memory in years. I buried it. But it felt good to get it out, ya know?"

I relate to the catharsis, even though my memory was the opposite of buried. It's been clawing out of its grave every night for months.

Tess speaks up next. "He told me that my mother abandoning me at such a young age was not my fault. And that my anxious attachments don't serve to make me feel loved. He said that I should build an attachment to my true self instead."

I know Tess well enough to guess which memory she just lived through.

"It was the day she left. She said we were out of milk for the mac and cheese, so she needed to run to the store. I waited and waited, all alone. The water boiled over on the stove. When I checked the fridge, I found a full gallon. But I refused to accept it, refused to call anyone. I waited for days, so sure that she'd come back for me. The neighbors finally called the cops when they smelled the gas."

Tess wipes the tears from her eyes.

Luna nudges Jared. "Tell them, J."

He's anxiously twisting the gold chain around his neck until he finally relents. "Okay, fine. I don't remember every word Pax said like you weirdos do. But he knew that the General...my father...

taught me how to be a real man. With his fists. Pax said that it was time for little Jared to heal."

I never knew Jared was a military brat. That explains how triggered he got by the Marine in the bar.

"I saw the only time I ever fought back." Jared points to the surgical scar on his chest. "The time I almost didn't survive. Fucker broke a rib, punctured a lung." He takes a deep inhale of the hot steam rising off the water. "But I'm still breathing."

Luna sniffles and places a kiss on Jared's cheek. It's not often I get to see the sweetness, the genuine love between these two.

"You're up, babe," Jared says and takes a swig from his flask. "This is the worst drinking game ever, by the way."

Luna takes a moment to compose herself. "Pax told me that my sister's addiction was not my responsibility. He said that trying to fix others will not make me whole."

She's being sincere, but it's hard not to sense a performative edge in Luna's words. Like she's walking the aisles between yoga mats or recording an Instagram Live.

"Then, I was transported. I was back in the hospital with her after her second overdose led to liver failure."

The mention of a hospital reminds me of the vengeful Mr. Fox and Dr. Mohai's warning to lay low. I'm laying as low as I can now as I listen to Luna's story.

"I begged the doctors, 'Please, whatever she needs, just take it from me. Take every organ, drain every last drop of blood and give it to her if it might help her get through this.' They didn't, but she survived. Unfortunately, she didn't stay clean. I just wish I could…"

Luna starts crying, can't go on. Jared wraps his big arms around her and presses his lips to her forehead.

"Hannah?" Tess asks. "What about you?"

I clear my throat, prepping the CliffsNotes. "He said that Ben's death wasn't my fault. And then I was back on the mountain. The day he died."

I know they won't press me for any more specifics than that. They know the story, or at least part of it. A version of it. After all, it was the reason Tess dragged us all out here in the first place.

"Well, what the fuck, Tess?" Jared asks. "Did you give this guy our whole life stories when you signed us up or what?"

"I didn't even know half of these stories, Jared. All I gave him was our names, that's it."

"So, how did he know?" Miles asks.

My instinct is to lean into reason. "I mean, he didn't necessarily *know* the memories, right? He just kind of...prompted them. If you google my name, you'll find plenty of headlines."

The "Hiker Returns without Fiancé" stories plagued me for weeks after I emerged from the wilderness.

"But not the rest of us," Luna says. "He was talking about family dynamics, behind-closed-doors stuff."

"What if he already gave us the answer?" Tess asks. "What if the spirits are communicating with him?"

"Come on," Jared says. "You actually believe that shit?"

"I absolutely believe in the spirit world," Tess says. "I believe there are energies at work beyond what the human mind is capable of understanding."

"Fuck that," Jared says. "I think he drugged us, made us hallucinate. The whole room was filled with smoke."

Luna shakes her head. "That was sage, Jared. Just like the leaves I burn to cleanse your apartment every weekend. You definitely can't get high off it."

"Whatever." Jared takes a swig from his flask. "This place is wack. I say we jump ship. Drive back to town and hit the bar. Manifest some fucking fun. Miles, you bring the Molly? If they're not drugging us, we can at least drug ourselves."

"I mean, yeah, I brought some." Miles throws a furtive glance my way. "Just in case. But I don't think we should mess with it out here. Especially not after that experience. You take it under the wrong conditions, you could slip into serious sensory overload."

"Oh, come on." Jared is about to drink from his flask again when Luna yanks it from his hand and straddles him. She places the flask on the poolside and puts her hands on his cheeks.

"Hey," she says. "I'm glad we're here, doing this together. And I'm so, so proud of you."

I've never seen Jared so vulnerable. He looks like he's going to cry, but he shoves it all back down with a dismissive shrug. "Whatever you say, babe."

I'm still processing the fact that for once, I'm not alone in my hallucinatory experiences. Does this mean my visions of Ben aren't so crazy after all? Are all human beings just vessels for spirits like Pax described? Is my very logical brain really buying these woo-woo thoughts?

Gratefully, Miles interrupts them as he swims up in front of me.

"Be honest. Are you judging me for bringing ecstasy to a wellness retreat?"

"Not judging," I honestly reply, "and I can't say I'm surprised, given your line of work. I'm just trying to square it with the 'all grown up' talk back at the saloon."

"I actually have to stay pretty clearheaded now that DJing parties is a real job. So I save the responsible drug use for very rare special occasions. And I don't know, I guess..." His cheeks go flush, and he floats to my side like a nervous kid who can't look me in the eye. "I guess I had an instinct that there might be something special about this weekend."

His shoulder brushes mine, instant electricity. Now I'm the one blushing, remembering that special night when something almost happened between us. When hands touched hands on the dorm hall floor.

Miles looks into my eyes. "I was worried we lost you back there."

"Yeah. Sorry if I scared you guys."

"It's okay. But I was about ready to dive into your subconscious and fight your demons."

"Oh yeah?"

"Oh yeah." Miles holds up clenched fists. "I'd fuck up Freddy for you."

"You'll fuck up your thumb punching like that." I gently pull his tucked thumb from inside his fist, moving it to the outside. "Now you're ready to rumble."

"Where'd *you* learn to fight?"

"I took a self-defense class last year. Through Groupon."

"Ah, physical *and* financial discipline." Miles bows his head in reverence.

"Damn right. LA's a scary place after dark." I've heard enough horror stories and had a few close calls myself.

"Well, you certainly look like you can handle yourself." Miles winces at his own words. "Okay, that sounded way creepier than I intended."

"A little creepy," I say. "A little cute."

It may just be the hot springs, but I feel a little lightheaded when Miles looks into my eyes.

"He's ready for you," Kimi announces from the side of the pool. She places a stack of towels on the ground. "Please dry off completely before entering the yoga studio."

As Kimi walks away, Jared hops out of the pool and starts drying himself. "Kimi's a real charmer, huh?"

"Jared," Luna says, "don't be ignorant. Native Americans are a very reserved people."

"Luna," Tess says, "don't be ignorant. Indigenous people are not a monolith."

"Oh my God, Tess, I was defending her. You know, there *is* such a thing as being so progressive you're actually oppressive."

Tess steps up to Luna's face. "If you want to feel oppressed, I can—"

"Okay." I step between them. "Let's all take a beat. We've just been through a really trippy experience. But we're here to unwind together. So, can we maybe leave this tension outside before we head into yoga?"

Everyone nods in silent agreement as they finish drying themselves. I don't know how I became the peacemaker here, but I'm mostly just protecting my own peace.

As we walk through the door, I see Kimi standing just inside. She delivers a very cold "Namaste," and I can't help wondering if she heard that entire exchange.

I avoid her gaze, knowing my friends' behavior is not my responsibility.

I'm not here for them. I'm here for me.

I'm ready to be fully embodied.

14

"WELCOME, YOGIS," PAX SAYS AS WE ENTER THE STUDIO. HE'S still wearing the white linen jumpsuit that seems to be his constant uniform, like a ghost who never changes. I wonder how he can always look so clean and smell so fresh while we all look like stinky little desert rats.

"Do we have time to change into proper attire?" Luna asks in her bikini.

"The only proper attire for yoga is the skin you live in," Pax responds. "Help yourself to mats and props."

We all walk to the cubbies in the back of the room where the mats and props are waiting. Luna moves a little faster than the rest of us, rushing back to claim her spot directly in front of Pax's mat. Jared stumbles up and unrolls his mat right next to hers, so close that it's actually touching.

"Space out, babe," she tells him.

He gives an exaggerated sigh and drags his mat across the floor.

I unfurl my mat far away from Jared, not wanting to catch any of that energy. When my bare feet step onto the firm rubber surface, I realize it's been a long time since I've last practiced. I'm feeling a little self-conscious until Pax speaks.

"We'll be doing a very easy flow today. Remember, this is not about doing yoga well or doing it right. It's about finding what feels best for your individual body. Let's start on all fours with some cat cows, shall we?"

Following Pax's instruction, I get down on all fours and start moving my spine, curving up and down in slow movements.

I'm reminded of how I met Ben in a yoga class. He was the only guy in a class full of women, so it was hard to miss him. Before and after every class, everyone fawned over him, including the teacher.

But not me.

I just watched from afar, kept to myself. Still, I did find myself going to that same class at the same time every week. Maybe it was because it worked with my schedule, but it really didn't. I actually had to speed from the hospital through rush-hour traffic every Wednesday to make it in time. So yeah, maybe I went every week just to see him.

One day, as we were grabbing our props, Ben's hand touched mine on a bolster.

"Sorry," he said. "You take it."

"No, it's fine."

"Why don't we share?" he joked. "I'm Ben."

"Hannah."

"Well, Hannah. At the risk of sounding like a total stalker, I have a confession to make."

I felt no threat, no weirdness. Only excitement as he confessed: "I've been coming to this class every week for the last two months just to see you. Truth is, I actually hate this class. It kicks my ass into a sweaty mess until I'm sore for days after. So, will you save my exhausted muscles any more strain and let me know if you'd like to get a coffee with me sometime?"

I was dazzled by him back then, but now, I wish I could go back to that exact moment and warn him. "This doesn't end well for you. If you date me, you will die."

Of course, what I said instead was "Yes. Let's give that body of yours a break."

We spent three hours at the coffee shop getting to know each other and only left because the frustrated barista kicked us out. Ben didn't try to take me home that night, didn't even kiss me. He took his time, shook my hand, and respectfully requested a second date.

That one was a picnic at Echo Park Lake. While Date One was mostly surface level, Date Two unearthed the deeper stuff. The family dynamics and darkest fears. It turned out we had a lot in common. Two black sheep nuzzling closer and closer.

On Date Three, Ben invited me to his place for a home-cooked meal. As soon as the food went into the oven, I jumped his bones and we fucked on the living room floor like eager teenagers. Ben's roommate came home early, nearly catching us ass-naked as we hurried into the bedroom. The dinner never did get eaten; we were only hungry for each other.

The roommate situation became a hassle on both ends, so it didn't take long before we were moving in together. That's how everything was with us—constant forward motion. There was no friction, no questions about what we were doing. It was all so easy, so fluid. We just kept accelerating onward like an express train with no expressed destination. My favorite thing about the relationship was that I didn't have to *think* about the relationship when we were together.

Now that Ben's gone, I think about it every day. Searching my memories for the signs in small moments. Hunting for the red flags I'd somehow missed as we hurtled toward our fateful end.

"Transitioning now into downward dog," Pax announces.

"My favorite position," Jared says, speech slurred.

The whole room seems to be in collective agreement to ignore him.

I push my body back, bending at the hips. It really does feel good to reconnect with my body. I've felt so dissociated lately, and the Xanax probably hasn't been helping with that. Yes, it quells the anxious thoughts, but after one day at the retreat, my buzzing brain is already starting to slow through natural means.

"And flowing into up dog," Pax says.

I move forward, giving me a clear view as Pax approaches Luna. "May I give you an adjustment?"

"Yes, please," she responds.

Pax straddles her back and puts his hands on her hips. "Try to position yourself slightly forward here, and don't be afraid to thrust those hips. Feel the difference?"

Luna groans in response. "Oh yeah. That feels right."

Jared watches the whole time, face going a deeper shade of red. It could be the strenuous exercise, but I suspect it's pure rage.

"Back to plank," Pax says, "and up now to warrior one."

Jared attempts the transition but stumbles off his mat with a "Fuck."

Miles shakes his head. "Maybe lay off the flask, Jared."

"Maybe lay off my dick, Miles." Ever creative with the phallic comebacks.

"It's okay to lose your balance," Pax assures him. "That's all part of the practice, and there's no need to be embarrassed."

"I'm not embarrassed," Jared says. "I bench one eighty, bro." He tries to get back into the pose, but his arms start flailing.

"Our impulse is to flap our arms wildly when trying to regain balance," Pax observes, "but the chaotic movement only serves to throw us further off axis."

"Thanks for the tip, Paxman." Not a hint of gratitude in Jared's voice. "No hands-on adjustments for me?"

"Would you like an adjustment?"

"No. I'd like you to keep your hands to yourself."

"Jared." Luna's tone is as firm as her visible abs.

"Verbal adjustments it is," Pax says. "Moving now into long-legged forward fold."

I drop my upper body forward, but I feel compelled to crane my neck up to watch the shitshow unfolding at the front of the class.

Pax comes up behind Luna for another adjustment, draping his body over her back. "Make sure to keep your back straight even as you bend forward."

"Okay." Jared jumps off his mat. "That's enough of that."

He charges toward Pax like a bull, throwing a clumsy fist. Pax deftly dodges the swing, and Jared tumbles to the floor.

"As I said," Pax says, "chaotic movement."

Jared jumps up again, but Luna steps in front of him. "What are you doing, Jared?"

"What is *he* doing?"

I can feel my blood boiling at this agro-male bullshit. The petty jealousy is only masking a deep insecurity, but it's all toxic in the end. Violent. Luna isn't the most stable person in the world, but she can absolutely do better than the macho idiot she's been glued at the hip to for seven years.

Pax looks Jared in the eye. "Is this stirring up some emotions for you, Jared?"

"Yeah. It's stirring up some fucking rage."

"Good. That rage is exactly what we need to purge from your system before it consumes you whole."

"Oh, you wanna purge? Let's purge." Jared takes another threatening step toward Pax, but Luna shoves him back.

"Stop!"

I can't hold back anymore either. "Jared, do you really have to ruin this for everyone?"

"Hey, I didn't ask to come to this fucking place."

"Great. You don't want to be here, and nobody wants you here, so why don't you just take a fucking walk?"

"But I'm not the one—"

"Go!" I shout, pointing to the door.

Jared looks around at the rest of the group, who stand in silent agreement. I hold my cold glare on him.

"Fuck this." Jared storms out of the yoga studio like a child throwing a temper tantrum.

Luna's face is flush. "Pax, I am so sorry."

"Such base aggression poses no threat to me," he says. "I think the meditation session was an emotional shock to his system."

"I'll go get him." She moves toward the door.

"No." Pax puts a hand on Luna's shoulder. "Let him have his own experience. You are all entitled to your own. But I sense that tensions are high now, so why don't we dial it back? We'll engage in restorative yin yoga for the rest of our session. Please flow into extended child's pose. I'll join you for this final release."

This sounds like a great idea as I watch Pax get down into the pose.

I spread my knees wide and rest my forehead on the rubber mat. Breathing deeply, I force my eyes closed.

"Get comfortable," Pax says. "We're going to stay in this pose for a long…long time."

He starts humming a peaceful tune.

It's a soothing sound, hypnotic, but I'm buzzed on my own anger now.

If Jared keeps up his bullshit, he's going to ruin this weekend. I finally feel like I'm healing, like something is shifting inside me.

Unblocking. Releasing.

I don't want it to end now.

I squeeze my eyes tight, wishing Jared would go the fuck away for good.

15

JARED STORMS OUT OF THE YOGA STUDIO, ADRENALINE peaking in his blood. If this stupid place had a weight room, he could go put in a solid set to break through all the tension. That always helps calm him down when he gets too worked up. Pump through the pain. But he's trapped in the middle of the fucking desert with no kettlebells in sight, so the sauna will have to do.

He opens the hatch door and climbs inside the big wooden drum. It's kinda claustrophobic in here. Pulling the clunky metal valve allows the steam to start flowing inside from the hot springs, filling the barrel pretty damn quickly.

Shit. The vent.

He pulls the sliding wooden panel, about the size of a mail slot, creating an escape route for all that steam to slowly filter out. Taking a seat on the wooden bench, he sucks in hot air.

Taking slow, deep breaths. Thinking about his actions.

Jared is being an asshole, and he knows it. He needs to apologize to everyone, especially Luna. Hannah, not so much. He still feels weird about what happened out there in NorCal. Ben was a good dude. They had a few guys' nights together, got wasted and vented about their women. Even hit the weights once or twice. Dude was strong, and it was nice to have a guy to talk to about all that relationship stuff. So it really sucked when he died. Not to mention the fact that Hannah's story of what happened out there seemed pretty sketch.

But Jared doesn't care about Hannah. He cares about Luna.

He just gets so scared sometimes. Scared that she's finally going to wake up, realize she's wasted seven years of her life with him and leave. If she does, it probably *will* be for some spiritual guru like Pax. Someone who's into the same shit she is. Someone who's the total opposite of Jared.

Who is Jared anyway?

Just a sad little army brat who felt neglected by his daddy. He got a reputation in high school as the prankster because he loved the attention, was starved for it. That identity followed him into college, where he suffered through fraternity hazing rituals without batting an eye. The General had done worse. Jared just couldn't wait to get on the other side to engineer some pain himself. When he was frat president, his punishments became notorious, putting those freshmen maggots through hell. Recycling the abuse his father had taught him, had *shown* him. Instilled in him.

The truth is, Jared plays dumb because it's easier than admitting the truth. He knows at his core that he's just an insecure people pleaser. He wants everybody to love him, even if everything he does makes them hate him. It's better than not getting any attention at all.

He *is* really good at his job, though. Taking high-powered executives out on the town, all the cocktail bars and strip clubs, securing big deals in the coke-fueled midnight hours. But even *he's* getting sick of his own shit by now. At twenty-six years old, how much longer can he keep going like this? Isn't it time to grow the fuck up?

Maybe this retreat really is providing him with an opportunity. A chance to stop and reflect on who he is and who he wants to be. A chance to change, to be a better man who feels deserving of Luna's love. Then he might not be so fucking jealous all the time.

At the very least, he knows he doesn't want to be like his father. He doesn't want to get drunk and fight with anyone who looks at him sideways. But that's exactly how he's been acting this weekend. His fraternity brothers would've cheered on his bullshit, but Miles, Hannah, Luna? They're real friends. They call him out when he needs it because they really care, and he doesn't want to ruin the experience for them this weekend.

Whoa. That was a whole lot of thinking.

Jared comes back to earth in the sauna and takes a deep, cleansing breath.

This was a good idea. The steam helps clear his mind and relax his muscles, even better than a bench press would have. After a solid sweat sesh, he'll come out of this barrel a new man.

He'll stop being such a dick, embrace this retreat and have fun with his friends. Not the kind of fun he's been whining about (because he really does want to cut back on the drinking) but the kind that comes from genuine connection. It's all here at Avidya, and he's hungry for it.

Damn, the steam is getting intense.

Jared looks up and sees that the sliding vent is closed.

He's sure he opened it, but maybe his drunk brain is confused?

He rises from the bench and pulls the slider open, taking a deep breath of fresh air through the square opening. Lowering back onto the bench, he feels good. Confident. Things are going to be diff—

THWAP.

The sliding vent snaps closed.

What the fuck? Could that have been the wind?

No, there isn't any wind out here in the desert. He stands again and pulls the vent open, staring out at the mountain landscape.

THWAP.

The slider slams shut in his face.

This isn't wind. Someone is out there.

"Okay, very funny. Is that you, Miles?"

Jared deserves to be fucked with, but the claustrophobia is really setting in now. He tries to open the vent again, but it's stuck closed from the outside. He coughs, steam filling the room.

"Not cool, man."

Jared reaches for the steam valve and pulls it shut, but it's a little too late for that. The barrel is filled with steam that has no escape. The only place it has left to go is into Jared's lungs as his breath quickens.

"Fuck. This isn't funny, guys!"

He tries to open the sauna door, but the latch won't budge. Someone is blocking it from the other side.

"Let me out of here!" he screams. Jared is all for a good hazing, but this is quickly moving beyond a little prank. He's starting to go dizzy as he shoulders the door, but every movement is making him more tired. He stumbles over to the slider and starts punching it, trying to bust through the wood by pure force.

The slider suddenly snaps open with a *THWAP*.

Jared catches a glimpse of a face out there through the steam. Oh, shit. Is that the Marine from the bar? The fucker ducks out of sight too quickly to be sure.

Jared pushes his mouth to the slot, gasping for fresh air.

He pulls in just enough breath to start threatening. "When I get out of here, I'm gonna—"

His words are cut short when something is shoved into his open mouth. A wriggling lump, rough like sandpaper scraping the inside of his cheeks. He hears the rattling tail before he feels two sharp fangs sink into his tongue.

Jared falls backward against the bench seat, pulls the rattlesnake from his face, and tosses it across the wooden barrel.

He stumbles for the door, hearing the angered *hisssss* following on the floor close behind.

"Help!"

Banging against the door with balled-up fists, his strength is quickly sapping. He feels frail as his tongue swells up inside his mouth.

"Pleath! Howp!"

Those fangs sink into his leg now, piercing the flesh of his calf.

Jared falls to the floor, the worst place to be because the snake bites into his neck. He grabs it by the tail and pulls, but the squirmy fucker takes a chunk of flesh with it before he slams it against the wall. A satisfying crack tells him that he's killed the damn thing, but he isn't out of the woods yet.

He can actually feel the venom coursing through his veins. Like that time his lifting partner convinced him to try steroids. Just that one time, despite what everybody thinks. Only instead of amping him up like the 'roids did, the venom is draining him, making his eyes flutter. He can barely breathe now, but salvation suddenly comes.

The sauna door cracks open, a line of white light bursting through.

The steam floods out, and Jared follows, crawling across the wooden floor, out of this barrel of death. Fresh air never tasted so good as he tumbles to the ground.

He pulls himself across the stone pavers, trying to cry for help, but his throat is swelling up behind his thick tongue. Only raspy breaths can squeak through.

Jared's just about given up when he feels two hands hook under his armpits, lifting his body.

Thank God. Someone is here. Someone is helping him, pulling him away from the sauna. Maybe it really was a prank gone too far, but it's over now, and they'll get him the help he needs.

But why are they dragging him toward the hot springs?

"No" is all he manages to squeeze out before his whole upper body gets dropped into the pool.

His arms and legs flail wildly, but Jared can't break free of the grip that's now pressing him under. Fingers clench his head, keeping his face below the surface. Forced to chug salty hot water, he can't help thinking *this* is the worst drinking game ever.

He tries to scream, but the scalding liquid just fills his lungs, searing him from the inside out.

When the bright light comes in those final moments and his whole world turns to fire, he feels something like enlightenment. There's only one thought left, one dying wish as Jared's soul leaves his blistered body behind.

He hopes he'll see his father in hell.

16

"I THINK THAT WILL CONCLUDE OUR PRACTICE FOR TODAY." Pax's words stir me back to consciousness.

Had I actually fallen asleep in child's pose? There were no dreams or nightmares during that very intense nap. Just another enveloping blackness that I'm still shaking from my vision, feeling a little hungover.

I sit up and look around the room as everyone else stretches their way out of the pose, too. Rubbing my strained arms, I can't believe a few easy vinyasas were enough to make my muscles scream. But it's the good kind of pain. By the end of this weekend, I'll be back in a consistent practice.

Luna bows toward Pax. "Namaste. I better go find Jared."

"Give him my warmest regards," Pax replies with the first hint of sarcasm I've heard from the man.

Miles squeezes his legs together as he hurries out the door after her. "Yeah, I've gotta...go."

"Yes, expel the toxins that we've brought to the surface," Pax calls after him.

I'm rolling up my mat when Pax approaches. "How do you feel, Hannah?"

"Honestly? A bit sore, but definitely rejuvenated, too." My skin feels inflamed, sweat dripping down my back. "And warm, very warm. I've done hot yoga before, but the desert heat out here is intense."

"It's sad, isn't it? Civilization tries so hard to recreate what is already offered by nature. Meanwhile, the machinery used to heat those yoga rooms is polluting the very nature it's trying to emulate."

I nod, which sends sweat dripping into my eyes for a startling sting. "I don't usually sweat this much."

"That's a good sign," Pax says. "You're rinsing your pores while improving your circulation. That red glow means a healthy blood flow is returning to your body." He lifts a palm toward the side of my face, hovering an inch away, as if cradling my aura. Heat emanates like a furnace off his glistening skin. "I'm happy to see it."

Tess hovers over my shoulder. "Thanks for a great flow, Pax."

"You provided the flow. I was merely a guide. Until dinner." Pax bows and leaves.

Tess turns to me. "Okay, so he's a bit weird."

"A bit, yeah."

"But toilet snakes aside, this place is pretty great, right?"

"You were right," I say. "It's exactly what I needed."

Tess pushes her ear forward. "Sorry, one more time?"

"You were right, Tess. You are always right, and you always know exactly what I need."

"That's right."

She hugs me, and I tolerate the physical affection for as long as I can, which isn't very long. "Okay, sweaty-sweaty!"

"Not letting go!" Her arms squeeze tighter. "Never letting go!"

I squirm out of Tess's grip with a laugh. "No showers at this place, huh?"

"Wanna dip back into the hot springs with me?" she asks.

"Nah, I'm gonna take a little breather before dinner. See you then."

I step outside just as the sun is setting behind the mountains. Almost like it was waiting for me to bear witness. Time passes so quickly out here with the night falling hard on the heels of dead daylight. But I don't mind. I walk barefoot back to my yurt, letting the sand slip between my toes, thinking about how every grain is made up of the same atoms, the same energy that I am.

Pax's oneness talk isn't all bullshit, really. It's scientifically sound. I've just never felt so grounded, so connected to everything.

I've never felt so at home.

By the time we all regroup for dinner, I'm absolutely voracious. I can't believe how quickly I've acclimated to eating raw food, but I'm shoveling seeds and greens into my face before anyone else even gets to the table. Feeding my insatiable hunger, I feel strong and full of untold energy.

Pax settles down across from me with an approving nod. "It's important to refuel after the energy we expended today."

Miles lowers into a seat beside me. "God, I would kill for a cheeseburger."

"You should," Pax says. "If you wish to consume the flesh of another being, you should participate in every step of the process. From execution to gutting and stripping the—"

"Second thought," Miles interrupts, "I'm good with granola." He pops a handful into his mouth.

Luna is rubbing her arms as she approaches. "Have you guys seen Jared?"

I sure haven't, and the silence in his absence has already been such a relief.

Tess cranes her neck up from the table. "He's got to be moping around here somewhere."

Luna shakes her head. "I thought maybe he went for a walk to cool off, but he's still not back yet. I looked everywhere."

A thought pops into my head. No, that would be low, even for Jared. Still... "You don't think he would've..."

I don't even finish my sentence before everyone is on their feet, heading through the main hall toward the entrance of the retreat. Passing under the big stone arch, we all discover that my suspicion is *not* in fact too low for Jared.

The Range Rover is gone.

"Are you serious, man?" Miles kicks at the tire marks.

"He ditched us," Tess says.

Pax exhales deeply. "Perhaps I pushed him too hard too soon."

"No," Luna says, touching his shoulder. "This is not your fault, Pax."

Pax puts his hand on top of Luna's, and I can't help wondering if Jared's jealousy was valid. Is something going on between these two?

Luna turns back to the group. "Jared's just trying to teach me a lesson, guys. This is what he does. Disappears for a night and then comes crawling back the next day. He's probably getting wasted at the saloon, just like he said. But he'll be back in the morning. Trust me."

"Or he won't," Pax says.

"Why would you say that?" I ask.

Pax holds his palms together and starts his sermon. "The reality of enlightenment is that some people are simply not ready to fully open themselves. To transcend. If the rest of us remain attached to those who are stubbornly earthbound, they will act as stones, weighing us down. Sinking us into their own depths of despair. Then we will never reach the heights that we are destined to achieve for ourselves."

"That's all well and good," Miles says, "but this whole situation raises a really important question. What if something happens while we're out here? I mean, what do we do in case of an emergency? There's no phone or any way of contacting the outside world?"

"I do keep a satellite phone in my yurt, in case of an absolute emergency." Even mentioning technology seems to leave a bad taste on Pax's tongue, like a poison he's eager to spit out. "But I assure you, it won't come to that. You're all very safe here."

A sudden wind blows, causing the torches to flicker around us.

"We have a rather arduous journey ahead of us tomorrow. I suggest we all get some rest. If Luna is right, then we'll be seeing Jared bright and early."

As we all walk back into the retreat toward our yurts, I overhear Pax speaking softly to Luna.

"I hope you'll remember your intention, Luna. To achieve new levels of flexibility. Perhaps Jared's departure is giving you that opportunity to stretch toward new goals, without him."

"Maybe you're right." Luna smiles at Pax. "Thanks, Pax."

Honestly, Pax *is* right. Luna's better off without Jared. We all are.

A wet sloshing sound draws my attention to the hot springs as I pass. Kimi is mopping up water that's been splashed all over the ground next to the pool.

"What happened here?" I ask.

"Looks like your friend made quite a mess before he left us," Kimi responds.

"I'm sorry. He's a mess of a man. Feel free to let him have it when he gets back."

Kimi suppresses a scoff. "I won't hold my breath."

That's when it occurs to me. "Hey, didn't you have his car keys?"

Kimi drains the mop head in the bucket with a hard squeeze before answering. "Your mess of a man must have stolen them from my yurt."

"Right." I resist the urge to clarify that he's not *my* man, opting instead for a "Good night, Kimi."

"Sweet dreams," she replies.

A shiver ripples through me as the temperature drops steeply, and I enter my slightly warmer yurt through the animal skin flap door. It wouldn't have been hard for Jared to break into Kimi's equally secure yurt, but something still feels off about him leaving so suddenly.

Even stranger is the guilt I feel about it.

Had I somehow used the power of intention to manifest Jared's untimely departure?

It's a ridiculous thought, and I dismiss it as quickly as it came. Maybe Pax's schtick is rubbing off on me a little too easily.

Either way, I don't want to waste another thought on Jared. He's already drained enough energy from this experience, and I just want to focus on moving forward.

I feel a sudden urge to shed my clothes like a snake shedding its skin, to be au naturel beneath my wool blanket.

I'm praying that my yoga nap didn't ruin my sleep, and it doesn't.

The darkness welcomes me back like an old friend, all bundled up in sheep's clothing.

17

AN EARTHY FRAGRANCE WAFTS INTO MY YURT, AWAKENING me the next morning. I come outside to find Kimi mixing something in a big cauldron over a fire as the others begin to gather.

"Welcome to another glorious day at Avidya," Pax announces. "While most of our work is done here at the retreat, it's time now to leave behind even these small comforts. Today, we will be taking a pilgrimage into the wilderness. We'll hike through the day and spend the night on the earth beneath the stars."

After yesterday's restorative yoga, my body feels ready for more physical movement. I'm just glad I packed my hiking boots.

"Where are we hiking to?" Miles asks.

"You will see when we get there," Pax responds, ever cryptic. "But it's not about the destination. It's about the journey."

The guru is full of clichés, but that was a really bad one. Like, Doctor Grady level. I'm actually looking forward to unpacking this whole experience with him when I get back, showing him how much I've healed.

"It's ready," Kimi says. She scoops the mixture from the cauldron into clay mugs and starts distributing them.

"Very good." Pax turns to the group. "Kimi is a member of the Chemehuevi Indian tribe. Her ancestors were hunter-gatherers."

I swear I see Kimi's eyes roll at Pax's words as she hands me a mug. It must be pretty painful for her, hearing this white guru give a history lesson about *her* ancestors.

"They were survivors who thrived on this very land," Pax continues, "long before the names of Joshua Tree or 29 Palms were established."

"Are," Kimi corrects him.

"I'm sorry?"

"We *are* survivors. You haven't gotten rid of us yet."

"Of course. My apologies." Pax's face goes flush at the error. "When one endeavors to exist beyond time and space, the past and present tenses are sometimes blurred."

Kimi ignores the excuse and takes control of the narrative. "The Chemehuevi cultivated this land with the Serrano for years in the Oasis of Mara until the prospectors invaded and pillaged it."

I suddenly remember the Chemehuevi Indian Burial Ground I saw before I dipped into the mining museum. Two stark histories resting side by side with no one there to contextualize the conflict between them. Now I understand why Kimi might be harboring some resentment toward Pax, toward this whole town. But then why would she be working here, for him, if that were the case?

"In honor of this history," Pax says, "I will be taking a humble step back in leadership today and passing the reins to Kimi. She will be our shaman for the spirit journey ahead."

Pax takes a literal step back as Kimi rises behind the cauldron.

"We won't be serving breakfast this morning," she says. "It's important to drink this on an empty stomach."

Miles sniffs the mug, filled with twigs and leaves and hot water that's turned dark brown. "Oh, shit. Is this ayahuasca?"

Kimi shakes her head. "The ayahuasca plant is indigenous to South America."

"Right, of course," Miles says. "Peyote then?"

"This is a mix of local plants and herbs," Kimi says. "But if you're asking if it's psychoactive, then yes. Prepare for a trip."

"Speaking of which," Pax says, "I'm afraid I must ask you all to sign a waiver." He passes around pieces of parchment with fountain pens. "It relays your consent to engage in therapeutic treatment with organic hallucinogens."

Tess looks at the waiver. "Legal waiver doesn't really mesh well with the whole 'beyond civilization' vibes, huh?"

"A tacky necessity, I admit," Pax says. "But you might think of it less as a legal document and more as a written intention. Sign your name and commit to the journey ahead."

I've always been wary of hallucinogens, especially after seeing plenty of shroom-headed college kids trip their way into the ER on the verge of mental breakdowns. But that was way different from what's being offered here: a controlled experience with a trusted guide.

Still, given my recent spate of nightmares and blurred realities, this might be a really terrible idea.

Then again, I have felt a lot more grounded since arriving at the retreat, so maybe I need to keep trusting the process. Maybe a drug-induced spiritual experience will help flush out the rest of these haunted memories and visions, leaving me cleansed and free.

Either that, or it will bring them flooding back with a vengeance.

What would Dr. Grady say? He'd probably advise against it, especially since I just quit the Xanax cold turkey rather than slowly detoxing like he suggested. But my psychiatrist isn't here, and I can decide for myself.

"Hey." Tess interrupts my internal debate. "You know you don't have to do this part, right?"

"I know." Something about Tess's words only makes me want to do it more, so I quickly sign the waiver. "But this is what we're here for, right?"

"This is what we're here for," Tess agrees, signing the waiver, too.

Miles doesn't hesitate to sign his. "I'm so ready for this."

"Do you think we could wait for Jared to get back?" Luna asks. "This is exactly the kind of fun he was looking for, and I just know he would love it."

"Is he still not back?" I ask, not wanting to sound too excited about it. I can only imagine how much more annoying Jared would be while tripping on hallucinogens. He'd just ruin the experience for everyone else, like he did in yoga.

"No," Luna responds. "I'm sure he's just sleeping off his hangover at a motel or something. But he'll probably be driving back here soon, and I don't want him to come back to an empty retreat."

"I'm sorry, Luna," Pax says. "But the elixir has already been brewed, and there is no time like the present. Why don't you leave him a note and let him know we'll be back by sunrise tomorrow?"

"Okay." Luna deflates as she uses a spare sheet of parchment to write out her note.

"Your handwriting is impeccable," Pax observes. "There is a real power and confidence in your curves."

"Thank you," Luna says, blushing. "I write all the sale tags at the yoga studio."

"I only wish that I could steal you away to serve here at Avidya."

"Don't tempt me, Pax." Luna grins back coquettishly.

One minute Luna's frowning over her missing boyfriend, the next she's fawning over her gray-haired guru. Maybe this is all part of her and Jared's jealous little games. When Jared finally does return from the lesson he's trying to teach her, Luna will have another one waiting for him. A lesson in the shape of Pax's linen-clad arms wrapped around her.

Either way, I'm not going to waste any more energy trying to figure it out.

"Let us all lift our elixirs," Pax says, taking center stage once again, "and toast to transcendence."

We all clink mugs and down our drinks. I nearly vomit from the taste, bitter and earthy with all the textures of mud and sticks.

"The elixir should peak once we arrive at our destination," Kimi explains. "The walk will accelerate the process and keep you grounded in your bodies. Make sure to drink lots of water." She distributes animal skin canteens to everyone. "We'll be providing food, but you'll want to pack clothes for a cold night. We leave in ten minutes."

I head into my yurt to gather my things. I haven't been on a real hike in ages, and as cheesy as a spirit journey sounds, I think it might be fun. I pack my backpack just like Ben taught me. Soft items on the bottom, heavy items in the middle, hugging the spine. Easy access to important items, like maps, on top.

Of course, I don't have a map for this journey into the unknown.

On my way out of the yurt, I notice a spiderweb in the corner. Stepping a little closer, I see that something is already caught and wrapped up like a Christmas present, but the predator is nowhere in sight. I consider clearing the web, but Ben always taught me not to mess with nature.

When you mess with nature, nature messes back.

I leave the web as it is, letting the universe take its primal course.

18

AS WE TREK THROUGH THE DESERT, THE RETREAT FADES INTO the horizon line behind us. Kimi leads the way while Pax brings up the rear, keeping us all fenced in like cattle. We're in the middle of nowhere, surrounded by vast stretches of sand, but a strange claustrophobia settles in over my shoulders.

Luna, on the other hand, is chipper as ever. "This reminds me of a yoga retreat that I went to in Abu Dhabi."

"Because sand?" I ask, increasingly impatient with her desperate flexes.

"Never mind," she responds. "You had to be there."

Luna just has to be everywhere, a jet-setter fueled by Mommy's credit card. I envy the generational wealth that keeps her afloat, along with the flexible work schedule. Only people of a certain class can afford to pay for yoga teacher training in the hopes of competing for paltry part-time teaching gigs. The whole scene reeks of privilege.

Of course, Luna doesn't have to rely on her family's money

anymore now that she has Jared, the successful advertising bro. Or at least she used to.

I catch myself on the odd thought.

She used to?

Why would I think that way? Jared will come back, of course. The heat is just getting to me.

Miles takes a deep swig from his water bottle. "How much longer?"

"We're almost there," Kimi assures us.

Miles turns to me. "How you feeling?"

"A bit...off?"

"Yeah. Same."

It's hard to tell if the drugs are kicking in or if we're just on the verge of heatstroke. Or both. We're closing in on a field of giant boulders, moving through the mazelike structure until we emerge into a clearing at the center.

"This is where we'll set up camp," Kimi announces.

I look around at the Stonehenge-like circle of tall, thin rocks as we drop our bags. "Are these natural formations?"

"Very much so," Pax affirms. "But that doesn't mean they aren't intentional. Some believe this location to be an energy vortex. A sacred place where the forces flowing in and out of the earth are so powerful, our limited human perception might call it *super*natural."

Tess's eyes are aglow as she puts her hand on one of the stone structures. "I can feel it vibrating."

"Elixir's probably kicking in," Kimi says.

I'm definitely starting to feel it now, seeing the sturdy rocks go a bit wobbly.

"Kimi and I will set up camp," Pax tells the group. "In the meantime, the best way to experience a true spirit journey is to go off alone into the wild. Connect with the land. Open yourself to whatever it has to offer you. Isn't that right, Kimi?"

"Sure." Kimi nods absently as she starts to build a fire pit.

Pax really can't help grabbing the microphone. "The goal," he explains, "is to find your spirit guide. Your primal mentor."

"And what, exactly, does that look like?" Miles asks. "A talking coyote?"

"Your guide is personal to you," Pax says. "It will take the shape of whatever you need most to carry you toward the next stage of your growth."

I turn to Tess. "Is this the kind of true spiritual experience you were hoping for?"

"Fuck yeah, it is. You feel it, right? This place is powerful."

I rub my arms as I look around at the towering stones. Tess must sense my unease because she takes my hand.

"Hey. We don't have to fly solo out here. We can stick together if that would feel better."

"No." Her clingy reassurances are starting to wear on me. "You don't have to hold my hand through this whole retreat." I pull my hand away, then try to soften the blow. "I mean, you should have the experience you came here for. Go. Find your spirit guide."

"Right. Well. See you on the other side, I guess." Tess has a strange look in her eye, and I wonder if I've hurt her feelings as she slips into the space between two round boulders.

Everyone goes off alone in different directions, so I do the same.

Time moves like molasses, and my vision is just as goopy, everything blurring and wiggling at the edges. I'm not sure how long I've been out here before I come across a large opening in the rocks.

Not just an opening but a gaping black hole.

The entrance to a cave?

"Hello!" I call, and the word echoes back.

As I creep inside, the cold air clings to my skin. I trip over something in the dirt, catching myself on the cave wall so I don't fall flat on my face.

It's hard to see in the dark, but I crouch down and touch cold iron.

Train tracks?

No. Minecart tracks.

I've found one of the hundreds of old mines the old man at the museum mentioned.

"Haaannaaah..."

The voice in the dark is barely a whisper.

Ben's voice? I can't tell, but I freeze and listen for...

Tiny squeaks above my head.

When I crane my neck back, a swarm of leathery wings descends and flaps around me.

Bats.

I rush back toward the light, birthing myself out of the mine and back into the sunshine. Dropping to the dirt, I curl into a duck-and-cover pose as the winged rodents screech and flap over my head. I wait until the sound dies down to peek through my fingers. Not a trace of the bats against the blue sky. Because they all flew away, right? Not because I imagined them?

I'm starting to regret drinking that elixir when I see something in the dirt that I'd missed on the way in. An old plank of wood. Lifting it to eye level, I wipe the dust and read the words that are roughly carved into it.

DEAD MAN'S DUE

This isn't just any mine.

This is Waylon Barlow's mine.

Screeeeeeeeeeek.

A new sound comes from the mineshaft now as the old man's rhyme returns in my head.

"*In the dark of Dead Man's Due...*"

Screeeeeeeeeeek.

Not animal or human, but metal scraping on metal. Growing louder until a shadowy figure bleeds out of the darkness.

"*Waylon Barlow waits for you...*"

The miner wears old suspenders and a big old hat, just like the mannequin in the museum.

"*He'll hack you up without a trace...*"

Dragging a pickaxe along the minecart track, moving toward me.

Screeeeeeeeeeek.

When he gets close enough, I can see his face clearly. But it isn't his face.

"*Pick your bones and steal your face...*"

He's wearing the bloodied skin of another person over his own.

No way is this really happening. This is just a hallucination, triggered by the drugs.

No way is Waylon Barlow lurching out of the mine toward me right now.

I squeeze my eyes tight, wishing it away.

Screeeee—

The sound suddenly stops. Did it work?

I exhale and open my eyes, only to see Waylon Barlow swiping his pickaxe sideways at me. As I throw my hands up to shield my face, the sharp iron point slices across my forearm, sending me stumbling back.

Blood drips down into the dirt as I clutch my arm and realize...

This is really happening.

I don't have the breath to scream, but I turn and run. Scrambling up a large rock, I feel my fingernails scrape against stone as I pull myself up and away. At this height, I have a view of the vast boulder field and the desert beyond, but I can't see camp anymore.

Had I already wandered that far?

Barlow crawls up behind me, and I scream, backing away from him. My foot almost slips off the edge of the rock.

I turn and realize I'm trapped up here. Unless I jump.

The cold iron swipes inches away from my back as I leap across the gap. My chest slams on the edge of the boulder across the way as my fingers drag against the sandpaper surface. I barely manage to pull myself up, scraping my legs as I scramble over the top of it, then down the other side.

I start running through the boulder field, a maze of orange rocks. "Help!" I scream.

Barlow ducks out from behind a rock up ahead. I skid to a stop in the sand, swiveling back and running in another direction. He stays close, breathing heavily through his flesh mask. I can hear the pickaxe *clink*ing and *clank*ing off the walls of stone.

Taking a hairpin turn at a crossroads, I find a small space beneath a boulder overhang, and I duck and roll beneath it. Hiding like a scorpion in its hovel, I hold my breath as I wait, listening.

Those old boots step through the sand around me, then move out of sight.

I slide out from under the rock and dash through the maze, screaming over and over again, praying this is just another nightmare that I'll soon wake up from. It feels like the stone walls are closing in, like I'll never escape as I dart around a sharp corner and slam into a body.

A helpless "No!" erupts from my throat.

"Hannah?" But it's not Barlow I've run into. It's Miles. "Are you okay?"

He looks at the blood dripping down my arm, and I can't find the words as I collapse against his chest. Miles takes off his plaid shirt and drapes it over my shoulders, holding me close.

"It's okay," he whispers. "You're safe. It's me."

19

I'M STILL SHELL-SHOCKED AS I SIT BESIDE THE CAMPFIRE with the rest of the group huddled around me. Kimi pushes the logs around, sending embers into the night.

"Stay close to the flames," she says.

Tess shakes her head. "I think we should head back to the retreat. I mean, this feels like an emergency situation, right?"

"It's not safe to travel in the dark," Kimi says. "We'll leave at first light."

Pax stands on the other side of the fire. "I'm deeply sorry this happened to you, Hannah. Kimi should have warned everyone just how intense the hallucinations can be. But it's all perfectly normal, isn't it, Kimi?"

Before Kimi can answer, I speak up. "It wasn't a hallucination. I was attacked."

I show them the gash on my arm that I'd been hiding under Miles's shirt.

Tess lets out an "Oh my God" at the sight.

"We need to treat that," Kimi says. She opens up a medical pouch and crouches down beside me. "What caused this?"

"A pickaxe," I say. "An old one."

Kimi cocks her head. "Somebody attacked you with a pickaxe?"

"Sweetie," Luna says, voice dripping with false sympathy, "you've got scrapes all over you, probably from scrambling up and down those rocks. Are you sure that's not what caused it?"

"How do you know I was scrambling up and down the rocks?" I ask the two-faced yogi.

"I said 'probably.' And you don't have to attack me for asking a reasonable question," she says, dodging *my* reasonable question and diving straight into her own victimhood.

Kimi cuts open a piece of aloe plant and squeezes the cold goop on my wound. "This will help with pain and inflammation, but you should get a tetanus shot as soon as possible."

"I'm up-to-date on all my shots," I say. "But I appreciate you, Kimi."

"So, this person who attacked you," Miles says, gratefully validating my story. "What did they look like?"

I'm tempted to say his name, but they'll probably all think I'm crazy. Still, I can at least give a description. "They were dressed like an old miner. Overalls and a wide-brimmed hat."

"Did you get a look at their face?" Pax asks.

"Yes, but..." and here comes the craziest part, "they were wearing somebody else's."

Miles blinks hard. "They were wearing somebody else's...face?"

"I'm sorry," Luna says. "But that sounds like a bad horror movie. I mean, what is this, *The California Pickaxe Massacre?*"

"I found a mine entrance, Dead Man's Due." I'm finally ready to name the devil who attacked me. "I think maybe it was—"

"'Waylon Barlow waits for you.'" Kimi quotes the rhyme as she finishes wrapping my arm.

"You know the story?" I ask.

"Everybody in 29 Palms knows the legend of Waylon Barlow." She stokes the flames again.

Tess shrugs. "Okay, well, some of us are in the dark here, so would you mind sharing with the class, Kimi?"

Kimi leans back against a rock. "Hannah seems to know it."

"The man at the museum only told me the start. Some mean bank robbers dug a gold mine?"

"Mean's a nice way of putting it. They were fucking animals." The F-bomb startles everyone as Kimi continues. "They struck gold but got greedy. Dug too deep."

"And what, dug straight to hell?" Miles asks.

"Some folks think so, yeah. There was a cave-in. Somebody tied a fuse too short, the dynamite blew too quick, and all five members of the Barlow Gang got trapped inside."

I look around at my friends. Five of us came to this retreat together. Now we're down to four.

"Those men were in there for weeks before anybody knew. Before a team finally cleared the rubble to rescue them. Only, there wasn't much left to rescue. Just Waylon Barlow and four human skeletons, gnawed to the bone."

"Oh God." Luna clutches her stomach. "He *ate* them?"

Kimi nods. "Kept the face of his last kill, though. He was wearing it when the rescuers showed up. Barlow was out of his damn mind, totally dissociated. Told them to leave him alone with his gold. They tried to help, but he came at them, swinging that pickaxe. Protecting his treasure. He took one man out before they finally shot the crazy bastard, sending him tumbling back down the mine shaft. Never to be seen again. Legend has it he haunts this land now. Hunting down any prospectors who come for his gold."

"Well, that's fucked," Tess says.

Pax clears his throat. "A primitive story, no doubt. But it's clear that Hannah has encountered her spirit guide."

"I'm sorry," I say. "You think my spirit guide is a murderous cannibal miner?"

"I think you heard the tall tale of Waylon Barlow, and some part of you bonded with his spirit, clinging to this story of death in the wilderness," Pax says. "The unconscious mind is a powerful thing, and you summoned the specter of a ruthless survivor for a reason."

I can see the painful parallels he's drawing to my own life. "But I didn't even know the full legend until just now. How could I have imagined it if I hadn't even heard it yet?"

Luna chimes in. "It sounds like you heard enough of it, Hannah."

"I think I've heard enough of *you*, Lauren," I clap back.

She bristles at her real name.

Kimi stifles a laugh. "I knew you weren't no Luna."

Luna crosses her arms. "My parents named me Lauren, but Luna is the name I've been called to by the universe. I'm a Pisces moon, so I'm very sensitive to messages from my lunar mother."

Kimi stands, tossing her stoking stick to the dirt. "Well, maybe the message you need to hear is 'stop stealing—'"

"That's quite enough," Pax says, firmer than I've ever heard him. "Hannah, as destabilizing as it may have been, you had a true breakthrough today. One that we can debrief on tomorrow. But I think we're all a bit worn out from the trip, so right now, the best thing we can do is rest and head home in the morning."

Debrief? The term feels very officious and un-Pax-like.

Still, I'm ready to stop talking about the horrible experience.

As everyone gets ready for bed, I try to make myself comfortable on the desert floor. But I just keep seeing Waylon Barlow, hearing that *screek* every time I close my eyes.

"Can't sleep?" Tess asks beside me.

"Tess, I swear it was real."

"And I don't want to invalidate that, Han, I really don't. But I also don't know what 'real' means to you right now, and I'm not sure that you do either. I mean, I believe in spiritual forces, sure. But I don't believe some undead maniac with a leprechaun complex can actually hurt you."

I can't help a small laugh of relief at how absurd it sounds out loud.

"On the other hand," Tess continues, "we know you'd been seeing things *without* the mind-altering hallucinogens. So it makes sense that your trip would feel doubly real under the circumstances."

Tess is the only one here who knows about the night terrors. The haunting. "But this was different. This wasn't..."

"Ben?"

I nod.

"How do you know that?" she asks. "I mean, it could've been anyone beneath that flesh mask, right?"

"You think my hallucination is wearing a disguise? Just how many layers of crazy do you think I am?"

"None at all. I think that when we suffer from serious trauma, we're haunted by it. And a haunting can take different shapes at different times. But you can trace it all back to the same cause. The truth you're refusing to look in the eye." Tess takes my clenched hand and gently unfolds it. "It's time to let go of whatever you're holding on to. You blame yourself for Ben's death, don't you?"

I haven't told Tess everything about that day. How could I? But it's hard to deny the guilt that weighs me down.

"It's my fault, Tess." I start my confession, desperate to say more. To come clean.

"No, it's not. Ben took you out to that mountain because he loved you, and he wanted to spend the rest of his life with you. And he died, and that sucks. But you're alive. So start acting like it. Because you deserve to be happy, Hannah."

"Is that why you've been pushing Miles my way?" I've seen the secret glances and quiet encouragement Tess has been giving him.

"Who, *me*?" Tess blushes.

"Subtlety has never been your strong suit."

"You and I both know he's always had a thing for you. So I figured I would float him your way, see if you bit. I just want you to explore all of your options."

"What if I don't?"

"If you don't want Miles?" Tess perks up a little. "That's okay, too. But maybe you're finally ready to think about what it is you *do* want."

Tess scoots a little closer in the darkness.

"No," I explain. "I mean, what if I don't deserve to be happy? To be alive? What if I can't heal and move on, and I'm just haunted forever?"

"Hey. You are not crazy or broken or cursed. You are human." She reaches into her bag and pulls out a small glass vial. "I bought this at Ineffable. I think you could use some."

"Essential oils? Do you really think these things work?" In the medical field, we tend to view this stuff as snake oil.

"I really do." Tess pours a few drops onto her fingertips and rubs it onto my temples. "This one is for clarity of heart and mind." I can't deny that I feel some instant relief. "Why don't you hold on to it?" She hands me the bottle.

"Thanks, Tess."

"Don't stay up too late."

Tess rolls over, and I stare into the flames. Touching my bandaged arm, I look at the blood-red scratches all over my legs and wonder if it really is possible that I dreamed up the entire encounter. Had I just manifested Waylon Barlow from that mine shaft with my own drug-addled mind and chased myself into a scraped-up mess like Luna said?

Yes, it felt real. But so did the saloon bathroom-stall attack.

Did ice-axe-wielding Ben just morph into pickaxe-wielding Barlow in my mixed-up mind?

I wish I wasn't doubting myself so deeply, but it's somehow better than the alternative.

Better than believing some vengeful spirit is really out to kill me.

20

MY INSOMNIA COMES HURTLING BACK WITH A vengeance.

After two perfectly restful nights at Avidya, I don't sleep a wink in the desert. I just lie there wide awake beneath the stars, blazing bright above. I swear I can hear them burning, screaming in the night sky from light-years away.

Pax was right. I feel totally destabilized, dysregulated by whatever the hell happened out there. Any sense of peace and security I've built up has been replaced by shredded nerves.

The trek back out of the wilderness the next morning is slow and awkward. Nobody really knows what to say about my experience, and I feel utterly alone with it. By the time we all arrive back at the retreat, I'm spent and exhausted.

Luna, on the other hand, is energized with hope as she rushes into her yurt. When she returns without Jared, all that hope melts from her face. "I guess he's still not back."

"It's early yet," Pax assures her. "I'm sure he'll return before the end of the weekend. In the meantime, you look tense, Luna." Pax rubs her shoulders.

"Yeah. Sleeping in the dirt really messed up my alignment." She moans under his touch.

"Perhaps a massage is in order," Pax suggests.

"Perhaps Jared had a good reason to leave," I say, louder than intended.

Luna cocks her head, ever the ingenue. "What's that supposed to mean?"

"Hannah," Tess warns, "just leave it."

"No. I'm sick of this. She acts like I'm the crazy one while she plays sick little mind games right out in the open."

"What mind games?" Luna asks.

"You're always the victim in your passive-aggressive 'poor-me' routines. Jared might be the perfect pawn, but someday even *he's* gonna catch on to your bullshit and leave for good. Maybe that day has finally come." I didn't realize I had the energy for that kind of outburst, but apparently it had been building up inside, in need of release.

Luna just stares back, ice cold in the aftermath. "You want to talk about playing the victim, Hannah? I tried, I *really* tried to be there for you after Ben died."

I point my finger in Luna's face. "Do not say his name."

"After. Ben. Died." Luna punctuates each word like she's stabbing me through the heart. "But you were too selfish to realize it. You just wanted to stew in your misery."

"Guys, come on." Tess tries to step between us, but Pax puts a hand to her chest.

"Let them air their grievances," he says. "We're here to cleanse toxicity in all its forms."

Oh, I have plenty of toxins to spill. "I'd rather own my misery than whitewash myself with toxic positivity, Lauren."

"My name is Luna!"

"Yeah, yeah, your name is Luna, and your spirit animal is a fucking unicorn, and the whole world is made of magic sparkles and fairy dust. Grow up."

Luna bites her tongue, closes her eyes, and takes a meditative breath. "That hurt, Hannah. You have hurt me."

"You don't know what hurt is, you privileged prima donna." I feel dizzy, possessed. Why am I spewing all this hatred?

Luna's lip trembles. "I think I need to go flow this out. I'll see you all at dinner."

She sulks away as Pax turns to me. "That was very brave of you, Hannah."

"Wrong B-word, Pax." I've never felt so bitchy, and the shame settles in quick.

"Wow," Tess says. "That was harsh."

"I know. I just... I didn't sleep well, and...maybe I should go apologize."

I start toward the yoga studio, not exactly sure what I'm going to say, but Tess stops me. "Harsh, but necessary."

"Really?"

"Hannah, that girl's been getting away with her bullshit for years without anybody ever calling her on it. Shit, she probably only keeps Jared around because he draws all the fire. I say well done."

I still feel guilty about it.

Until Miles nods. "I gotta agree. You spoke the truth. Besides, Luna will bounce back all smiles in no time."

He's right about that. No way Luna won't be spinning my attack in a positive light, thanking me for the growth opportunity the next time I see her.

"Speaking of refreshing," Miles adds, "I'm thinking a hot springs bath to wash off all the dirt would feel pretty amazing right now. What do you say?"

I can feel Tess watching out of the corner of my eye, and I'm sorry to disappoint my cupid, but I'm really not in the mood for romance. "I think all I need right now is a serious nap."

"Totally, I get it," Miles says. "Catch you at lunch then." He peels his sweaty shirt off, and I try not to stare as he walks toward the hot springs pool.

Tess turns to me. "You sure you want to pass on that?"

"I'm sure."

"Okay." Tess gives me a kiss on the cheek. "I'll be in my yurt if you need anything."

"You're the best."

Opening the flap of my yurt, I collapse onto the mattress. Even after my outburst, I can still feel some rage bubbling in my blood. But maybe that's a good thing. Pax said emotions would come up so that we could purge them.

I came here to heal, but I only feel crazier now. I can't stop picturing Waylon Barlow chasing me, can't shake how real it all felt.

Maybe Pax was right about that, too. Maybe I was just projecting the miner imagery and the story I heard at the museum.

Between the drugs and the heat, it's possible that my hallucinations are growing more vivid, twisting and evolving. Rooted in memories of axe chases in the wilderness.

I twist the engagement ring on my finger. The self-soothing gesture works like a charm as I fall into the blackness of sleep, only to find myself dreaming of that day on the mountain.

"Hannah?" Ben asks. "My knee's going numb." He laughs, still holding the engagement ring out in its little box.

"Ben, I...can't." The words fall from my chapped lips without a thought. It isn't a matter of thinking. It's just the truth, tumbling down and crashing on my boyfriend's head like a landslide.

The look on Ben's face is unlike anything I've ever seen before. I know I just destroyed him, killed him, but he doesn't look sad or hurt. He just looks angry.

Ben snaps the box shut and pushes back up to his feet. "Why?" is all he can muster.

"I don't know," I respond, head swimming. I really don't know. Not with my brain, not in a way that I can convey to him in this moment.

"Is there someone else?" A logical question.

"No."

"Fuck, Hannah. There has to be someone else." He's pacing now. The wispy clouds are moving fast behind him, reminding me that we're so high above ground level.

"There's no one else, Ben, I just…"

"You just don't love me," he snaps back.

"I *do* love you."

"But you don't want to marry me."

"I guess not." That's all I know. When I saw the ring, and he asked the question, my gut said no. It's all so confusing. Am I making the right decision or sabotaging the best thing in my life?

"That's fucking bullshit," Ben says.

His face contorts in a strange way. Like he's wearing a mask, wearing someone else's face, and it doesn't fit anymore. I've never seen this side of him before, but maybe I always sensed it. The real Ben, hiding just beneath the surface of the nice boy all the while. Maybe this is why I said no, why my gut spoke up to warn me.

This isn't self-sabotage. It's self-preservation.

"We've never even talked about marriage," I say.

"We've never talked about a lot of things." Ben is staring off into the distance now.

The clouds around us are darkening. Being this high on the peak means being vulnerable to lightning strikes, and I'm scared for so many reasons. I feel exposed, defenseless. Like I could be struck at any moment.

"It's getting scary up here," I say. "Can we go home now?"

"Yeah, I'm going home. But I don't know where you live anymore."

He starts strapping the crampons onto his boots as I put a hand on his shoulder.

"Ben, come on. Don't be—"

Ben swats my hand away. "Don't touch me." He pulls the ice axe from his bag, spinning to point it in my face. "We're done."

Slinging the bag over his shoulder, he starts trekking back down the mountain, fast. Running away from me, away from the whole situation.

I rush to strap my crampons back on, too.

"Wait up!" I call.

Clenching my own ice axe in a cold grip, I hurry to catch up.

Trekking down in the snow is much more dangerous than hiking up. Gravity is not my friend, but that's what the ice axe is for. It'll come in handy if I slip. A quick swing of the blade planted in the snow will keep me from falling, from tumbling endlessly to the bottom of the mountain.

Even then, I knew I should've let Ben go. I never should've chased after him, ice axe in hand. I should've let his "we're done" be the end of it.

But it's not the end of it.

I run, I stumble. The axe flails in my grip as I chase Ben down the mountain, screaming his name. "Ben! Ben, don't leave me!"

Trapped in this lucid dream, I wish I could rewrite history.

But all I can do is watch as the nightmare unfolds all over again.

There's no way of stopping the bloodshed to come.

21

LUNA GRABS A MAT FROM THE CUBBY AND UNROLLS IT IN THE empty studio. She's grateful to have the space to herself because she really needs to get centered. Especially after Hannah spent the entire spirit journey centering *her*self.

No, don't focus on Hannah.

Focus on Luna.

She starts with a plank. Shifts to down dog.

Flowing into up dog. Hop to the front of the mat.

Halfway lift. Forward fold.

Up to mountain pose.

The spirit journey was supposed to give everyone their own opportunity to find themselves, to connect with something greater. But Hannah's crazy hallucinations robbed Luna of that opportunity.

They're all here for Hannah, to help her move on, so why is she being such a bitch? So judgmental and ungrateful and downright mean.

Was Luna flirting with Pax? Yes, of course she was. But flirting is just a harmless expression of loving abundance. Jared does it all the time with waitresses and bartenders, right in front of Luna's face.

Who is Hannah to question their relationship? They know who they are, and they're secure in their bond.

At least Luna *was* secure until Jared's latest disappearing act.

Luna tries again to block out the anxious thoughts and focus on flowing all the emotions right out of her body.

Step up into warrior one. Crescent pose.

Back into a chaturanga.

The kinks in her back are already starting to work themselves out, but her anger bubbles up again.

This time, it's directed at Jared.

Yes, he's pulled a stunt like this many times before. A big selfish baby waiting for Mama Luna to ease his wounded pride. She just can't believe he still hasn't come back yet.

What if he's really hurt? What if he needs her and she's being neglectful?

No. Jared is the neglectful one, not her.

Pax said that she has to stop trying to fix other people. That includes Jared.

Warrior two. Reverse warrior.

Back to warrior two. Triangle pose.

It also includes her sister, Annie.

The last time Annie relapsed and disappeared, Luna found her in a tent off the Venice Boardwalk. She was screaming and pulling her hair out while Luna tried to talk to her. Annie claimed that she wasn't homeless, that she chose to live that way. Luna tried to convince her to come sleep at her place. There's plenty of room since she and Jared still aren't living together after six years of dating.

He keeps saying he needs his own space, but any time she goes to his bachelor studio, there isn't much space to be found. Just dirty laundry scattered everywhere while he plays video games on his giant TV. For all she knows, that's exactly where he is right now.

Jesus, why aren't they living together yet? Isn't that a clear sign of a dysfunctional relationship?

Maybe Hannah's right.

No, Hannah is fucking crazy. Why isn't anybody else seeing that? She went off the deep end after Ben died, but everybody is acting like she's this sad little girl in mourning. Luna's tired of sugarcoating it, like she does everything. Hannah's nuts, just like Annie.

Why would she rather live in a tent than her own sister's apartment?

Revolved triangle. Warrior three.

Maybe Pax is right. Annie is on her own path now.

Maybe she'll be just fine without Luna's help.

Luna wishes Annie could be with her now, here at this place. Experience the healing that Avidya has to offer. She can picture Annie walking the labyrinth maze, speaking her intention to the spirits: *Sobriety!*

Maybe here, she could finally find herself, just like Luna is now.

As she does another sun salutation with her eyes closed, Luna hears the shuffling of feet behind her. She turns to see the aerial straps swaying in the breeze.

There are so many open doorways and windows in the room,

but there's no breeze out here in the desert today. So what caused those straps to move?

Maybe it was the spirits, guiding her toward them. Telling her that this is what her body needs right now. She listens to their guidance, puts her legs through the loops, and hangs upside down, closing her eyes.

Luna steadies her breath, getting into a meditative state as the blood flows from her limbs to her head.

She's too deep in the flow state to feel the presence stepping in front of her now. To see the hands that grip the pickaxe, holding it underhand and extending the point toward her belly button. She pierced it in high school but hasn't worn a navel ring in years. Not since she heard women giggling at her during her first-ever yoga class. LA yogis can be so judgmental.

The pickaxe hovers there for a moment. It could thrust forward at any second to give her belly a fresh piercing she'll never recover from.

The iron point slowly drags through the air an inch from her stomach, straight down the middle of her ribs, toward her neck. So close to opening her up and spilling her guts out onto the yoga studio floor.

But the weapon just lingers there, pointed at Luna's throat.

She breathes in, unaware.

Breathes out, oblivious.

The pickaxe is poised to stop her breathing forever. To slice the artery where all her blood is flowing now, unleash a geyser of red that will paint the wooden floors in wet crimson.

All of this is happening just outside of Luna's embodied awareness.

Still, she's present enough to hear a *creak* on the floorboards.

She opens her eyes, but nobody's there.

Maybe the sound came from somewhere outside, or simply from within, thanks to all that blood in her head.

She untangles her legs from the aerial straps and moves back toward her mat, shaking off a chill.

Luna is ready to flow anew.

She moves through a few more sequences.

Plank, chaturanga, up dog, down dog.

Her practice over the years has left her body feeling strong and sure. It's her emotions that she wants to strengthen. She's realizing now as her brain bounces from Jared to Annie to Hannah that yoga has been her avoidance crutch for too long. If she really wants to bolster her practice, she needs to sit with all the feelings that come up.

She slips into child's pose, intuitively embracing the restorative posture and closing her eyes in search of clarity.

What comes next is akin to a spiritual awakening.

She's done with Jared. Even if he does come back to the retreat, she'll tell him, right to his face. *It's over.*

No more childish games, pushing and pulling in toxic cycles.

Moving forward, Luna only has space in her life for healthy cycles.

This place really has changed her. She's ready to become the best version of herself.

In fact, maybe it's time to embrace her real name.

Lauren.

Kimi was right. She shouldn't be appropriating other languages, other cultures. It's just that Lauren has so much baggage that comes with her. All the embarrassing shit she did back in her sorority days when she was desperate for outside approval. She moved to LA to reinvent herself, but she's doing that now, here at Avidya. She doesn't need a fake name to become a new person.

Clarity courses through her consciousness, a deep warmth settling into her muscles.

She feels strong in this new intention as she pushes up into upward facing dog, keeping her eyes closed, her legs straight and strong behind her, her back arched and propped up with firm arms.

If she did open her eyes in this moment, she might see Waylon Barlow crouched down in front of her, inches from her face. She might even catch a glimpse of the cold eyes behind the flesh mask, staring through the holes where eyelids once were.

But she doesn't open her eyes in this moment. She takes one more breath in, one more breath out, and by the time her perfect lashes flutter open, there's nothing to see in front of her.

Because Waylon Barlow is standing behind her now, straddling her body with a leg on either side of her slender frame.

What she feels next is cold iron against the middle of her back, the pickaxe head pressed perpendicular to her spine. A hand reaches forward and wraps around her face.

"Wha—" she cries, unable to finish that single syllable before the hand pulls back with brutal force. Those thirty-three vertebrae she studied in yoga teacher training all *pop* with blinding clarity as her spinal column snaps like a flimsy stick of incense. Her head rests between her feet now, body bent backward.

She coughs blood, splattering her face and dripping down to the yoga mat.

The energy drains from every chakra as she settles into shavasana. Lauren's final corpse pose.

22

I CAN STILL FEEL THE CHILLED MOUNTAIN AIR CREEPING under my skin when I jump awake in the hot yurt. I sit up and twist my torso, back aching from that sleepless night in the dirt. Maybe I should follow Luna's lead and do some yoga.

I really shouldn't have snapped at her like that. Clearly, I'm the crazy one, not her.

Dreaming about Ben cemented that what I experienced in the desert was nothing more than a hallucination. A fucking terrifying one, but the drugs were clearly to blame for that. Dr. Grady always said that demons can manifest in many forms, and Pax had been saying something similar all weekend.

Waylon Barlow is just another manifestation of my demons, my mind trying to work out what happened that day in the snowy wilderness. Expunge it from my brain. If I'd been brave enough to confront my spirit guide, if I'd ripped that false face off, Ben probably would've been staring back at me behind it.

I'm not eager to rejoin the world of the living as I exit my yurt.

Pax sits at the table, waiting patiently for the group to join him. I don't really want to sit alone with him after I awkwardly implied that something was happening between him and Luna, so I awkwardly wait out of sight instead. Or at least, I think I'm out of sight.

"I don't bite," Pax says, turning to grin at me. How did he know I was there?

I reluctantly move toward the table but don't sit. "I wanted to apologize." *Want* is a strong way of putting it. More like I feel the need to, just to smooth things over. "If I made you uncomfortable with my accusations…"

"Hannah, I assure you. Nothing you or anyone else could ever do has the power to make me uncomfortable. I am responsible for my own comfort, as you are for yours. So, tell me. Do you feel more comfortable after your rest?"

"Not really, no."

"That's quite all right. Sitting with discomfort is all part of the process." He pours some hot tea into the same mugs we used for the spirit journey. "Just plain mint tea, I promise."

I take the offered mug, sneaking a sniff before taking a sip.

"You know, it's counterintuitive," he says, "but drinking hot tea in hot weather can actually cool the body down."

"I know. The body stops storing its own heat and releases sweat."

"Right," he says. "You're a doctor."

"How'd you know that?" I definitely don't remember telling him.

"You still seek the answers that I've already given you."

"Right," I say. "The spirits told you."

"You may doubt my words. But do not doubt your own experience. You know, in Tibetan Buddhism, intensely focused meditation is said to produce a tulpa. A mystical being manifested in the real world as a materialized thought-form."

It's hard to suss out all the pseudoscience vocabulary, but is he suggesting that my spiritual run-in at Dead Man's Due *was* real?

"But I digress. We were talking tea." Pax raises his teacup, returning to the thermal dynamics that led us down this road. "If you'll indulge me a metaphor, what really happens is that your body stops resisting its environment. It's the struggle that creates more suffering. Once your body becomes one with the heat, there's no more need to fight. Harmony is achieved."

"Is that what we're doing out here?" I sip my tea. "Searching for harmony with the spirit world?"

"That's right. But some spirits prefer chaos."

"Hey." The voice over my shoulder makes me jump a little and spill my tea as I turn to see Tess. "Feeling better?"

"A little," I reply. Tess sits next to Pax at the table, so I decide to finally take a seat myself. "I guess I owe Luna an apology, huh?"

Could I just blame it on being cranky and hangry? I'm definitely the latter as I reach for a handful of almonds and start munching.

"It's probably a good idea to clear the air with her," Tess says, "but it'll have to wait. I just went to get her for lunch and found this in her yurt."

Tess places the parchment on the table. I lift it to read the message aloud. "Jared came back. Rented an Airbnb in town for us to make up. Back Sunday to pick you up. Have the best time! xo Luna."

"Wow," Miles appears behind me and slides into the seat next to me. "That's flakey."

Something more than hunger stirs in my stomach as I lower the note. "I don't know. Jared came back, and they both just left without saying a word to anyone?"

"I mean, it's pretty classic behavior from those two." Tess digs into a bowl and serves herself some sunflower seeds. "Also, you did a pretty good job of making them both feel unwelcome before they dipped."

My hands tighten around the mug. "You're saying this is my fault?"

"Not talking fault here. Just saying."

"Okay, but how do we know Luna really wrote this note?" I ask.

Miles takes the parchment and looks at the swooping scrawl. "You know anyone else who writes like this?"

I remember now that Pax had specifically commented on Luna's unique handwriting.

"Besides, why would somebody forge a note like that?" Tess puts the back of her hand to my damp forehead. "You sure you're okay, Han? You feel a little warm."

"It's just the tea."

I focus my attention on Pax now. He's stopped eating and is staring straight ahead, gripping his wooden utensils with white knuckles.

"Pax, did Luna say anything to you or Kimi before she left?"

Kimi speaks for herself with a "nope" as she leans against a wooden post.

Pax finally addresses the group. "It's disappointing when people don't follow through on their commitments. I can only hope that your friends' departures don't cast a pall over the weekend. We still have so much in store for everyone. But perhaps we should take the rest of the day to rest. If you'll excuse me."

Pax's knife and fork clatter to the table as he stands to leave.

"Maybe Waylon Barlow came for them, too," Kimi offers, palming a handful of almonds into her mouth.

"Can you *not* with the ghost stories?" Tess replies. "My friend was seriously traumatized by that trip you orchestrated."

Kimi stifles a laugh and looks me in the eye. "I'm so sorry for your trauma." She walks away from the table, leaving us three remaining retreat attendees alone.

Maybe Jared and Luna did just up and leave. Or maybe something scared them away.

"So," Miles asks, "what do you guys want to do with our free time?"

I don't feel very free at Avidya anymore as I push away from the table. "I've got some reading to do."

I remember Pax mentioning that there's a small library on the premises.

But *library* is a strong word for one bookshelf, brimming with dusty spines. I start scanning all the spiritual texts, old and new. From ancient Sanskrit collections that look like the first and only handwritten editions to Eckhart Tolle books you can pick up at your local Barnes & Noble. Pax really is covering all his mystical bases.

Back when I was in med school, I spent hours upon hours studying in the library for years upon years. I know that if I want to understand what's happening here, I need to educate myself.

I keep searching until I find what I'm looking for.

The Joshua Tree Gold Rush.

Flipping through the book, I find the chapter on Dead Man's Due Mine. It doesn't look exactly like the one I entered, but these photos were before the cave-in. One photo features that hand-carved sign I found in the dirt, so now I'm certain.

Reading up on Waylon Barlow provides even more upsetting details. It turns out he and his gang didn't dig the mine themselves. They enslaved the local Chemehuevi to do all the work. The photos show Indigenous people chipping away with pickaxes in the dark.

I go back to the bookshelf, searching for more history when I find *Indigenous Life at the Oasis of Mara.*

This book provides a history of the land and its people, something Kimi had alluded to.

Flipping it open, I read about the sacred caves where healing rituals were performed by tribal medicine men. These were the very same caves that white settlers had invaded to dig for gold, forcing Indigenous folks into labor, deep in the mines where so many of them died.

The Chemehuevi were already settled at the Oasis of Mara when the white colonizers came, bringing death and disease with them. There's even a passage about the burial ground I saw in town. In truth, the colonizers wiped out so many native people here that the entire valley is a graveyard.

I don't want to admit it to myself, but I feel the pall of death stretching over this whole retreat. There's so much history here, so much pain and collective trauma.

So many spirits.

I feel dizzy as I close the book, trying to force all the puzzle pieces into place while my imagination runs wild. It's a dangerous spiral that will surely only fuel more nightmares, more hallucinations. Am I really starting to believe that restless ghosts like Waylon Barlow—like Ben—could manifest in the real world to terrorize the living?

The evidence in my hands is too compelling to ignore. I just need some perspective from someone with way more insight than me.

There's only one person who can help me understand what's really going on at Avidya.

23

I TAKE THE BOOKS FROM THE LIBRARY AND GO IN SEARCH OF Kimi's yurt, which is set away from the others. When I find it, I see smoke drifting through the crack in the flap.

Peering inside, I spot Kimi sitting on the floor, her back to the door. She's hunched over and whispering in a sing-song fashion as smoke rises from in front of her.

What is she doing? Burning secret herbs? Casting a spell, some ancient ritual?

Is Kimi the shaman responsible for summoning an evil spirit from the land to attack me?

I burst through the flap with a confident "What are you doing?!"

Kimi spins to face me with a startled "Fuck!" The joint falls from her hand to the ground.

Wait. *That* was the source of the smoke?

Kimi quickly retrieves the joint, shaking her head. "You trying to make me burn the whole damn place down?"

"I'm sorry. I thought I heard…"

"Huh?" Kimi pops the AirPods out of her ears, releasing a heavy beat. "What are you doing in my yurt?"

Kimi had been singing along to music. Not reciting a spell.

I'm instantly flush with embarrassment. "I..."

"Close the flap, bro." Kimi rushes to shut the door flap behind me. "Before he sees us."

"Is that weed?" I point to the joint in Kimi's hand just to confirm.

"No, it's an ancient blend of mystical herbs." She smiles. "Just fucking with you. Yeah, it's bud, and it's fresh as fuck." She extends the joint to me. "You look like you could use some."

I shake my head. "No more mind-altering substances for me, thanks."

"Suit yourself." Kimi takes another hit.

"So...I'm confused," I confess, unsure of exactly how to phrase it.

"Why? Because I'm not the docile native servant girl you thought I was?" Kimi exhales smoke. "It's a performance, Hannah. Pax thinks all this kabuki theater makes the experience more authentic."

So Pax's penchant for the theatrical goes well beyond the smoke-and-mirrors show he performed that first night.

"My name's not even Kimi," Kimi says. "It's Kimberly. My mom grew up watching too much *Power Rangers*."

"Wait... You're named after the Pink Ranger?"

"Beware the pterodactyl, bro." Kimi flaps her arms with a "*Kaw! Kaw!*"

I can't help laughing, relief flooding my system. But I'm also mortified that I'd fallen so easily for the stereotype and then made even more racist assumptions about sinister rituals. "Wow. I feel like an idiot."

"You're not an idiot." Kimi takes a seat back on the floor, putting on her best Pax voice. "You're just deep in avidya."

I lower to the floor across from her, trying to process just how much this place has gotten into my head and under my skin. "Can I ask you a question?"

"Shoot."

"Do you like it here?"

"Oh, I fucking hate it." Kimi pulls deeply from the joint. "You know, yurts originated in Central Asia with the nomadic Mongolian people. That gong Pax loves to bang is from western China. There are Buddhist figurines set up in front of tapestries of Hindu gods, not to mention ancient artifacts from about six different Native American tribes. It's a gross-ass cultural appropriation buffet out there."

"So why work here?"

"Why does anybody do anything they don't want to do? Fucking capitalism. You wouldn't guess it from his one-with-the-earth vibes, but Pax is loaded and pays me well. Beats slinging frozen lemonade at Coachella, that's for sure."

"I get that." We've all worked jobs we hate with shitty bosses. I lucked out with the nurturing Dr. Mohai as my attending physician while other interns got stuck under domineering megalomaniacs.

"Can I ask *you* a question?" Kimi asks.

"Sure."

"Those people you came with. Are they really your friends? Because y'all don't seem to really like each other all that much."

"Of course they are." I say it on defensive reflex, but I can't help imagining how unfriendly we all look from Kimi's perspective, especially after two of us bailed. "I mean, they *used* to be. We've kind of been...estranged for a while. But that happens, right?"

Kimi shrugs. "Wouldn't know. I don't really fuck with friends. Prefer to fly solo."

"Like a pterodactyl?"

"Damn straight." Kimi smiles. "Anyway, I'm pretty sure your girl Tess has a thing for you."

"What?" It catches me off guard, and my instinct is to deflect. "No way. We've just been super close ever since college. Maybe a little enmeshed, if I'm being honest."

"And your lips never enmeshed in college?"

"That doesn't count." There was that one night when we killed the peach schnapps after our footy photo shoot. Friendly snuggles turned to sweet smooches, but it definitely wasn't a thing.

"Whatever you say." She puts the joint to her grin and takes a drag.

I'm seeing a whole new side of Kimi, a side that feels strangely comfortable and familiar. It makes me feel like I can actually let my guard down. "Screw it. Pass me that joint."

"Attagirl!" Kimi hands me the joint. "What do you got there?" She points at the books I forgot I was carrying.

I blush all over again as I hold up *Indigenous Life at the Oasis of Mara*. "I was reading up on what all those gold miners did."

"Fucked up, right?"

"Understatement of the century." I take a deep pull of the weed.

Kimi absentmindedly flips through the pages. "Wild how one evil fuck like Waylon Barlow gets to be a local legend with a cute little nursery rhyme. But thousands of my ancestors just disappear without a trace, and it's like this quiet, unspoken history. Sometimes I want to scream it from the mountaintops."

I think about Ben's funeral, how everybody was saying the nicest things about him. How I stayed quiet, couldn't speak, even though I wanted to scream the truth.

"So," I say, "I know you don't believe Pax's spiritual bullshit. But what *do* you believe?"

"Oh, I believe this whole valley is filled with the spirits of the dead." Kimi takes a hit. "But I do not believe they'd be wasting their precious time trying to communicate with white folks through energy vortexes."

I laugh, which makes Kimi laugh and cough on smoke.

After recovering her breath, she goes on. "I think the only question that matters is what *you* believe. Because if it's real to you, then it's just fucking real, right?"

"You mean, do I really believe the ghost of Waylon Barlow chased me through the boulder field?" The weed is hitting as I take the book back and close it, shaking my head. "I'm starting to think I'm not healing as fast as I thought I was. I guess it really was just a trip from the ayahuasca. Sorry, not ayahuasca. What was it again?"

Kimi looks hesitant to speak. "Fuck it," she says, stamping out the joint. "That shit was chamomile."

"...chamomile?"

"It was tea, with some dried twigs mixed in for dramatic effect. There were no drugs, Hannah. Just a placebo."

"I don't understand." I've now graduated to uncomfortably high as I try to wrap my brain around what Kimi is telling me. "Why would you do that?"

"It's not me," Kimi says, voice lowering. "Listen, it's fun to rag on Pax. But you should know that this place is not what you think it is."

There's a rustling outside the yurt, and Kimi's whole body goes tense.

What is she so scared of?

She pulls a burlap sack from the corner, filled with all of our cell phones, and hands me mine back.

"Here. I think you should hold on to this."

Footsteps outside the yurt now. Kimi shoves the bag away.

"Why? Kimi, what's going—"

"You need to get as high as you can."

I shake my head, already too high. "I don't need any more—"

"Kimi." Pax's voice makes us both swivel to face the yurt entrance, where he stands with his hands on his hips. "You know it's not in our practice to mingle with guests. They need to have their own experience."

Kimi nods, her confident voice suddenly faded. "Of course."

"Hannah, may I ask what brought you to seek Kimi's counsel?"

I jump to my feet. "I was just asking her about this book I found in the library."

Pax takes the book from me and flips through it. "Ah, yes. It's important to have a sense of the history of the land. Why don't you take it back to your yurt and we can discuss it at breakfast tomorrow?"

Pax is giving summer camp counselor vibes, and I'm tempted to play the unruly camper. But now does not feel like the time to push back.

"Right," I say, opting not to make waves. "Good night."

Stepping out of the yurt, I linger outside and listen.

Pax speaks in an urgent whisper. "If you breathe another word to any of them when I'm not present, there will be consequences. Do you understand?"

"Yes," Kimi replies.

"Good. I will not have you ruin everything I've built. Christ, it stinks like weed in here."

I hear Pax's footsteps and quickly swing my body around to the side of the yurt, watching him exit into the darkness.

As he enters the building, part of me wants to go speak to Kimi again, but I don't want to get her in any more trouble. So I follow Pax instead.

He walks down the hallway, and I'm rushing to catch up as he turns the corner. When I get to the main entrance, he's nowhere to be found.

The water is flowing down the mirror, into the pool of crystals, and Pax has disappeared.

I go back to my own yurt and turn on my cell phone. There's no service, and my battery is low. What good is this going to do? I turn it off.

I feel like I should be warning Tess and Miles, but warning

them about what? I've got more questions than answers as I try to connect the dots between this phony retreat and the dark history here.

My eye catches on the corner, where the spider is consuming its meal.

Taking a step closer, I see there are three more flies caught in the web.

Just waiting to be eaten.

24

TESS SITS ON THE FLOOR OF HER YURT WITH HER SKETCH PAD in her lap. Inspiration thrums in her chest, and she knows exactly what she needs to draw. Her hand grips the black charcoal as it grazes along the blank white canvas. Starting with the oval shape of a face she knows so well, filling it in with those perfect features.

The piercing eyes. Adorable nose. Plump lips.

She gets lost in her love affair with creation until she finally holds it up to admire her piece.

A portrait of Hannah. Beautiful.

Tess plants a kiss on the paper.

She's too taken with her own work of art to notice the flap quietly parting behind her as Waylon Barlow enters. Standing over her shoulder now. Admiring her work with her.

Barlow grips his pickaxe, waiting patiently for Tess to sense the presence standing behind her. She does, but she's too scared to turn.

The charcoal trembles in her hand.

She opens her mouth to scream as Barlow swings down hard.

The tip of his pickaxe crashes down through the back of Tess's skull. It punctures through her brain and slams down against her bottom teeth with such force that her whole jaw rips off its hinges, the gory bone plopping into her lap.

Tess's tongue flaps wildly under the iron spike that juts from her ragged face as she stares at the sketch, where red blood drips down Hannah's charcoal face.

It's ruined now.

As Barlow yanks his pickaxe from Tess's head with a horrific *slurrriiip*—

I jump awake in my yurt. Pawing at my own face, I find my jaw intact.

Another vivid nightmare, this one not even about me.

I could hear Tess's thoughts, feel her emotions. But they weren't real. Were they?

No, Kimi had simply planted a seed by prying with her personal questions, and I'm just back on my bullshit with more—

"Bad dreams?"

The voice gives me my second startle of the morning, sending my head swiveling to see Pax standing just inside the door flap.

"What are you doing in here?" I pull the blanket up to cover my body. I'm wearing a full sweatsuit in the cold weather, but I still feel naked under his gaze.

"We've been calling for you, Hannah." Pax steps closer to my bed. "You slept straight through the horn. I heard you crying from just outside and grew concerned. You were thrashing on your bed when I entered. I was tempted to give you a gentle shake to bring you back to us, but I felt I should let you endure whatever battle you were engaged in."

I shudder at the thought of Pax touching me while I wasn't conscious. "I'm a deep sleeper."

"What were you dreaming of, I wonder?" He advances farther into the room and takes a seat at my bedside. "Dreams often carry messages from our collective unconscious. Connect us to others in ways deeper than we can imagine. Tell us things we might otherwise wish to ignore in our waking life. They can be rather informative if we know how to interpret them."

"I find them to be less informative than they are invasive. Kind of like a man entering my bedroom without permission." I'm not going to tiptoe around him anymore. Especially not after what Kimi told me last night.

"Point taken." He smiles. "I sometimes forget my boundaries."

"Living as you do beyond time and space." I just can't resist echoing his bullshit back to him.

Pax nods, and his smile shifts into a smirk. The kind you give when you realize that the person you're talking to isn't buying what you're selling anymore.

"I'm only here to help you, Hannah. I think we should discuss your experience in the desert. Best to unpack these things while they're still fresh."

"You're right. Maybe I should unpack it. With my psychiatrist." I don't like lying helpless in bed while he sits beside me. It makes me feel like an injured patient, giving him all the power. I toss off the covers and stand up, surprised to see that I'm not actually wearing my sweatpants. Turns out I slept fully clothed in yesterday's jeans and shirt, full of dust and dirt. Embarrassing in its own way, but not enough to dampen my demand. "I need to use the satellite phone to call my doctor."

My cell phone might not be useful for making calls, but I can at least pull Dr. Grady's phone number from my contacts before the battery dies for good.

"As I mentioned," Pax responds, standing to face me, "it's only for emergencies."

"This *is* an emergency. A mental health emergency." I don't like admitting that to Pax, but if it gets me what I want, it's well worth him thinking I'm crazy. He probably already thinks that anyway. I need to talk to someone outside of this strange bubble I've found myself in, and I really do want to unpack that Tess dream with Grady. I've never dreamed as another person before, never disassociated so deeply in my nightmares. Waylon Barlow stepping into the spotlight of my psyche feels like an evolution of my symptoms that's worth addressing.

"Hannah." Something about the way Pax says my name just annoys me. He can make anything sound condescending. That's how he exerts his control, isn't it? Makes people feel smaller, less than. "I think you'll find that if you just embrace the healing I'm offering you here, you'll have no need for Western psychological manipulation."

"Right. Because psychological manipulation isn't part of the *dharma* here, is it, Guru Pax? I would love to unpack some of *your* methods."

"I am an open book." Pax extends his arms wide in a pathetic bodily metaphor.

"All of these practices of yours. Where did you learn them? Where did you study?" I spent six years in medical school, but I doubt Pax has anything like that under his belt.

"I traveled the world, from one community to another. Taking bits and pieces from every culture I encountered. With their blessings, of course." It sure sounds like he's trying to justify the cultural appropriation Kimi had flagged. "But in the end, nothing trained me quite like the year I spent living out here, alone. I spent many nights sleeping at the center of the stone structure we all journeyed to."

"The one near the entrance to Dead Man's Due Mine."

"Yes. But it was so much more than a materialistic dig site before that. I was brought into contact with something much larger than myself, given a clarity that connected me to all things. It's this experience that I hope to impart to every soul who comes to Avidya. But in order to reap the full benefits, it's important to keep the lines of contact with the outside world severed."

"You do realize that's like Cults 101, right?" Incidentally, that's also the name of a podcast I listen to during my breaks at the hospital. They review cases where leaders use tactics like "Target. Love bomb. Isolate. Control."

"So, is that your theory?" He seems genuinely amused. "That I've targeted you and your friends for my cult?"

"Maybe." I'm trying to play it sly, but I haven't actually fleshed out my theory yet. It's mostly just vibes.

"Where exactly *is* this cult? I don't see anybody else out here."

I'm quiet in response, so Pax keeps talking.

"Even so, let's take those tenets you've presented and work with them, shall we? What if my goal was to help you *target* your deepest trauma? To shower your inner child with *love*? To *isolate* all of those limiting negative beliefs and help you regain *control* of your life? Would that make me a cult leader?"

"That all depends."

"Depends on what?"

"On what you really want from us."

Pax lets out a deep sigh. "I can see that your defenses are up. Understandably so. It's a vulnerable process we're engaged in. That's why I've scheduled something a little different for today."

I want to grill him now, ask him about the placebo ayahuasca trip, and keep pushing for the satellite phone. But I know it's better to hold off and put him on the spot in front of everyone else.

"So," he asks, "will you be joining us today, or do you need some more time to rest?"

"Yes. I'll be joining you today. May I have some privacy first, please?"

"Of course. My apologies again for crossing your boundary. It will not happen again."

I doubt that very much.

"I do think you'll enjoy today's activity," Pax says. "Perhaps you'll find that my methods can actually be quite, dare I say, fun."

As he heads out of the yurt, every muscle in my body releases the tension. I'm tired of Pax dancing around every question without giving any sense of clarity. He didn't even deny that he fancies himself a cult leader, did he? He straight up embraced the principles.

I don't know exactly what he's up to, but Kimi said very clearly: *This place is not what you think it is.*

If this place isn't a healing retreat, then what the hell is it?

25

I LEAVE MY YURT TO FIND MILES AND TESS CHATTING OUTside. Some part of me feared the dream had been real, so I rush up to hug Tess and can't help asking: "Are you okay?"

"Of course I'm okay." Understandably, she looks at me strangely. "Are you?"

I put my hand to her cheek, double-checking that her jaw is fully intact. "Not really, but I will be."

"Okay, be cryptic then."

Pax and Kimi are busy setting up three easels with big blank canvases.

"Oh, hell yes," Tess says, rushing up to run her hands along the wide array of painting and drawing supplies. "We're in my element today."

Miles peers over his easel at Pax, who stands in front of us with the sun blazing directly behind his head like Jesus fucking Christ. "Please tell me we're not doing a nude painting."

"No," Pax says. "Our artistry today will not be bound to the constraints of the human form. However idyllic it might be," he adds, striking a pose in his perpetually crisp pantsuit.

It actually gets a laugh out of Tess and Miles, but I'm no longer amused. I was the first to fall for Pax's schtick, but now I need to pull back the curtain and expose the Wizard of Woo-Woo.

"Today," Pax says, "we will engage in the divine act of creation. A blank canvas is the most beautiful thing in the world. Existing in the pure state of possibility, it reminds us of how we entered into this universe. Free from the attachments and traumas that ensnare us now."

The blank white rectangle stares back at me, but I see no possibilities. Only emptiness.

"I want you to paint without thinking," Pax says. "You have all the colors, all the textures you could possibly need at your disposal. Channel something from your spirit guide, through your hand and out the bristles of your brush. Let them guide your creative soul."

I squeeze a blob of brown paint onto my palette and drag my paintbrush through it. Leaning toward Tess, I speak in a hushed whisper. "Pax is full of shit."

"What do you mean?" Tess reaches for a piece of charcoal, just like in my dream.

I shake it off, knowing that charcoal is Tess's favorite medium. This isn't a sign of anything. I just have to stay focused on the task at hand.

"Watch this." I raise my brush. "Question, Pax."

Pax seems preemptively annoyed, which is great. I want to catch him a little off-kilter. "Yes, Hannah."

"How do we know which tool to use for our art?" I motion helplessly at the box full of pencils and crayons, brushes and chalks.

"Tune in and listen to your spirit guide. Let it guide you out of primal ignorance toward your chosen instrument."

"Right. Well, my spirit guide gravitates toward a pickaxe, but I'm not totally drawn toward that instrument right now."

"Of course," Pax says. "Perhaps we can find you a more fitting guide for this next leg of your journey."

"I'm game." I shrug. "Load me up on that chamomile and send me back out into the desert. I'm sure I'll come back with a whole gaggle of spirit guides."

Tess raises an eyebrow at me. "Chamomile? What are you talking about?"

"Pax?" I cross my arms. "Are you ready to speak your truth? Or should I?"

Pax tenses and throws a sidelong glance at Kimi. She avoids his gaze, fear etched in her brow.

"It seems someone has spilled the proverbial tea," Pax says. "For optimal therapeutic reasons, I had hoped to reveal this at the *end* of our time together. But yes, the mixture you drank before your spirit journey had no hallucinogenic properties."

"I'm sorry..." Tess lowers the charcoal to her side. "What?"

"It was my intention to teach you," Pax says, "to *show* you that you don't need drugs in order to have a spiritual experience."

Miles scratches his head. "That's pretty sneaky, man."

Yes. It's working. The tides are turning against this culty asshole, and my friends are standing beside me.

"I understand that by your standards, I did not tell the truth," Pax says. "But what I'm guiding you toward here is a much greater truth. To achieve this sacred goal, I must create certain illusions in order to dispel the old ones."

"And the waivers?" Miles asks.

"All part of the illusion," Pax says. "Do you see now the weight that a flimsy piece of paper can wield? You signed on the dotted line and created the experience you desired."

Tess chews this over for a moment. A very long moment. "That is pretty cool," she admits.

"Pretty cool?" My hands start to shake. I can't believe she's just accepting all his dodgy answers and half-truths. "Tess, come on."

"What? He showed us the power that material things have over us. We just accept all these made-up systems, these authorities that tell us how to live our lives."

I have no tolerance for this argument because I know where it leads. It's the anti-vax anthem that gave me two years of hell at the hospital. The stress of that time still lives in my frayed nerves as I try my best to temper my anger at Tess.

"Systems are based on science," I say as calmly as I can. "Not spirits."

"I couldn't agree more," Pax says. "Society has been possessed by narrow-minded thinking for far too long. It's time for an exorcism."

Tess and Miles are both nodding, and I want to smack them both upside their bobbleheads. This can't be happening. I must be trapped in another nightmare, one where my friends have been replaced by alien idiots.

"Now, Miles," Pax says. "Tell me about your work."

The canvas in front of Miles is covered in watercolor paints, all bright blue and green.

"I guess I'm trying to paint music," Miles says. "Synesthesia, ya know? Like, what the notes would look like if I could see them, all flowing together. But that's kind of hard to do."

"Don't try to *do* anything," Pax says. "Just let the music flow through you. Don't paint what you see. Paint what you *feel*."

I take the opportunity to check in with Tess, trying hard to understand. "So, you're really okay with him lying to us?"

"It's an engineered experience, Hannah." Tess shrugs, working away at her easel. "You just got a step ahead of the guru and spoiled it for the rest of us."

"The guru is up to no good."

Tess scrapes away at her canvas. "I think maybe you're just using Pax as a distraction from the real takeaway here."

"Which is what?"

"If the trip wasn't real, then whatever you saw out there in the desert *was* just in your own messed-up mind." Tess throws her blackened hands in the air like she just dropped a hot truth bomb at my feet.

It feels more like an arrow piercing straight through my heart. "So you *do* think I'm crazy."

"I didn't say that." Her shoulders fall, exasperated, like it's just so much work putting up with me. "I think you're having the experience that Pax wants—"

"I don't give a shit what Pax wants." I grit my teeth and give up the fight. "Forget it."

I'll have to shift my method if I want to catch Pax with his linen pants down in front of everyone, so I focus on painting something special. It's time to hold a mirror up to this monster.

"Hannah, come on." Tess tries to reopen the conversation, but I just ignore her.

Pax glides behind Tess now, looking over her shoulder at the canvas, just like Waylon Barlow did in my dream.

"This is...extraordinary," Pax says.

I don't want to give Tess the satisfaction of looking at her work, but I sneak a peek out of the corner of my eye. The abstract charcoal pattern looks like two human forms entwined as one. A monstrous entanglement.

"Well," Tess says, "I should confess that I have an MFA." She flaunts it every chance she gets, acting like the fine arts are a higher calling than my path into science and medicine.

"It shows," Pax responds. "And those late nights sketching here under the spirits' guidance have clearly paid off."

I can't stop myself from interjecting. "If only the spirits could pay off your student loans."

I immediately regret taking that cheap shot as Tess's jaw drops. I just get so frustrated with how disconnected she is from reality sometimes, and I wanted to remind her that the real world still exists outside of this retreat, but I'm clearly becoming my worst self out here.

Pax puts a comforting hand on Tess's shoulder. "I'm feeling a lot of love coming off the canvas."

"Yeah, I guess that's what I'm trying to channel today." Tess glares at me. "Whether it's felt or not."

I avert my eyes to my own painting, focused on finishing my masterpiece.

Pax looks Tess in the eyes. "Love need not be accepted to have an impact on the recipient."

Tess's eyes well up a little. "Thank you, Pax."

He steps behind me now. "Oh my." The guru's face falls, just like I hoped.

Waylon Barlow fills the canvas in his big round hat and overalls, raising his pickaxe high with blood dripping from its pointed edge. But was it Waylon Barlow who attacked me? Or just Guru Pax dressed up for more spiritual theater?

"What do you see?" I ask Pax as he stares at my crude painting.

"It's not what I *see*. It's what I feel, which is rather frightened."

"Is that what you want *us* to feel? Frightened?"

"I'm afraid I don't follow you." He's not taking the Rorschach bait.

"No, you want *us* to follow *you*. You're in control here, right? So what's the end game?"

Pax entwines his fingers. "Control is an illusion, Hannah. You are all free here."

"Bullshit." My fingers clench around the paintbrush. "I signed up for healing, not gaslighting."

"Hannah..." Tess starts, but I have no patience for her, for anyone anymore. I'm sick of everyone lying to themselves and painting me as the identified patient.

I point my red-dipped brush at Pax. "If we're free, then why don't you give me the satellite phone? I want to report my friends missing."

"Missing?" Tess says. "They left a note, Hannah. You need to relax."

"Oh, but we're not here for relaxation, Tess. We're here to transcend, right, Pax? To move from ignorance into self-knowledge."

I take a step toward Pax, who stands rooted and strong.

"That's it, Hannah." He smirks a smirk only I can see. "Step into your truth."

"You want to know my truth? My truth is *fuck* this place and *fuck* you, guru!"

I stab my brush through the canvas, piercing Waylon Barlow through his false face and dragging the handle down to rip a hole straight between his legs.

Tess and Miles gasp, but Pax is silent as I toss the brush to the ground, red paint staining my fingers.

What the fuck did I just do?

I move away from the group, but Miles steps in front of me. "Hey, are you—"

"Don't, Miles." If he asks me if I'm okay, I'll scream. Even though I'm very much not okay and want nothing more than to let him comfort me, to feel his arms wrap around me. But I'm a raw nerve of confusion and anger, and all I know how to do in this state is push people away. "If you think I'm here for a hot desert hookup, you're wrong, so give it up already."

His sweet face melts as he steps out of my way, and I walk off alone with a red right hand.

26

I SLIP INTO THE HOT SPRINGS BATH AND LET THE WARM water soothe my tense muscles. I really need to get my shit together and stop snapping at people, because it's not helping my case at all.

But what exactly is my case? What do I know for sure?

Two of my friends are gone.

Yes, there's an explanation for that, but it just doesn't sit right.

Especially after I was attacked outside the mine by Waylon Barlow. There were no drugs to blame for that, but there *is* a precedent for me seeing things that aren't really there. I wish I could trust myself, but the lines have gotten so blurry out here in the desert, and my memories already feel like distant dreams. Was I confronted by a costumed creep, a spirit of the land, or just another Hannah hallucination?

One thing's for sure: Pax lied to the group about the drugs. Unfortunately, everybody else seems fine with that red flag, so I guess I just have to let it fly.

That's hard to do when Kimi tried to warn me about Pax, and then I basically heard him threaten her to keep her mouth shut.

This place is not what it seems.

Was Kimi just talking about Pax's slippery methods? Or does he have some bigger ulterior motive?

I suspect the latter. The way Pax spoke to me, the way he glared at me. There was something menacing in it.

I take a deep breath of hot steam rising off the water, then start walking in laps around the edge of the pool. The movement helps stir my brain.

Okay. So, if I'm determined to figure this shit out, what's the first thing for me to do?

I need evidence, some kind of tangible proof. The universe must be listening as my foot grazes something on the bottom of the pool. I dunk below the surface, pawing at the ground until I grab the thing, rising back above the water with a gold chain in my hand.

Not just any gold chain. This is Jared's necklace. I remember him anxiously playing with it after the sound bath.

How did it end up at the bottom of the pool?

The chain is broken—not unclasped, but broken. The kind of thing that might happen during a struggle.

When Jared left the yoga studio the other day, he said he was going to the sauna. That's when he disappeared.

I climb out of the pool and wrap a towel around myself as I open the sauna door.

The haze clears as I look around inside, lowering to my hands and knees under the bench seat, searching for more clues.

That's where I find a sliver of dried skin, about the size of a stamp.

Snakeskin?

As soon as I rub it between my fingers, it dissolves into meaningless crumbles, like it was never there at all.

A snake in a sauna sure seems like a recipe for a bad time.

I step out of the barrel and remember seeing Kimi cleaning up the area right after Jared's disappearance.

Your friend made quite a mess.

Another M-word starts swirling around my mind now, one that I really don't want to consider. Was Kimi covering up not just a mess but a murder?

But if she's in cahoots with Pax, then why would she help me, warn me?

Unless she was intentionally misleading me. Maybe she's only in it for the money, just like she said.

My brain keeps pinballing like I'm trying to crack the code of a true crime series. But I'm always wrong when I guess the guilty party in those.

I just need to connect some more dots to make sense of it all.

What about Luna? She went to do yoga by herself before she disappeared.

I head into the yoga studio, exploring every corner, looking for some kind of clue. Some kind of evidence that Luna had been here, that something happened before she disappeared. I need something concrete that I can show the others, but I don't find a damn thing. It's all pristinely clean, nothing out of the ordinary.

Until I count the yoga mats in the corner.

One of them is missing.

Would Luna have taken one with her to the Airbnb? No, she

brought her own and left it in Jared's car. I saw it when we were loading in for the trip.

Something isn't right. Something is being covered up.

That's what paranoia sounds like, doesn't it?

But is it paranoia when you have hard evidence?

No, a broken necklace and missing yoga mat aren't evidence of anything.

Pax lied, but maybe Tess is right about him. Just because he's a disingenuous guru doesn't mean he's a murderer.

Is that really what I think is happening? Murder?

No, that would be way too crazy.

But maybe Jared and Luna have been secreted away somewhere for deeper brainwashing.

Maybe Pax is like a New Age Scientologist starting his own religion out here in the desert. He gets his hooks in at the retreat, then sends them off to a larger compound, where they all eat from bigger and bigger communal bowls.

Of course, there's no evidence to support any of this speculation, so I'm back on the hunt.

The sound bath den is next. This is where we all had our first spiritual experience together. I head over to the shelf where bundles of leaves and herbs are resting, all labeled with little placards.

White sage. Mugwort. Palo santo.

These are all familiar herbs that I've seen sold on Abbott Kinney. Luna said it was nothing more than sage that Kimi was burning that day, but as I lift each bundle to smell, none of them have the aroma that I remember.

Until I come across one labeled *Divinorum*.

This bundle of dark leaves looks just like the one Kimi was burning. I lift it for a sniff, and it immediately brings me back.

This is it. This is what we were all inhaling when we had our intense hallucinatory experiences.

Divinorum.

Something about the name rings a bell, but I can't place it. It sounds Latin, like a drug.

I flip through my encyclopedic medical school knowledge but turn up empty-handed.

Who else would know drugs?

Dr. Grady.

I wish I could talk to my psychiatrist now, get his guidance, but how can I call him without the satellite phone?

I pull my cell phone out of my pocket and turn it on. The battery is down to its last bar and there's still no service.

"You need to get as high as you can."

Kimi wasn't talking about the weed we were smoking that night. She was giving me a coded message just in case Pax was listening, which he was. If I want to get cell phone service, I'll need to get high, gain more elevation to catch the signal.

I use my phone to snap a photo of the divinorum leaves and placard before heading out of the sound bath den. I have to find a way to get my SOS call out before my phone battery dies and my only lifeline dies with it.

27

THE RETREAT IS NESTLED BETWEEN TWO LARGE MOUNTAINS, so if I want to get high like Kimi suggested, I'll have to prepare for a proper summit hike.

My first since Ben's death.

I pack plenty of water in my backpack and start the journey. The rocky terrain here is nothing like the icy slopes of Northern California, but it's just as treacherous. It only takes five minutes of trekking before one wrong foot sends a rock sliding out beneath my boot, and I slam face-first against the dusty earth.

My whole skull is throbbing, but I can't give up.

I spend an hour slipping and scrambling up toward the sky, stopping to check my phone every hundred yards or so with no luck. Probably best to keep it turned off and just push all the way to the top. That takes me another half hour, but I make it.

As I tip my canteen, the last drops of water spill onto my tongue, leaving nothing for the hike down. People often think that ascents are the hardest, but it's going down a mountain that you have to worry about. Fighting gravity as it tries to pull you down faster than your feet can keep up is how most people end up tumbling to their death.

I shield my eyes from the sun, which is so much closer up here, taking in a full view of the retreat in the valley below. It looks abandoned with nobody out and about anymore. They must have all returned to their yurts for an afternoon rest after I totally killed the buzz.

I'm not going to beat myself up for that because it will all be worth it.

Turning my phone back on, I lift it high. Still no signal.

"Come on, come on..."

I walk around the perimeter of the peak, careful not to step too close to the edge.

Looking out at the desert below, I have a vision of the snowy valley that fateful day, when I chased Ben down the mountain...

I close my eyes and shake it off.

No. Stay in the present. Focus on the mission.

Climbing onto a small boulder at the edge of the mountain gives me an extra few feet of lift, and my phone catches a bar of service.

"Yes!" But is one bar enough?

My text notification chimes with a message from an unknown number.

Your internship is over, incompetent bitch. I'm coming for you.

The threat throws me off balance for a moment. A quick google of the texter's area code tells me it's a Houston number, which tells me it's Mr. Fox.

Shit. Is he actually crazy enough to come after me? What if he—

My phone vibrates with a low battery warning. I don't have time for more theorizing.

Pulling up Grady's contact info, I look at his smiling face again. I should have called him when we pulled over for the dead rabbit, when my body tried to send me a warning from the universe by way of a crippling panic attack.

I won't make the same mistake twice.

My thumb presses *Call*, unsure of exactly what I'm going to say or how I'm going to say it.

It rings one. Twice. Three and four times.

"Please, please, please answer."

If the call goes to voicemail, I'll never—

"This is Dr. Grady."

"Grady!" I gasp. "Oh, thank God."

"Hannah? Is that you?" His voice sounds garbled. "I can barely hear you."

That one bar of signal is working as hard as it can, but I'm afraid it won't be enough.

"I need your help." I speak quickly, no time to think, to censor my tumbling thoughts. "Either I'm losing my mind or something really bad is happening."

"Happening where? Are you still at the retreat?"

"Yes, but two people have already disappeared."

"What do you mean, disappeared?"

"Disappeared, Grady. They were here, and now they're gone. I mean, Luna left a note, but I found Jared's necklace in the pool, and Pax pretended to drug us but didn't, and I found this...this herb..."

"Hannah. Slow down."

Damn it, I sound unhinged. Just focus on the most important details.

"I saw something, some*one*. They attacked me. This local legend, an old miner with a—"

Clink.

My words crash to a halt as I look across the valley toward the source of the echoing sound.

Waylon Barlow faces me from the peak across the way, standing patient and still in broad daylight. As if I summoned the thoughtform myself, just like Pax suggested. As if the figure from my painting crawled off the canvas and up the peak just to mock me from a distance. A dark mirror image challenging my fragile sense of sanity when I'm trying so desperately to keep it stable.

He swings his axe into the rocky earth once more.

Clink.

"Hannah?" Grady says through the phone. "Are you there?"

"Go away, go away, go away," I whisper across the valley. The wind sweeps my words away, and only Grady can hear them.

Clink.

"Are you talking to me, or is someone else there?" he asks through the phone.

Barlow lifts his pickaxe and points across the valley at me. A threatening gesture, even at this distance.

"Hannah," Grady says. "You're scaring me. Talk to me."

Clink.

"Someone's trying to kill me, Grady. He's staring at me right now. Unless…" I hesitate to finish the thought, but it's one of the reasons I'm calling. Isn't it? "Unless he's not really there at all."

"Okay," Grady says, locking into a confident tone. Psychiatrist to the rescue. "I want you to listen and do exactly as I say, Hannah. Just so you know you're not alone, I'll do every step with you, okay?"

Clink.

I'm frozen, can't answer.

"Hannah, okay?"

"Okay."

"Okay. Close your eyes."

I hesitate to take my eye off the killer, but he's a mountain away. He can't really get me, can he? My eyelids resist as I force them closed.

Clink.

"Take three deep breaths as I count them off. Three. Two. One."

I feel each breath settle my nerves.

"Now open your eyes."

When I do, Waylon Barlow is gone. The mountaintop across the way is barren.

"Is he still there?" Grady asks.

"No," I respond, finally ready to accept that he never was. There's no costumed killer or theatrical performer. Just another manifestation of my broken brain. It makes sense that talking to my psychiatrist now would trigger the vision again, even if it is taking this strange new form of Barlow instead of Ben.

"Good," Grady says. "You're safe. Now, start at the beginning. What's going on out there?"

I look down at the empty retreat again, not sure where to begin. I've lost the thread on the paranoid narrative my mind had tried so hard to weave.

Staring at the rocky desert floor beneath, I see it's a long way to the bottom. Long enough to make for a quick ending if I leap far enough out and don't go tumbling against every rock on the way down.

Maybe that would be best for everyone.

"I'm so tired of this, Grady." I sigh into the phone. "I'm tired of not trusting my own mind. I just want it to be over."

"Don't talk like that, Hannah. Please. You have so much to live for."

"Do I?" My life has felt empty for a long time. Now that I've had some time away from work, I know that Grady was right. It's been nothing more than a busy distraction from the void of my existence. I can't imagine plugging back into the hospital grind, not after the awakening I'm having out here. Not after realizing how dangerously unstable I really am.

What difference would it make to anybody if I threw myself down to the rocks below?

"Everybody thinks I'm crazy," I say. "I'm starting to think so, too."

"I don't think you're crazy," Grady responds. He always sounds so sincere. I picture him pacing his office now in his New Balance sneakers, and it brings a little light to my dark thoughts. "What were you saying about drugging?"

"Right." I remember now why I was calling him in the first place. Pulling the phone from my ear, I text the photo to Grady. "I just sent you something. I need to know what it is."

"Okay, I just got it. Hm, I'm pretty sure this is... Give me a second. Doing a quick google here. Yeah, it's known as the 'sage of the diviners.'"

"So, it really is just sage."

There you go. I'm crazy. Might as well jump.

"Well, it's not just any sage," Grady says. "*Salvia divinorum* has psychoactive properties."

"Salvia?" I've heard of that drug before, seen it. Not in person, but in viral videos on YouTube of people taking a hit and immediately nosediving into a hallucinogenic state.

"When you inhale the smoke," Grady explains, "you can have a very quick trip, maybe fifteen to thirty minutes."

Holy shit. Pax *had* drugged us. Just not when we were expecting it.

If he can be that manipulative, who knows what else he's capable of?

"Grady." My hand trembles on the phone. "He's drugging us."

"What? Who is?"

"The psycho fucking guru. He gave us a placebo when he said we were taking hallucinogens, but he actually drugged us during the sound bath. Shit, he even had us sign waivers to cover his ass retroactively. Like a fucking magician using misdirection."

"Okay, I don't like the sound of this, Hannah. Where are you, exactly?"

"I don't know. We're in the middle of the desert, north of 29 Palms. At the end of Dead Man's Due Road. There are two big mountain peaks, and we're in the val—"

Beep-Beep.

The call drops as my phone battery dies.

I stare at the black screen, my lifeline to the outside world gone.

Standing exposed on the mountaintop, I want to break down and cry. Exhaustion racks my weary bones as I look down. Some part of me still yearns for the sweet relief of the big leap. The final *release* of giving up.

Thankfully, my higher self is stronger.

I refuse to die at this stupid place.

But if I want to get out alive with my sanity intact, I need to convince my friends that I'm not crazy after all. Even if Waylon Barlow is only in my head, it's clear now who put him there. Because Pax is in my head too, in *all* of our heads. It's time to flush the fucker out.

I start my descent back down the mountain, taking every step with extra caution.

I can't afford to fall.

28

BY THE TIME I MAKE IT BACK DOWN THE MOUNTAIN, I'M parched. Refilling my canteen at the communal tap, I gulp down water until I feel replenished. But I'm still not ready for what I have to do next. Heading toward Tess's yurt, I have to find a way to smooth things over.

"Tess?" I ask through the flap. "Can I come in?"

"Sure." Not a ton of enthusiasm in her tone.

When I enter, Tess is standing in front of an easel, sketching with charcoal. It's an eerie recreation of my dream. Only in this staging, I'm Waylon Barlow.

Tess doesn't turn to face me, so I just dive in with a tentative "Hi."

No response. Just more scratching away at the big white canvas.

I'm desperate to blurt out everything I've learned, but that didn't go so well with Grady. Tess was clearly wounded by my words, so I'll have to start there and ease into it.

Taking a step closer, I'm partly expecting to see my own portrait being sketched on the canvas, just like in my dream. What I see on the canvas instead is something much darker and more abstract. The shape looks something like a human heart, ripped in half with torn veins and ventricles fraying outward.

"I'm sorry for what I said earlier," I say.

"Why? It's true. My art doesn't pay the bills, and I'm okay with that. But the fact that you thought it was a dig tells me that you've been quietly judging me." Tess finally turns to face me now, tears welling in her eyes. "And that's a shitty feeling, Hannah."

I take a step toward her, desperate to fix this. "I lashed out, okay? I was feeling alone and unheard, and I just wanted to hurt you, so I said something stupid."

I'm being honest, but that doesn't mean Tess has to believe me.

"You've been lashing out at everyone this weekend," Tess says. "We're not in college anymore. We're grown-ass adults. It's time you started acting like it."

How had the tables turned so quickly? The weekend started with Tess and me laughing about how childish Jared and Luna were. Now, the lovebirds have jumped ship, and Tess is lecturing me about *my* behavior. I feel my defenses go back up.

"What do you want from me? I came to this retreat, just like you wanted." As soon as I say the words out loud, something clicks. "Wait. You never actually explained *how* you got this exclusive invitation."

"I told you. I heard about it through a friend at the gallery, and she introduced me to Pax."

"So you met Pax *before* coming here?" I can't seem to turn off my suspicious mind.

"No, that's not what I…" Tess crosses her arms. "I thought you came here to apologize. Are you really interrogating me right now?"

"I came to talk to you about what's really going on here."

"What's going on, Hannah, is you're sick. And maybe it's my fault for not understanding sooner just how serious it is. But it's not like I didn't try to be there for you after Ben died."

"Why is everybody throwing that in my face now? I'm sorry I couldn't make you all feel better about how supportive you were being. I was in mourning, okay?"

"But that's just it. You're not mourning anymore. You're just giving up. I know you, Han. I can tell. You used to face everything with this bright strength. College, med school, everything. But lately, it's like you just want to crawl into a hole and die. What's it going to take to make you realize that you want to live?"

Coming hot on the heels of my mountaintop teeter, Tess's words cut deep.

"I do want to live," I say. "I want to live and get far away from the manipulative asshole running this retreat."

"What are you talking about?"

"Pax drugged us."

Tess laughs. "I'm sorry. But did you not just attack him for giving us a placebo? Which he then admitted to? I'm having a little trouble following your shifting conspiracy theories."

"He gave us a placebo for the spirit journey, yes, but in the sound bath, Kimi was burning salvia to make us hallucinate."

"So, now Kimi is the Big Bad, not Pax?"

I hadn't quite thought that part through. It was Kimi who

was burning the salvia. Could she have done that without Pax knowing?

"I don't think so. Kimi just..." I stutter, and Tess latches on to my faltering confidence.

"You don't even know which paranoid delusion you believe right now." Tess shakes her head. "I think you should go rest. Jared and Luna will be back tomorrow morning, and then we can all move on and stop pretending that we're still friends. This was clearly a big mistake."

It stings like hell to hear her dismiss our friendship like that, but Tess is clearly too hurt to hear me. There's no point trying to get through to her right now, so I just shrug.

"I guess you're right. This was a mistake."

"Glad we're finally on the same page." Tess turns back to her easel and rips the paper off. She crumples it into a ball and tosses it across the room. "Can you leave me to draw in peace now? It'd be nice if I could actually get something good out of this retreat."

Tess picks up her charcoal and goes back to sketching.

I keep my mouth shut and slip out of the yurt, away from my former best friend. Drifting past the labyrinth walk with all those spiraling stones in the dirt, I remember my intention word.

Release.

A noxious mix of pain and rage is burning in my gut, but I don't know how to release it all. I want to open my mouth like a dragon and torch the whole damn place.

Instead, I go back to my yurt to regroup.

"Hannah."

I flip on my heels with fists raised to find Miles lurking in the corner.

"Whoa," he says. "Sorry I scared you."

"What are you doing here?"

"I just wanted to apologize."

"*You* want to apologize? I was the asshole." I'd been so caught up trying to make amends to Tess that I'd almost forgotten how nasty I was to Miles, too.

"I was coming on too strong," Miles admits, "and that wasn't fair of me. I mean, it's no secret that I like you, Hannah. But there's a time and a place for that. And it's not when we're all feeling exposed and vulnerable at this retreat."

"Thank you for saying that." I sit on the edge of my mattress, grateful for the tender directness. "It makes me feel a little less crazy."

"You are definitely not crazy." Miles takes a seat next to me. "I've been thinking about what you said to Pax, and something does feel off. I mean, Jared and I have been friends for a long time. Running off like that isn't exactly out of character, but I would've expected him to be back by now with a case of beer, ready to party. And this place is Luna's dream—she wouldn't just bounce. If Jared really came back, she would have made him stay."

"Exactly!" Hearing Miles put it that way is such a comfort. I'm not the only person who thinks these cover stories are out of character, but the question still remains. "So, where the hell are they, Miles?"

"I don't know." He shrugs.

I dig into my pocket and put the broken necklace in Miles's hand.

"Jared's chain," he says. "Where'd you find it?"

"At the bottom of the hot springs pool. I also found out that Pax drugged us with salvia in the sound bath."

"Salvia? Holy shit." Miles runs a hand through his hair. "I should've recognized it."

"You've done it before?"

"Someone passed me a joint after a show once, and I didn't know it was laced. I tripped for like twenty minutes before bouncing back. That shit is intense, but it's actually legal in California, so it's not like he was dosing us with LSD or anything. But still..."

"Pretty sneaky."

"Pretty fucking sneaky," Miles affirms. "So, what do you think is going on?"

After working through every theory, there's only one that makes sense anymore. "I think Pax is trying to brainwash us, make us believe he's some kind of supernatural savior. He's been getting into our heads just so he can pit us against each other and separate us. What if he has Jared and Luna hidden away somewhere against their will?"

"What, like some kind of Shelly Miscavige situation?"

"Exactly." That's just one of many *Cults 101* episodes where suspected kidnapping and Stockholm syndrome were key ingredients for a loyal following.

"I'm not gonna lie; it sounds like a stretch to me." Even if Miles doubts me, the honesty is refreshing, especially when he follows it up with a game plan. "Either way, we need to get some answers. If Pax is being dodgy about letting us use that satellite phone, then I say we go get it ourselves."

"After all his lies, how do we even know he really has one?"

"Only one way to find out." Miles stands, and I think I'm thinking what he's thinking.

"Okay." A new energy floods my veins as I stand with him. "Let's go find out."

I'm so grateful to have Miles on my team, I could kiss him right here and now.

But he's right. There's a time and a place for such a thing, and now is not it.

Maybe later, though.

29

PAX'S YURT IS SET FARTHER AWAY FROM ALL THE OTHERS. FAR enough that you can't actually see how big it is unless you walk right up to it, like Miles and I are doing right now.

"Living a bit larger than the rest of us, isn't he?" Miles whispers.

"Guess he needs the extra space for his giant ego. Pax!" I yell into the yurt. "You there?!"

Miles cringes. "Not going the discreet route, then?"

"Seems like nobody's home," I say, hearing no movement inside. "If you see him coming, make a noise."

"What kind of noise?"

"I don't know. Whistle."

He shakes his head. "Can't."

"You can't whistle? I thought you were a musician."

"It's a sore subject."

He looks genuinely embarrassed by this musical deficiency as I put a hand on his shoulder. "Any sound will do, Miles."

I reach for the tent flap, but he grabs my hand. "Wait. Are you sure this is a good idea?"

"This was kinda your idea."

"Well, I kinda have bad ideas sometimes. I just don't want to put you in any danger."

"I'm perfectly capable of putting myself in danger. Just watch my back." I duck into the yurt before he can respond.

It's definitely roomier in here, but also messier than I expected. There are dirty clothes everywhere—jeans and T-shirts—which makes me think Pax only wears his white linen uniform when he's around us. A water-pump shower kit in the corner explains how he's always looking and smelling so fresh.

But what really draws my attention is the bed. Not a straw-filled mattress on the dirt like everyone else, but a full-framed off-the-ground bed. I flop onto it to confirm that yes, it's fucking memory foam.

Turning my head to the bedside table, I see an empty Snickers bar wrapper. This is somehow the worst offense. That hypocritical bastard is eating processed sugar before bed. But I'm not looking for evidence of Pax's hypocrisy. He offers that up in spades every time he opens his stupid mouth.

Hopping off the very comfortable mattress, I start my hunt in earnest.

Now that I know he's living in the lap of luxury out here, I'm confident he really does have a satellite phone. But where would it be?

I clock a bookshelf in the corner and rush over to riffle through the titles.

There are plenty of pop psychology books, including one by a famous holistic therapist who rose to fame on Instagram and has since been exposed as an anti-science nutjob.

But Pax doesn't have a social media presence, so what's *his* endgame?

I don't need any confirmation that he's performing tricks with smoke bombs and sleight of hand, but seeing *The Magician's Secrets* on his shelf seals it.

Persuasion: The Power of Influence tells me that he's a practiced psychological manipulator.

Then there's *The Illusion of Security: Controlling the Human Identity*.

I pull this one off the shelf, but before I flip through it, I notice a small black box on the shelf below, almost like a jewelry case.

Cracking it open, I find a small piece of gray plastic attached to a key ring.

An electric key fob, just like the one I use to buzz in and out of my apartment complex.

Why would Pax need an electric key at a retreat with no electricity? Maybe it's for his own apartment off-site, but—

"It's Pax! Hi, Pax!" Miles shouts from the other side of the flap. "Here you are, Pax!"

Least subtle alert system ever. I need to teach that boy how to whistle.

"Here I am." Pax's voice is too damn close for comfort on the other side of the flap.

I scan the yurt walls for an exit, pawing at the flaps of animal skin in search of some slit that I can slip through.

"How can I help you, Miles?" Pax's tone is already strained with impatience.

"I was wondering if you could give me another primer on the labyrinth walk."

"It's rather self-explanatory. I have faith that you can figure it out on your own."

My head snaps to the bed, remembering it's actually raised. I drop to the floor and slide underneath it, dirtying my clothes in the process. That's where I find the plastic Pelican case, like the kind Ben used to carry camera equipment in. I'm betting this one contains a satellite phone.

Unfortunately, it's too cramped down here to open it. I'm trapped with no choice but to wait while Miles is trying and failing out there to keep Pax occupied.

"But what if I get lost in the—"

"You'll find your way," Pax says. "I really must be going."

I listen as Pax pushes through the yurt flap and pads across the floor. He sits on the bed, and the mattress sinks down, pressing against my hip.

Pax's hand reaches down and paws beneath the bed, nearly touching my face.

Shit. He must be looking for the satellite phone.

I push the box within his reach until his fingers loop into the handle, pulling it out.

Holding my breath, I listen to the distinctive sound of fingers pressing buttons, an electronic *beep* accompanying each one.

He's using the phone right now. But who's he calling?

"Yes, it's me," he says. "No, the results with this group aren't as strong as I hoped." Pax doesn't sound like Pax anymore. The smooth guru tone is gone, replaced by a strange coldness. "But there are still three left. I have especially high hopes for one candidate who's absolutely ready to transcend. I'll let you know as soon as I'm finished with them."

The phone turns off with a beep, and I watch Pax's feet shuffle over to the bookshelf. The next sound I hear is that little box on the shelf snapping open.

He's looking for the key fob, but he isn't going to find it there.

Because it's currently clutched in my sweaty palm.

I can't stand the silence, the waiting, so I shift my body forward to peek out from under the bed, just in time to see Pax snap the box shut in frustration.

He tucks the satellite phone into his pocket before heading for the door flap.

"Miles!" Pax calls. "I'd like to speak with you."

As soon as Pax is out of the yurt, I snake my way out from under the bed.

Slipping through the tent flap, I make sure Pax doesn't see me. He's too focused on Miles, who's dutifully playing into his own cover story by stumbling his way through the labyrinth maze.

"Were you in my yurt?" Pax asks him.

"Was *I*...in *your* yurt?" Miles puts his hands on his hips, effortlessly unsmooth. "No, I have my own yurt. Why would I be in your—"

"Ready, Miles?" I interrupt the interrogation.

"Where are you two going?" Pax raises a brow in suspicion.

"We're going for a night walk." My hand slips into Miles's. "This retreat has really opened us up to possibilities."

I throw a loving smile at Miles.

Pax squints. "Is that right?"

"That's right," Miles adds. "I was just doing the labyrinth maze to ask for guidance from the spirits. They told me to lean into love."

I rest my head on Miles's shoulder. "Thank you, Pax."

Pax seems to buy it, at least for the moment. "I'm very happy to hear that." His gaze moves away from us to scour the retreat now. "Have either of you seen Kimi?"

"Not recently," Miles says, turning to me. "Getting chilly. I should grab my jacket." He leads me away from Pax, his fingers intertwined in mine. When we finally duck into his yurt, we both exhale with relief.

"That was a close call," Miles says.

I look down at his hand, still holding mine.

"Sorry," he says, retracting it.

"You're fine. It was a good cover, right?"

"Right, totally." We're both blushing in the knowledge that our cover came very easily. "Did you find the phone?"

"I did, and then I heard him use it."

"Who'd he call?"

"I don't know, but he was referring to us as 'candidates' ready to 'transcend.'"

"Cult," Miles says. "That's one hundred percent cult talk."

"I also found this." I show him the key fob.

"A door opener at a retreat with no doors," Miles says, echoing my thoughts. "Safe to say it doesn't work on any of these deerskin flaps, so what do you think it's for?"

"I don't know, but we can't go sneaking around all night looking for secret passageways all *Scooby-Doo*-like. Pax is already too suspicious."

After seeing those books on his shelf, I know we're dealing with a calculating psychological abuser. Which is both validating and terrifying.

"So, what do we do?" Miles asks.

"Seeing you in the labyrinth gave me an idea. We both believe that Jared and Luna didn't just take off back to town, right?"

"Right."

"Which means their car has to be around here somewhere. We just have to follow the tracks."

Miles puts on his jacket. "I guess we're going on that night walk after all." He touches the inside pocket with a furrowed brow.

"You okay?"

"Yeah, I just lost the…" He shrugs it off. "Not important. But we better stay hydrated." Reaching for his canteen, he takes a swig and brings it with him.

We duck out into the night and run into Kimi preparing dinner in the dining area.

"Hey," I say. "I've been looking for you, and so has Pax."

Kimi keeps her eyes averted. "You shouldn't have said what you said to him."

"Well, I don't really give a shit about him. He interrupted us the other night, and I need to know what's really going on at this place. You said it's not—"

"I didn't say a thing." Kimi's eyes keep darting from me to the wall of animal skulls. "The weekend is almost over. It would be best for everyone if you just saw it through and stopped making waves."

There's something pleading in Kimi's eyes. Something that makes me say, "Okay. Sure."

She brushes past me, whispering something in my ear.

As I head off into the night with Miles, he asks, "What did she say?"

I relay the chilling warning: "He sees everything."

30

THE PERPETUAL FLAMES ARE STILL BURNING OUTSIDE THE retreat entrance. I grab a torch, even though it doesn't do much to brighten the dark road ahead.

"Ready?" I ask Miles.

"I hear there's no time like the present." He takes a swig of water and offers his canteen to me, but my throat is too tight with fear to drink anything. "So, what's the plan again?"

"We're just following the tracks." I lower the flame to highlight the car tracks in the dirt. "This is where Jared parked. And it looks like the car backed up, turned around, and headed back toward town."

We start walking along the tracks in that direction.

"That doesn't exactly conflict with the narrative, right?" Miles scratches his head. "I mean, what if Jared and Luna really did head back to town? That's a long-ass walk in the dark for us, and what"—something rustles in the brush—"the fuck!"

Miles grabs me in terror as…a rabbit scurries across the dirt.

We both laugh in relief.

"Sorry," Miles says. "Guess I'm not exactly a fearless protector."

"I'm not asking you to be one." I thought I had that with Ben, the adventurous outdoorsman, but it wasn't real in the end anyway. "Take another look." I bend down to the dirt. "How many tracks do you see?"

Miles squints in the dark. "Two sets. Looks like the same tread."

"Right. Two, not four."

"Right. One car, in and out." Miles is a bit slower than I was hoping.

"One car that Jared drove in, then back to town...and then returned to pick up Luna before heading back to town a second time."

"Whoa." He looks genuinely impressed as he finally pieces it all together. "When did you turn into Sherlock Holmes?"

"I'm a doctor. It's kind of my job to crack cases by interpreting the presenting symptoms." The detective part of the gig has always been way more appealing than the people part.

"Well, you are very impressive. Always have been."

"Thank you, dear Watson."

Miles gives a cordial bow back. He's acting extra goofy tonight, but I don't mind a little levity. We keep following the tracks by the light of the torch until the moon breaks through the clouds and lights our path a bit more clearly.

Miles stares up with saucerlike eyes. "Damn. The moon is bright."

"Hunter's Moon, right? At least that's what Pax said. But I'm pretty sure we can't trust anything Pax says."

"Do you believe in aliens?" Miles asks, like it's the most casual thing in the world.

"Did you really just ask me that?"

"Well, if you'd rather keep speculating about the nefarious retreat plot, we can totally—"

"Yes, I believe in aliens. I mean, not like little gray men, but there has to be some kind of life out there." It's not a far-fetched belief. Just a statistical probability.

"I have this theory," Miles says. "Humans, we think this is our planet. But the earth is 70 percent water, right?"

"Right..."

"So really, it's a water world. Not like Kevin Costner with webbed feet on a jet ski, but just literally. The planet is mostly oceans. So what if *we're* the aliens, and the earth actually belongs to the fish and the octopuses?"

I could give him a million biological reasons why that makes no sense. But I decide to play along instead. "Okay, so taking that a step further. Maybe Pax is a representative of that alien race. He's come back to collect us, to help us transcend back to the mothership before we kill this planet for good."

Miles claps. "There you have it, Holmes. I think we cracked the case."

"I hope so. Because the alternatives are way scarier."

After a moment of silence, walking under the weight of those alternatives, Miles speaks up again. "Keeping our mind off present circumstances, can I ask you something? And if it's totally inappropriate, you don't have to answer it."

"That's a pretty weighted lead-in, but sure. Go for it."

"How did you get through it? Losing your fiancé like that? It must have been awful."

It was bound to come up eventually. I steel myself before I speak. "Well, first of all, I didn't really get through it. I just worked harder, numbed myself on drugs, and kept pushing forward. I was kind of hoping to change tracks at this retreat, but here we are."

I stare down at the tire tracks, leading us farther into the darkness.

"I get it," Miles says. "It's way easier to disappear into drugs than to face shit head-on." There's a moment of silence before he adds, "And second of all?"

"Huh?"

"You said first of all."

I didn't mean to set myself up like that, but I guess I have nothing to lose. Maybe it's finally time to tell someone the truth.

"Right. Well, second of all, I guess, is the fact that...Ben wasn't my fiancé."

Miles stops short, and my heart sinks like an anchor in my chest.

"What?" His gaze is locked in on the engagement ring on my finger. "Tess told me that he proposed to you that day."

"He did. But what Tess doesn't know, what *nobody* knows...is that I said no. I lied to everyone. I guess I felt like I couldn't come back with no body *and* tell everyone that I turned down his proposal. By the time I changed my mind and wanted to tell the truth, it was too late. The story just...stuck."

"So, what's the real story?" The question is a fishhook, latching on to a memory in my brain, and Miles is slowly reeling it up to the surface. "What happened after you said no?"

"Ben, wait!"

I rush to catch up with him, but he's better at walking in crampons than I am. My footfalls are clumsy. I trip and fall, swinging my ice axe into a tree. It catches in the wood, preventing me from hitting the ice face-first and sliding all the way down.

"Please!"

Ben just keeps going, doesn't even care.

I chase him the whole way down the mountain, finally reaching him at the bottom of the trail. "Just wait!"

He spins on his feet. "I'm done waiting for you, Hannah. I've wasted years of my life with you. If you don't want to spend the rest of our lives together, then what the fuck are we even—"

The sound of an animal huffing draws our attention to the tree line.

A herd of elk has gathered, creating a stunning tableau. Two calves sniff beneath the snow in search of grass with their mother and big-horned father. The sight of these majestic beasts pulls the air from our lungs.

For a timeless moment, all the tension between us disappears, and it feels like everything might be okay. Maybe these creatures appeared just in time to remind us that our problems are meaningless in the grand scheme of things.

Ben takes out his camera and starts toward them.

I put a hand on his arm. "Don't get too close."

"Don't tell me what to do," he spits back, pulling from my grasp.

Ben was the one who always warned me about getting too close to wild animals, but he's being stubborn now. He's ignoring me out of spite. Deep down, I know that the more I try to stop him, the harder he'll push back.

So, I let him go. I watch as he inches closer and closer to the herd, his camera *click-click-click*ing away.

I feel it in the air. A shift in the energy of the herd. Something is wrong.

The father elk raises his head in Ben's direction. Hearing the *clicks*, sensing a disturbance.

I see this, all of it, but Ben doesn't. His camera is held up close to his face, focused on the mother and her calves, paying no mind to the father. Even though he always warned me that you have to pay attention to the protective father.

I could yell to warn him, I *should* yell.

But I don't. I'm silent. Like a meditative practice, I am merely an observer.

Some part of me wants it to happen. Some part of me manifests it.

The moments that follow collapse on each other like a series of dominos.

The father elk takes off across the snow, stomping and kicking up white dust.

Ben lowers his lens and turns to run back toward me. His eyes lock into mine, begging me to meet him halfway, to save him.

But the elk is too fast. The beast lowers its head and thrusts upward into Ben's back.

Majestic horns erupt from his chest. One of them shoots out near his collarbone, the other somewhere through his ribcage. His body is skewered on the elk's heavy head for a moment before it rears back and discards him into the snow.

I'm frozen as the father turns back to his family, guiding them back into the woods with bloody horns. I wait until every little beast disappears beyond the tree line before rushing up to Ben's body.

He sputters blood in the snow. "Han...Han..." Probably trying to say my name, but in the moment, I think he's asking for my hand. I pull his glove off, then remove mine to wrap my warm fingers around his. He looks so frail, so pathetic. Eyes pleading in those final moments.

I can't find words, but I want to do something to ease his pain. I reach into his pocket and take out the jewelry box. Holding my hand in front of his eyes, I slip the ring onto my finger.

A tear slides down Ben's cheek, colliding with blood. The visible breath from his mouth disappears. Part of me dies with him, replaced by something colder. Darker.

The ring feels instantly tighter around my finger as my dissociating mind commits to the tragic story. My boyfriend proposed, and I said yes, of course, but then he died in a terrible accident.

That's what I'll tell everyone, because I can never tell them the truth.

Only I just did.

I told Miles everything.

31

THE DESERT FEELS COLDER THAN EVER AS I WAIT FOR MILES to speak.

He just stares at me, frozen in horror at what I just revealed, and I'm fully prepared for him to call me a killer and run far, far away. Shame pulses through my whole body until he finally opens his mouth and speaks the last words I ever expected to hear.

"I'm so sorry, Hannah. That must have been awful for you."

"Awful for *me?*" I must have misheard him. "Ben died, and I could have saved him."

"No." Miles shakes his head. "Ben made his own choice. And the way he turned on you out there, it sounds like a really scary situation. People talk about the fight-or-flight response, but there's another one. Freeze. That's all that happened, Hannah. You froze, understandably."

It's a more compassionate view of my own inaction than I've ever had for myself. But it's true, isn't it? Ben made his choice. All I did was let nature take its course. I thought maybe he'd learn a valuable lesson in that moment. I just didn't know it would be the last lesson he ever learned.

"And after all that," Miles says, "you still carried his body down the trail all that way?"

"Not all the way." My legs still remember every crunching footfall of the journey. "I gave up, Miles. I left him out there."

"You made a choice, just like he did. You chose to save yourself. The only difference is that yours was the right choice."

Some part of me knows it's true, that it was the only way to survive. Another part of me wonders if I ever really did escape the wilderness. Maybe my whole life after that day has just been a frostbitten fever dream, and my body still lies twitching in the snow, clutching its final burst of warmth before a cold death.

"You know what I think?" Miles says, taking a step closer to interrupt my terrifying thoughts. "I think you're still carrying him."

I feel a phantom pinch in my shoulder, like the rope is still slung over it.

"Maybe it's time you really let go," Miles says.

My mantra word drifts back into my mind as I stare into Miles's eyes. He looks so handsome in the moonlight, so soft and welcoming.

Release.

I grab him by his scruffy beard and kiss him. I can't help it. Now is clearly not the time for romance, but I need to feel some kind of joy in the darkness. It's the first time my lips have ever touched another's since Ben died, and it gives me new life. New purpose. I have to get out of this desert nightmare so I can finally start over.

As I pull back, I see a dopey smile on Miles's face and feel the same grin creeping across my own.

"Whoa," he says, real Keanu-like.

"Yeah." I'm at a loss for better words myself as my eyes land over his shoulder, where the moonlight is glinting off something hidden behind a large boulder. Something black and shiny.

"Holy shit." I pull away from Miles. "It's Jared's Range Rover."

I rush up to the car and peer through the windows at the empty seats.

"We found it," Miles says. "We actually found it!" He sounds overjoyed before his tone shifts into abject dread. "But what the hell is Jared's car doing out here in the middle of nowhere?"

"I don't know." I move around to the trunk, where the word SEMPER is freshly carved into the paint. "But this is one hell of a clue."

"Fuck." Miles runs a hand through his hair. "Do you think it was the Marine?"

"It makes sense, right? I mean, Jared really pissed him off." A shiver ripples down my spine as I remember the look in Dennings's eye when he spit against the car window at me.

"Wait." Miles squints. "What exactly are we saying now?"

I stare at the carved-up trunk, thinking out loud. "What if our cult kidnapping theory is wrong? And the person I saw dressed up like Waylon Barlow was real? Like a trained soldier with a grudge, picking us off one by one."

Miles's eyes go wide. "You think Jared and Luna are *dead*?"

"I don't know." I jam the stick-end of the torch into the dirt, then put my hand on the trunk handle. "But this would be a fine place to hide the bodies."

My fingers tremble, afraid of what I might find inside by the flickering firelight. I'm fully prepared to see Jared's and Luna's corpses, twisted and piled up together in their final embrace.

When the trunk opens, two big lumps are waiting inside.

Not their bodies. Just their bags. I catch my breath and start searching through them.

"Okay, so their stuff is here," Miles says. "That's good, right? Maybe the car broke down and they had to hoof it into town?"

"And they just left the keys behind?" I pull the car keys out of Jared's bag. It sure seems like someone was tidying up all the evidence together when they made Jared and Luna disappear.

"Fuck!" Miles is losing his cool, and it's starting to trigger me. Like Ben all over again.

"Hey. I need you to stay calm, okay?"

"Right, okay." Miles spots Jared's flask poking out of the bag. He grabs it and takes a swig, then offers it to me.

I shake my head. "I also need you to stay sober, Miles. Please."

"Yeah, sorry, of course," Miles nods. "Just my nerves are a little rattled, that's all." He chases the booze with a swig from his water bottle.

I'm starting to think he's not so great under pressure as I close the trunk and get into the driver's seat. Miles climbs into the passenger side, sweat dripping down his face.

A twist of the key brings the engine roaring to life.

"Car seems fine to me," I say. "So there goes that theory."

The radio kicks on, and Taylor Swift's voice fights through static. "*Down bad!*" Miles sings back to the speakers. "God, I love this song. She's so underrated. I mean, I know everyone loves her, but then everyone loves to hate on her too, so like...underrated, man."

I stare across the car at him, baffled by the bizarre behavior. "Look, I'm happy to talk aliens and Swifties some other time, but maybe not right now?"

"It's just, we were having such a good time together before we found this car, and it's all a little too intense for me right now, and I just really love this song." He turns the knob to make it louder. "Can we just take a moment to, like, soak it in?"

Miles runs his hand along the leather seat. I flip the volume knob low.

"Miles, what is going on with you?" He's been acting weirder and weirder, and it's really freaking me out. "We don't have time to soak it in. Our friends are missing."

"I don't want to think about that." His hand moves from the leather console between us to graze my arm. "Your skin feels so smooth. Why don't we just forget all this scary stuff...and lean into love?"

Miles leans over the console to kiss me, but I waste no time in smacking him across the face.

It startles his eyes wide open. "Ow."

I look at his saucer pupils, and it finally dawns on me. "Miles. Are you high?"

"What?" His face contorts like he's trying to solve a complex puzzle. "Wait. The Molly."

My whole body vibrates with fury. "You took the Molly? Are you fucking kidding me?"

"No." He shakes his head. "Did I?" Miles is fumbling over his own words now. Because he absolutely is high.

"Jesus. You haven't changed at all." I thought he was different, that he'd grown up since college, but it turns out he's the same party boy after all. And I'm in the middle of nowhere again with a two-faced man showing his true colors.

"It's not my fault," he says.

I need an ally in this moment, and Miles is useless. An immature child taking zero responsibility. But I'm most mad at myself. "I can't believe I fell for your bullshit."

"Hannah." His eyelids are fluttering wildly. "Let me...explain."

"Get out." My voice is firm. I can't deal with this right now. He betrayed my trust, and now I have no one.

"What?" Miles mumbles.

"I'm driving the car back, and you're gonna walk it off." I reach over him and open the door. "If I spend another second with you right now, I'm going to lose my shit, and it's taking every ounce of my energy just to hold it together. So please, Miles. Get out of the car."

"No way." He shakes his head, a stubborn glint in his eye that makes me shudder.

"Miles..."

"Hannah." He lunges over the console again, hands gripping my shoulders. "You can't—"

My fight response kicks in as I shove him back against the door. "Out!"

"Okay, okay!" Miles holds his arms up in surrender and stumbles out of the Range Rover. He turns back to me, looking dazed and confused. "How will I get back?"

"Same way we came. Take the torch and follow the tracks." I toss his canteen at him through the window. "Drink some water, sweat it out. I need to go warn Tess."

My foot hits the pedal, and I speed off.

I feel bad abandoning Miles like this, but he abandoned me first, showing a side of himself that felt frighteningly familiar. I can't believe I actually let my guard down and kissed him.

It was a stupid mistake, one I wish I could erase.

Taylor Swift is still singing softly about cosmic love, but I punch the *Off* button, driving in pained silence as my hands shake on the wheel.

When I get back to the retreat, I leave the car out front and rush through the main entrance, heading straight for the only person left I can trust.

I burst through the flap of Tess's yurt to find her casually reading a book in bed.

"Tess."

"Hannah?" She sits up straight. "Are you okay?"

I'm having trouble breathing, my heart racing as I try to speak. "We found it. Jared's car, we found it."

"What?" Tess leaps from the bed. "Where?"

"Just up the road, hidden behind some boulders. Somebody started to carve *Semper Fi* into it. I think maybe that Marine from the bar came after us."

I rest my hands on my knees, gasping for air as Tess rubs my back. "Stay calm. What do you mean, 'started to'?"

"It was just the first word. Maybe he..." I'm processing that detail for the first time now. If a Marine was planning on killing someone, why would they leave such a glaring clue behind? "Maybe someone stopped him. Maybe he's just another victim. That means someone else could be...killing..." With every step forward, I'm stumbling two steps back. "We have to..."

I'm hyperventilating as Tess lowers me to the bed. "You have to lie down, right now. You're having a panic attack, Hannah. Close your eyes. Deep breaths."

"We can't..." I writhe on the mattress, my body fighting my brain. There's no time for this.

"Stay here," Tess says. "I'm gonna find help."

"Careful," I utter, watching helplessly as she slips back into the night. "Please...be careful."

My eyes flutter as I see the book resting on Tess's bed beside me.

Bound: A Spell Guide for New Witches.

32

"HANNAH!" MILES CALLS AFTER THE RED TAILLIGHTS FADING in the distance. "I swear I didn't take anything!"

But he's already second-guessing himself. *Did* he take a pill and just forget somehow?

His brain might be a bit scrambled right now, but he does know what he's feeling.

Very high on Molly.

The torch flame flickers, casting a beastly shadow against the big boulder.

Miles jumps out of his skin until he realizes the shadow is his. He has to laugh it off as he pulls the torch from the ground.

"Okay," he says aloud, trying to stay composed. "You're scared of your own shadow, but it's fine. You're fine."

Holding the torch creates a new fear as the flames dance inches from his face. He has to be extra careful because drugs and fire do not mix well.

But that fear takes a backseat when the flame sheds light on something else, hidden behind the boulder. The Rover had been blocking their view of it before Hannah took off.

A combat boot sticks out from behind the rock, toes pointed up. There's a person back there. Why is there a person back there?

"Hello?" Miles asks.

Silence.

He trembles as he approaches to see why he got no response.

The Marine is sitting in the dirt with his legs splayed out in front of him, his upper body propped up against the rock. At least Miles is pretty sure that's the Marine. It's hard to tell because the guy's face has been sliced off, leaving a dark red mask of muscles behind. The dead man's lidless eyes look a little too lively in the firelight. There's no way he could still be alive, though, because there's a gaping hole in the Marine's chest several inches wide. Bits of cracked rib bone are jutting out as Miles inches closer and can't help asking a very dumb question.

"You okay?"

Squeak.

A desert mouse crawls out of the chest hole, and Miles screams, then pukes all over the dead man's boots. When he finally stops puking, he takes several deep swigs of water from his nearly empty canteen. That's when he notices the chalky residue left on his tongue.

What the hell is that?

He tips the last drops of water into his palm to look at it under torchlight. Powdery blue silt. Like someone smashed up pills and...

Fuck. The Molly.

He'd noticed the pills weren't in his jacket before he and Hannah left for their walk, but he'd figured they must have fallen out in the yurt somewhere. Now he's convinced that someone ground them up into powder and put them in his water.

Why would anybody do that? That's so mean.

His eyes fall back to the faceless man with the hole in his chest.

That's way meaner. Whoever did that to the Marine probably drugged Miles and wants to put a hole in his chest, too. There's a killer out here, and Miles is alone in the dark, and he really doesn't want a hole in his chest.

His head is swimming in panic as he tries not to think about what it means to have five doses of MDMA coursing through his blood right now. The more he thinks about it, the more his anxiety will make his blood pulse, and the more his blood pulses, the more the drugs will kick in. Which is exactly what's happening now because he's freaking the fuck out. He's seen people overdose on far less at music festivals. Their bodies seize up, and they choke on their own tongues.

This is bad. Really bad.

Miles takes a deep breath. He just needs to get back to the retreat. To get help and to warn Hannah that somebody killed the Marine, which means that somebody probably killed Jared and Luna, which means that somebody probably wants to kill Hannah and Tess and Miles, too.

What if somebody already *has* killed Miles with those five doses?

No, he can't think like that. He still has a chance of making it back to the retreat for help. Maybe Kimi has a special herb that will make him throw up, some sort of organic stomach pump. Yes, it's all gonna be okay.

Miles clutches the torch as he walks back through the pitch-black night. Even the moon is scared and hiding behind a cloud now.

The desert air is filled with strange sounds, only amplified by the drugs. He swears there are monsters in the night, creeping up behind him. Tentacled octopus aliens slithering through the dirt, right on his heels. He can see them vividly in his mind's eye, but he won't allow himself to look back.

Miles walks with purpose, following the trail back toward the torch lights at the retreat entrance. Seeing them gives him hope, so he focuses on bringing his torch back to its little torch family.

The distance wobbles in and out, so close and then so far, and then so close and then so far.

He's sweating heavily when he finally makes it back across that seemingly endless desert and sees the Range Rover parked out front.

Good. Hannah made it back safely. He tosses the torch into the dirt and heads inside.

The water feature gushes before him, way too loud, and the liquid is moving in all directions at once. Shit, he's so damn high.

Miles stumbles past the wall hangings, which are all coming alive in a violent dance. The hunters chase their prey, catching and killing. He averts his eyes from the gory slaughter.

This is the worst.

When he rounds the corner, he stops short at the sight of something else, some*one* else.

Someone just like Hannah described.

At the end of the hall stands a figure dressed like an old-timey miner, wearing a human face that Miles now knows came from the Marine. Waylon Barlow playfully twirls the pickaxe like a helicopter blade in his hands.

"Hey!" Miles shouts, surprised by his own fearlessness. "You!" That follow-up could've used a little work.

The old miner calmly turns and walks through an open doorway.

Is Miles really seeing Waylon Barlow? Or is he just so high that he's latched on to Hannah's hallucinations?

He follows to find out, nearly tripping over a meditation cushion on his way into the sound bath den. His blurry vision can't lock onto the dark figure with the big hat. It keeps fading in and out of the shadows as Miles beckons.

"You want to dance?" Miles is a good dancer, people always tell him that. "Let's go, hat head." His verbal threats might be lacking, but he reaches for a gong mallet, ready to fight.

Miles stumbles through the space, determined to kill the killer and save Hannah. To show her that he isn't the fuck-up she thinks he is. He's ready to settle down and have little babies with her if that's what she wants. He even wrote a song about her called "Dorm Room Hearts."

Maybe he can grab that guitar in the corner and play it for her later.

Footsteps bring his wandering mind back into his body.

"Where you at, Barlow?" Miles asks, searching the dark.

His pulsing eyes finally land on not one but three miners,

standing beside the wind chimes with their iron pickaxes held against the dangling metal. Miles charges forward, but the miners bleed back into one figure, dragging the pickaxe across the chimes, causing them to *clang-clang-clang*.

The sound is piercing, worse than nails on a chalkboard. More like nails being driven straight into his ears as sensory overload kicks in. He yells as he stumbles forward, swinging his mallet and whiffing air as he knocks over the chimes, creating more unbearable sound. Miles falls to the floor, clutching his ears in crippling pain.

Barlow grabs Miles by his shirt and throws him into the center of the room. Miles feels everything so acutely, all the pain thrumming in his muscles as Barlow pulls him up by his hair and pushes his head down into the large sound bowl.

He can't see what's happening next, but the sound starts to warble around him as Barlow drags the rubber mallet around the bowl's edge. Miles doesn't know how many decibels are shuddering against his ear drums, but it's enough to cause permanent damage for sure. He screams against the noise, futile and flailing, until he feels his ear drums *pop* like tiny balloons.

Everything is silent now as he feels blood trickling out of his ears. Miles clenches his fist, thumb on the outside, just like Hannah taught him, and throws a punch backward.

His knuckles connect with Barlow's face, slipping against the flesh mask and knocking it off as the fucker stumbles backward.

It was a good punch, but the exertion is making Miles's heart race a hundred miles a minute, and he doesn't want to fight anymore. He tries to crawl away, but he feels a hand latch on to his leg and drag him across the floor on his stomach.

When the dragging stops, Miles rolls onto his back. The gong hovers directly above his neck. A big bronze disk with a sharpened edge, poised like a guillotine and suspended by two flimsy little ropes.

Miles squints up into the unmasked face of the miner.

It's not Waylon Barlow at all.

"Why?" he asks, unable to hear his own plea beyond a muffled hum.

In reply, the blood-faced killer places their hands on top of the gong and pulls down hard, easily snapping those retaining ropes. The heavy disk descends swiftly and slices straight through Miles's throat. It cuts through flesh and slides between the vertebrae to sever his spine.

Miles's eyes fill with colors, so many colors, and he can hear the full spectrum of the rainbow.

A blissful synesthesia before an endless silence.

33

THE COLD AGAINST MY FOREHEAD BRINGS ME SQUIRMING back from the darkness to Tess's bed.

She lies beside me, dabbing my head with a damp towel. "Easy, honey."

"I fell asleep?" My eyelids flutter, trying to ground myself.

"You were out cold when I came back." Tess puts the towel aside. The panic on top of the physical exhaustion from the day must've just sent my body into a forced shutdown.

"Did you find anybody?" I ask.

"No Pax, no Kimi, no Miles."

"Miles was with me." I sit up, not ready to explain what happened in the car. "He should be back here by now."

"Well, it's a total fucking ghost town out there." Tess gets off the bed, rubs her arms. "I'm starting to freak out a little bit."

I swing my feet over the side of the bed. "It's honestly a relief to hear you say that."

"Before you passed out, you were talking about a killer. You really think Jared and Luna are dead?"

"Why else would their car be stashed up the road with all their bags in it?" I'm actually hoping she'll counter with a better explanation, but no such luck.

"Shit," Tess says. "Could Pax really be capable of that?"

"I think so." I got distracted out there by the vandalized car, but Pax is clearly suspect number one. "Even Kimi is afraid of him. Maybe she's hiding out somewhere, or she got away. She said he sees everything."

Tess responds with a furrowed brow toward her sketchpad in the corner.

"What?" I ask.

"It's just that when we were painting, Pax talked about my late nights sketching here. I *have* been sketching every night since I got here…"

"…but how would he know that?"

"Either the spirits told him, or…"

Tess follows a straight line from her easel to a standing bookshelf on the far wall of the yurt, lined with little animal skulls. She examines each one until she gets to a rabbit skull and gazes into its hollow eye socket.

"That fucking creep." Tess exhumes a small black wire with a tiny camera on the end.

"Jesus." My stomach sinks. "There are probably hidden cameras all over the retreat. Kimi said this place isn't what we think it is. It has to be some kind of experiment, right?"

"Experiment for what?" Tess drops the little camera skull to the ground and stomps the bone to bits beneath her feet. "What the fuck is he up to?"

"I don't know. But we need to get out of here, Tess. I have Jared's keys—we can go right now. Miles is probably still walking back, so we can just scoop him on our way." I have to believe that, have to hope that I didn't leave him for dead in the desert.

I reach into my pocket and pull out a handful of keys.

"What's this?" Tess plucks the electric key fob resting atop Jared's car keys.

"I found it in Pax's yurt."

"This has to open a door around here somewhere, right?"

"I don't know, but I don't want to wait around to find out." I've officially moved past the "figure it out" stage into the "get the fuck out" stage.

Tess takes my hands. "Let's just take a step back from 'our friends are dead' and think through what we actually know. We found hidden cameras at a tech-free retreat. You found an electric key fob in Pax's yurt. Did you find anything else?"

"I overheard Pax making a call on his satellite phone. He was talking about getting results from the group."

"Okay," Tess says, "then maybe this is all just a big social experiment reality show, right? Like an open-air, spiritual escape room. Maybe we're just the last ones to figure it out and our friends are somewhere safe, watching and laughing while we get *Punk'd*."

"Maybe," I shrug, ready to believe Tess's serialized television theory over my serial killer theory. "So, what do you want to do?"

Tess dangles the key fob. "I want to pull the plug on this shitshow."

34

TESS AND I WALK DOWN THE MAIN HALLWAY THAT'S COVERED in murals and ancient artifacts. She pulls a stone hatchet hanging from a hook. "Just in case."

I can't believe we're actually arming ourselves for battle, but I reach for a stone dagger, black and cold in my grip. With my other hand, I hold the key fob along the wall as we walk. Hoping for, what? Some secret door to reveal itself?

"Do we really think this is going to work?" I ask, feeling foolish already.

"I say we do one sweep of the grounds," Tess says, "and if we come up empty-handed, we get in the rig and bounce."

"Okay. I'm just worried about Miles. I never should have left him out there alone."

"Why did you?" Tess asks.

"Well...we kissed..."

Tess stops and turns to face me. "He kissed you?"

"No, I kissed him. Which was nice, but then he started acting weird and scary. Turns out he was high on Molly."

"Really?" She starts walking again. "Ecstasy isn't exactly a 'take it alone' kind of drug. Why would he do that?"

"I don't know." I was so triggered in the moment, I hadn't really processed it.

"Didn't you say Pax was drugging us against our will?" Tess asks.

I'm following her train of thought now as I stop in my tracks. "You think Miles was dosed and didn't know it?"

In retrospect, that totally explains the way he was acting. Uncomfortably high and totally confused. I feel sick to my stomach, realizing I may have deserted Miles when he needed me the most.

"Hey." Tess interrupts my internal spiral. "We'll clear everything up when we find him." She puts a comforting hand on my shoulder. "Right?"

"Right."

"Keep at it." Tess motions to the wall, and I keep dragging the fob along it. "In the meantime," she says, "I'm more worried about Kimi. I don't trust her."

"But she's the one who's been trying to warn me this whole time."

"Then why hasn't she, straight up? She's being cryptic and sketchy at every turn. Maybe she only tried to warn you about Pax because she knows she's complicit."

"I'm sure there's an explanation." After that weed-fueled bonding session in Kimi's yurt, it's hard for me to accept that she might have ulterior motives herself. I like to believe I'm a good judge of character, but then...Ben.

"The explanation," Tess says, "is that this whole place is a team effort."

"Maybe she's just—"

Metallic crunching echoes from outside, like something is being smashed to bits.

Tess and I rush out to find Kimi, holding a pickaxe. She's chopping away at the hood of the Range Rover, puncturing through and striking the engine beneath.

"Hey!" Tess shouts.

Kimi looks up at us with wild eyes. She points the pickaxe at me, and my shoulders tense with the visceral memory of being attacked outside the mine entrance.

"You're not getting out of here," Kimi says. "I won't let you."

Tess raises her stone hatchet and rushes at Kimi, who dodges the swing and bolts at me. Kimi swings the pickaxe, but I duck and the iron point slams into the soft clay wall. It gets stuck there as Kimi releases the wooden handle, and I raise my stone dagger to her throat.

Seeing her eyes up close reveals a primal fear behind them. Kimi doesn't look like a killer; she just looks sad as she says: "I trusted you."

"Do it!" Tess screams, but I hesitate.

I'm not going to kill this girl, am I? Before I can decide, Kimi shoves me back and runs past me, deeper into the retreat.

Tess hurries up to me. "Why'd you let her go?"

"What did you expect me to do?"

"You've got a knife. Use it." There's a coldness in Tess's tone that I've never heard before. "I'm going after her. Go see if the car still works."

Tess runs off after Kimi, hatchet in hand.

"Wait!" I call, everything happening too fast. Out of the corner of my eye, I notice something by the water feature in the main hall. A glowing blue light emanating from the edges of the mirror, from behind the water.

I approach it from the side, realizing there's a small space back there, just large enough for someone to slide behind the mirror. Moving my body into the space, I hold the key fob against the wall.

Buzzzz.

A hidden door cracks open, pushing inward.

A secret room. *Scooby fucking Doo.*

My face is bathed in blue light as I enter.

It takes me a moment to process what I'm seeing because it's been days since my eyes have been exposed to screen light. The small room is a veritable control center with multiple computer monitors on a desk and an office chair in front of them.

I sit at the keyboard, place my dagger on the desk, and click the LIVE FEED icon.

The monitors are flooded with camera feeds of every yurt, labeled with each of our names.

Hannah. Tess. Miles. Jared. Luna.

It makes my skin crawl to know we've had no privacy this entire time. Pax has been watching us all. It doesn't feel like a reality show. It feels like something much more sinister.

I minimize the camera feeds and find folders on the desktop. Each one is labeled with our names.

Opening the *Hannah* file, I see a collection of data. Images and videos pulled from social media. Confidential contracts and tax documents. Health records from my stay in the hospital after Ben's death. Pax has access to every trace of my online existence.

Everything.

This is how he knows so much about us.

"I guess you're out of avidya now."

Pax's voice over my shoulder makes me shudder.

I swivel in the office chair to find him slumped on a cushy chair in the corner, drinking straight from a bottle of whiskey. His hair, normally up in a bun, is hanging down. Round glasses sit crooked on his drunken face.

Pax doesn't look like a guru in this moment. He looks like a loser.

"Who the fuck are you?" I ask. "And what is this place, really?"

"Name's Paul. Nice to meet you." He swigs from his bottle with a wince. Not just a loser, but a loser who can't handle his whiskey. "I'm a software engineer for a Silicon Beach startup. Or at least, I was. Specialized in data mining, digging deeper than anyone else would ever dare dig. But the real breakthrough came when I connected that skill to my own patented facial recognition software. One scan of the face and I can tell you everything you need to know about anyone on the planet. Revolutionary stuff, really. But some people are too scared to embrace a revolution, too scared to evolve."

Pax peels himself off the chair and glides over to my side.

"See, when I pitched it to my bosses, they told me I was crazy. That it was illegal and unethical. They fired me, those hypocritical assholes. I knew all the back-dealing bullshit they were up to, falsifying users to boost their IPOs, but *I* was the unethical one?"

He shakes his head.

"I felt lost, rejected. Found myself wandering down Abbott Kinney. Every other storefront was selling a spiritual awakening in one form or another. Buy this product, sign up for this service, and you will transcend your lowly human existence. That's when I had my own spiritual awakening."

Pax opens his arms wide.

"I realized that this was the key, the application for the brilliant software I had birthed. I could use my technology to create a profile on every participant and, under the right conditions, feed it back to them as a spiritual awakening. A brush with God."

"God being you," I say to the narcissist in hippie clothing.

"I'm not the cult leader you think I am, Hannah. I'm so much more sophisticated than that."

"Right. Drugging people against their will is very sophisticated."

"You all signed waivers. They just didn't specify *when* you would be exposed to drugs. I discovered that people open up more when they don't realize they're under the influence, which paves the way for the placebo effect later and helps taper them off safely. See, I've already got a few rounds under my belt, and I've made some tweaks along the way."

"You're full of shit." I shake my head at the bank of monitors. "All that spirit talk. This whole place is a lie."

"Replace 'spirits' with 'algorithms,' and it's all true. People do heal here, Hannah. If it didn't work, I wouldn't have competing offers from Google and Meta to host their corporate retreats. They've been monitoring my progress, and you're my last test group with the seed funding I was granted, off the books. Either way, I'm not going to let it all fall apart now."

"So you didn't get the results you wanted, and that's why you're wiping us out? Cleaning the slate to keep your pitch deck looking profitable?"

"Wiping you out?" Pax takes another swig of whiskey and places the bottle on the desk. "If my plan was to kill you, don't you think I would've done it by now?"

"Maybe I'm just harder to kill than you thought. It was you, out at the mine." I'm sure of it now. "Dressed up like Waylon Barlow."

"Have you been listening to anything I just said? I'm a data miner, not a gold miner. I hate to break it to you, Hannah, but you are legitimately crazy. Then again, you already knew that, didn't you? It's why you came here." He points at the stone dagger on the desk. "I mean, what were you planning on doing with that thing anyway?"

I shake my head, refusing his narrative. "I'm not crazy, and I'm not leaving here without my friends. You say you didn't kill them, so where are they?"

"I wish I knew because they're really fucking up my experiment here. I've never had so many goddamn flakes in one group before."

I use the mouse to highlight everything on the desktop and drag it over the *Trash* icon. "I will erase your whole psychopathic business plan in one second if you don't tell me."

"Okay, I think you need to take a meditative breath and relax. First of all, the universe will protect my work in this thing called the cloud. You can't just—" Pax lunges for the stone dagger, snatching it up and raising it high, but I grab the keyboard and *thwack* him across the face with it. Little plastic alphabet squares scatter as he collapses, knocking his head on the side of the desk before hitting the floor, out cold.

"Welcome to the cloud, prick."

I grab the dagger and rush back outside, leaving the pathetic Bond villain passed out in his lair.

35

PAUL'S BRAIN GROGGILY REBOOTS. HIS BODY IS SPRAWLED on the control-room floor, jaw throbbing from that keyboard he took to the face. Brushing broken keys off his chest, he pulls himself up by the edge of the table. Everything hurts. He grabs the whiskey and takes a slug, but it dribbles over his swollen lip as he shakes his head.

What an absolute fucking failure this retreat has been.

If he doesn't reel Hannah in and sort this shit out quick, he'll definitely have a lawsuit on his hands. He should've known better than to invite her after reading her file. Next time, no fucking crazies. If he actually gets the chance to have a next time.

Paul clicks through the camera feeds, searching. "Where are you, bitch?"

The yurts are all empty. He still can't believe so many participants jumped ship, but he refuses to blame himself. Kimi clearly stabbed him in the back. That ungrateful little diversity hire. Where the hell did she disappear to?

He'll sort her out later, but right now, he needs to find Hannah. When he clicks to the main hallway camera, he finally finds someone.

Paul wipes at his eyes, uncertain of what he is seeing.

The figure is dressed up like an old miner in a wide-brimmed hat, and that flesh mask looks fake as fuck. It's not a spirit out there, just a Spirit Halloween costume. Though he has to admit that Waylon Barlow is an inspired choice.

The figure grips a pickaxe in one hand and raises the other to flip a middle finger directly at the hidden camera.

It has to be Hannah, caught up in her own delusion. A regular Norman Bates playing dress-up and running around to wreak havoc without even knowing it. Totally fits her psych profile. Whichever personality is behind that mask, Paul isn't afraid to deal with the lunatic.

"Okay, psycho." He opens the drawer and pulls out his electric stun baton. He bought it after getting mugged on the Venice Boardwalk one night. Personal defense is a necessity. "No more games."

Paul exits the secret room and circles around the mirror, flipping the baton switch on.

But nobody's out there anymore. Waylon Barlow is gone.

Paul senses the presence behind him and spins on his feet. Up close, it's clear that the flesh mask is not fake after all. It's very fucking real. Paul has just enough time to see the frayed skin edges, to smell the reek of decay, before he catches the point of the pickaxe in his shoulder. He shoves Barlow, pushing his own pierced flesh off the pickaxe as he falls back, splashing into the water feature. Blood oozes from the wound above his collarbone as he crawls out on the other side of the pool and ducks back into the secret room.

He tries to close the door, but Barlow rams it, knocking him backward into his bank of monitors. Lights flash as everything comes crashing down in a heap of sparking wires.

Barlow swings the pickaxe down, but Paul rolls away, and the iron tip crashes through a computer screen with a crunching sizzle.

Paul scrambles back out the door, but Barlow is close behind, grabbing him by his linen shirt and throwing him back against the mirror. He splashes down into the water, shards of mirror raining down on top of him.

Paul pushes up to his hands and knees, jagged glass digging into his palms as he moves from tabletop position into a strong mountain pose. He really does like yoga; that part wasn't fake.

Paul raises his fists at Barlow, who stands outside the water.

"Come on." Paul beckons the killer behind that fake face. "Drop the axe and fight me like a man."

Barlow tosses the weapon to the ground. Paul spits blood, ready to fight. Until he sees the blue light. The stun baton that Paul lost in the melee is in Barlow's hand now. Electricity arcs between the silver rods.

Soaked to the bone and ankle-deep in water, Paul can feel himself sweating.

"Please," he begs. "I'm an empath."

He tries to move quick, but Barlow is already dipping the sparking baton tip into the pool below. Electricity surges through Paul's body, racking his bones and scorching his muscles. He hasn't eaten cooked meat all week, but that's what he smells as his body sizzles and spasms, then begins to fall. The last thing he sees is the amethyst crystal at the center of the pool rushing up to catch his face.

The purple point plunges through his open mouth and out the back of his crown chakra.

Brain matter dribbles down the crystal as Pax's consciousness transcends this earthly realm.

36

THE WALLS ARE CLOSING IN ON ME WHEN I FINALLY ESCAPE the compound, back out into the open air. Clouds above strangle the light of the moon, bathing the retreat in a cloak of darkness. My vision is still blurred from the unnatural blue light of the computer screens, everything hazy and shapeless in the night.

"Tess! Tess, where are you?!"

I need to find my friend, the only person left I can trust.

I have to warn her that it's Pax. It's always been Pax.

My foot bumps against a large stone, and I catch myself before kicking another one. I must have stumbled my way into the labyrinth maze, even though I can't see well enough to confirm it.

I clutch the dagger, taking tentative steps.

Something brushes against my back, and I spin to face…nothing.

My feet keep kicking stones as I try to navigate out of the labyrinth.

I catch a flash of Waylon Barlow's fleshy face mask in the dark, but it disappears just as quickly as it appeared.

How did Pax recover so quickly after I knocked him out cold? And why take the time to put on that stupid costume and keep up the ruse?

Unless I'm wrong.

Another gust of wind rushes in front of me, some kind of movement, and I swipe my blade blindly, striking nothing.

The sound of the pickaxe dragging across the dirt makes me spin and swing again, the stone edge of my blade slicing through only air.

The killer is toying with me. Treating me like prey.

I close my eyes—tapping into my primal instincts—and walk the path.

My feet touch no stones, intuition guiding me all the way into the center of the labyrinth. I can feel it; I've landed in the middle of the maze.

Ready to slay my demons, to be free of this nightmare, I speak my intention once more out loud.

"Release."

The next time I feel the wind rush behind me, I twirl and lunge with the knife.

This time, it finds its target, piercing through flesh.

But Waylon Barlow isn't there.

Tess coughs blood, confusion etched into her face. "Han...?"

"No..." I utter as my best friend drops to her knees in front of me.

I pull the knife out on instinct, despite my training. I should know better; I've *learned* better in medical school. Now the blood is flowing like an open faucet.

"No, no, no." I remove my sweater. "Stay with me." Creating a makeshift bandage, I wrap it tightly around Tess's torso, tying the fabric tight. "Pressure here." I guide Tess's hand against the wound, praying I missed her organs. "You're gonna be okay. I'll go find a first-aid kit."

Tess clutches the sweater, staring into my eyes. "Don't...leave me."

"I have to, I have to, but I'll be right back—I..."

Tess's eyes flutter and close, her body going limp.

"Tess, no!"

Time slows for a moment before footsteps draw my gaze up to see Waylon Barlow emerging from the shadows.

A relentless specter.

I grab the bloody dagger and run.

Darting past the hot springs pool, I see a body floating face down in the water. I don't need to flip him over to confirm, but I do it anyway. It's Jared, face swollen and blue. His jaw wiggles, as if he's about to speak from beyond the grave. Instead of words, a rattlesnake head squirms out from between his lips, hissing in my face.

I scream and scramble inside, finding myself in the yoga studio. Luna's twisted corpse is hanging from the straps in a tangle of angled bones. A broken marionette doll.

Dizzy with disgust, I force myself to press on.

My friends are dead.

The question now isn't just who killed them, but why? Why would someone stage them so callously, so theatrically? I'm clearly dealing with a cruel psychopath.

That cruelty gets confirmed when I hurry into the sound bath den and trip over one of the bowls. I fall to the ground as a round object rolls out of the bowl and bumps against my face. Lips touch mine, and I find myself staring into Miles's eyes, wide open in his severed head.

This is the final straw that brings vomit rushing from my guts and out of my mouth. When I finish puking, I wipe my arm across my face and stagger out into the main hallway.

I have to keep moving because Pax must be right behind me in his Waylon Barlow disguise.

But how could that be when his corpse is right here in the water feature with a purple crystal blooming from the back of his head? The water runs red around Pax's corpse, blood recycling through the pump and flowing down the front of the broken mirror now.

How can Pax be dead when he's the killer?

Isn't he?

If not him, then who?

I gaze through the flowing blood at what's left of the cracked mirror, seeing my own fragmented reflection. Gripped tightly in my hand is the bloody dagger, the one I just killed Tess with.

I glance down the hallway, waiting for Waylon Barlow to emerge in hot pursuit.

But the killer never comes.

Until I turn back to the mirror, and a spiritual awakening washes over me.

I'm not running from anything or anyone other than myself.

Standing in the reflection where I'm standing, clutching not the stone dagger but the iron pickaxe, is Waylon Barlow.

Me. It's been me all along.

That's the only thing that makes sense.

I knew it before I even came here, didn't I?

The retreat has transformed me, rid me of my ignorance.

I know myself now, my primeval nature.

A killer in disguise.

I close my eyes, trying to picture it, searching for the memory of killing my friends.

But I can't see it. File not found.

The sound of leaking air brings me back into my body, and when I look into the mirror, I only see myself.

I follow the sound back out front where the Range Rover has been mutilated.

By Kimi. That's right. There's still one other suspect left.

I hop behind the wheel and pray to whatever spirits will listen as I turn the key. The engine sputters pathetically but actually starts.

Yes.

Fuck what Kimi said. I *am* getting out of here alive.

I hit the gas, wheels kicking up dirt in my side-view mirror as I put the retreat behind me.

Not far enough.

Waylon Barlow jumps out from behind a rock, eyes wide behind the mask of flesh as he stumbles into my path like a deer in literal headlights.

Time slows down as I flash on the memory of Ben being gored by the elk. That unstoppable moment.

It's not too late to stop this one.

I tug the wheel to avoid another death.

Because I'm not a killer.

The corner of the bumper clips Barlow, knocking him to the ground as the car skids sideways. My foot slams the brakes, but it's too late. The boulder comes rushing up against the driver's-side door in a shower of glass, and darkness crashes over me.

37

"HANNAH. WAKE UP, HANNAH."

My forehead is pressed against cold leather. I lift it from the steering wheel of Jared's fancy new car, now crunched like a soda can.

"Hannah." A voice I know all too well cuts through the haze.

Blood drips from my hairline down into my eyes, and I wipe it away, looking toward the passenger seat.

There he sits. Frost peppering his eyelids. Elk horns jutting from his chest.

"Ben?" My brain is scrambled with confusion, but somehow, this moment makes sense. Of course he'd come to me in my moment of death. Come *for* me, like my own personal grim reaper.

"Am I dying?" I ask.

"No. You still have a chance. But you have to get out, now."

I look at those pointed horns, dripping blood. "I'm sorry. I should have warned you."

"I wouldn't have listened. You know that."

I do. But still. "Why won't you leave me alone?"

"Because you said yes." Ben reaches his cold hand out and wraps it around mine. He rubs his thumb along the engagement ring. Even though I hadn't actually said yes when Ben asked me to marry him, I did accept his ring, right before he died.

"No." I taste my own coppery blood as I withdraw my hand from his chilly grip. "My answer is no, Ben."

I can smell the gasoline. It's not safe here.

Ben frowns before a strange relief fills his frigid face.

"Then leave me," he says. "Get out of the car and live. Or else stay with me. Forever."

He smiles a bloodstained smile, illuminated by a fire that flickers to life under the hood of the smashed vehicle.

I shake my head. "I won't die with you."

Blood pulses into every limb, the will to live flooding my muscles as I turn away from Ben and push my weight against the driver's-side door.

It won't budge, the crumpled metal locked against the boulder.

When I turn back to Ben, he's gone. Smoke fills the cabin, creeping into my lungs as I call "help!" to anyone who can hear me. But there's no one left to hear me as my cry turns into a cough, a sputter.

My trembling fingers fumble over the button on my seat belt, finally pressing it and hearing the soft *click*. But there's no cathartic release. The belt is tangled above me, behind me, keeping me strapped to the seat like a straitjacket.

I wriggle my upper body free, squirming toward the passenger-side seat. My hand grips the handle to tug and push, but the door won't open.

The window is smashed open, so I wrap my fingers along the window frame. Shattered glass slices through my skin as I try to pull myself up, out.

It's no use. I can't escape this jagged death trap.

I'm going to die here. I've accepted my fate.

But someone else hasn't.

Two soft hands wrap around mine, lifting me from broken glass in a warm grip and pulling. I look up into the smoke, and another voice resounds outside the car, muffled by the sounds of mechanical mayhem.

"I've got you, Hannah."

It's not Kimi's voice. But who else is left alive?

I feel like a doll being tugged by a child, through the shattered window, out of the smoke and into the night.

Crumpling to the dirt, I cough and gasp at the air.

"Slow breaths—take it easy," the voice says.

It sounds so familiar, that cadence.

My eyes catch on their shoes first.

Scuffed white New Balances.

Am I just imagining my guardian angel rescuing me from my demons?

"I've got you." Dr. Grady scoops me into his arms and carries me away from the Range Rover wreckage, just as the flames consume that hunk of twisted metal.

"Grady?" He lowers me to the dirt below the light of a burning torch. "What are you doing here?"

"You called me, remember?" He's wearing his usual button-down shirt and khakis, now stained with blood from my banged-up head. "It seemed like a pretty serious SOS."

Of course. The phone call. When I saw Waylon Barlow, and Grady talked me off the ledge.

"I came straight to 29 Palms and started asking around about Dead Man's Due Road," he explains. "When I pulled up, I saw the car wreck."

I've never been more grateful to see anyone in my entire life. I'm pretty sure it's against the rules to hug your psychiatrist, but my arms wrap around him on instinct. He's stronger, more muscular than he looked back in his office.

"Thank you," I breathe. "Thank you, Grady."

"You don't have to thank me." He pulls back to look into my eyes. "But what the hell happened?"

"Waylon Barlow." My memory from before the crash trickles back. I look back to see the figure I'd clipped with the car sprawled out in the road now. "Please tell me you see that."

"You mean the old miner wearing overalls and a big hat and a severed human face?"

"Oh, thank God." It's real. I'm not crazy.

Grady helps me stumble over to the motionless body. I bend down and tuck my fingers under the flesh mask, peeling it away with a sickening wet sound.

"Who is that?" Grady asks.

I look at Kimi's bloodstained face. "Her name is Kimberly. And she killed all my friends."

"Not all of them." The voice comes from over our shoulders.

I turn to see Tess approaching, holding her bleeding stomach with one hand, clutching the stone hatchet in her other hand. Her eyes are wild in the firelight, like a witch who just broke free from the burning stake.

"Tess! I thought you were dead."

"Yeah, well..." Tess winces, blood seeping through her fingers. "You tried your best."

Grady steps in front of me like a human shield. "Get behind me, Hannah."

"Get real, Grady," Tess says, brimming with rage.

My head is spinning, probably concussed. "What's going on?"

"I caught up with Kimi earlier," Tess explains. "It wasn't her. That's what I was rushing to tell you when you put a knife in my gut."

"I thought I saw..."

"Waylon Barlow?" Tess says. "Yeah, I saw him, too. Out there by the labyrinth. But Kimi was with me. We were both coming to warn you. Kimi must have run off when she saw you were getting all stab happy."

"But she smashed up the car," I say. "She wouldn't let us leave."

"Because she found the other bodies, Hannah," Tess says. "She thought *you* were the killer, and she didn't want you to get away with it."

I turn to Grady, who's still helping me stay on my feet. "It's not me, Grady." I'm worried that my psychiatrist, my only lifeline, will abandon me.

"I know," Grady says, eyes soft with understanding.

"He knows..." Tess points her hatchet at Grady. "Because it's him."

Grady shakes his head, clutching me a little tighter. "Hannah. From what you've shared in your sessions about Tess, I think it's safe to say that your best friend is pathologically obsessed with you."

"Fuck you, shrink boy!" Tess advances aggressively, raising the hatchet high. "I will pathologically split your skull."

"A very sane threat," Grady coldly observes.

I step in front of Grady now, protecting him. "Stay back, Tess."

"Hannah." Tess stumbles, gripping her bleeding stomach as she looks up into my eyes. "Clear your heart and mind. You know the truth."

Tess's words pierce straight through the fog in my brain.

I take a deep inhale, exhaling my ignorance.

Fuck avidya. I'm awake now.

"Grady." I turn to face him. "When did you really get here?"

"Me?" he asks. The confusion on his face morphs into a brittle smile as he reaches behind his back. "I've been right behind you every step of the way, Hannah. I told you I wasn't going to abandon you now."

Grady pulls something shiny and black from the belt of his khakis, and I suddenly find myself staring down the barrel of a handgun.

"Perks of killing a Marine," he says with a shrug. "That and the extra face."

The world falls out beneath me.

Tess just shakes her head. "Fucking narcissistic sociopath."

"Instagrammers, I swear." Grady rolls his eyes. "You read a few pop psychology memes and suddenly think you're qualified to make a professional diagnosis." He aims the gun at Tess now. "Of course, in this case, you just happen to be right."

The *bang* echoes in my ears long after Tess's body has dropped to the dirt.

"Finally." Grady nuzzles into my neck like a sick puppy. "It's just the two of us."

38

"IT WAS YOU?" I ASK, ALREADY KNOWING THE ANSWER IN MY rattled bones. "All of it?"

"Impressive, right?" Grady smiles.

"Why?"

"Because I'm the only one who understands you, Hannah." He's never looked so deranged as he puts a hand on my cheek. "Every day I sit in that office listening to whiny bitches complain about their champagne problems. But you? The way you faced death and saved yourself? You're strong, Hannah, cold-blooded. Just like me."

I think back to the countless counseling sessions, my most vulnerable moments on display in his office. "You were never helping me."

"Actually, I was, by most psychiatric standards. I kept you medicated and dependent. Not just on the pills, but on me. I knew it was only a matter of time before you self-sabotaged at work, and then I'd really have you all to myself." He grinds his teeth. "But then Tess came in with this idiotic healing retreat idea. I was annoyed, to say the least, so my instinct was to discourage you. I didn't want her or anybody else stealing you away from me. But deep down, I knew it was too soon for you to reintegrate. I knew you'd crack under the pressure and come running back into my arms. Especially if I followed along and added a little gas to the fire."

I'm still struggling to connect the broken pieces. "And Waylon Barlow?"

"I popped into that museum right after you. The old man told me the tall tale, and it seemed like the perfect disguise. The perfect delusion for you to latch on to. Seeing Ben is one thing, but add another ghost, and you're off the deep end, questioning everything." I hate that he can narrate my mental breakdown so easily. Because he orchestrated it. "All I had to do was wait until closing to break in and steal the costume off that mannequin."

"But I was on the phone with you when I saw him…"

"AirPods. You see, it was just a matter of—"

"Sorry to interrupt," I say, "but this is the second time today that someone's mansplained their evil plan to me." Grady looks miffed by my dismissal as I carry on. "So, just to summarize. You went through this elaborate cosplay murder scheme just to make me feel more crazy?"

"To make you feel more *loved*, Hannah. This really is a wonderful growth opportunity for us. I realized that your friends were the only thing standing between you and me being together forever. If I could get rid of them, you'd have no one. Only me."

"You thought I would love you, even after you killed them?" I'm having trouble following the logic of a maniac, but that's probably a good sign for my own sanity.

"No, of course not. It wasn't just about eliminating them. It was about engineering new trauma. A horrific nightmare that I could save you from. Creating a trauma bond that would keep us connected forever." I've never hated the T-word more as Grady motions back toward the retreat entrance. "My initial plan was to frame Pax, until you called me and I realized he had a whole other scheme of his own. That was way too messy. But Kimi, she made the perfect patsy. The vengeful native." He looks down at Kimi's body, collapsed in the dirt. "I made her dress up at gunpoint and pushed her in front of your car. A lot of improvising on the fly, if I may pat myself on the back." He actually does pat himself on the back with the hand that's not holding the gun.

"Well, your perfect narrative is broken now."

"Only because you became more unhinged than I ever could've hoped for. I mean, when you stabbed your own best friend? I couldn't have engineered that moment more beautifully myself." He does a chef's kiss motion like the goddamn goober he is.

I seize the chance to lunge for the gun, but he sidesteps and throws his arm around my neck, pulling tightly from behind.

"I really do love your strong survivor energy," he says into my ear, squeezing tighter. "But I'm stronger."

There's no wriggling free, so I keep him talking, buying myself time for a better plan. "Okay, Dr. Grady. What's your updated treatment plan?"

"Something a little less delicate and a little more forceful. My professional opinion is that you're suffering from chronic schizophrenia. These delusions caused you to kill all of your friends, along with poor Pax and Kimi. By the time I got here to intervene, it was too late."

"Schizophrenia doesn't make people kill. Being an asshole does."

"You think a judge will care about your precious progressive hot takes? It's still called 'insanity' in a court of law. I gave you a chance for voluntary treatment, but you denied me. Your residency won't be so voluntary anymore, but you'll grow to appreciate what I've done for you over time. It's a wonderful gift."

That last word flips a switch in my brain. This idiot just unwittingly gave me a gift by reminding me of the one currently tucked in my pocket. I realize now that Tess was trying to signal me earlier. Quietly as I can, I slip my fingers into my pocket, but Grady pulls my hand up and twists me to face him.

"You could say thank you." He sneers. "Ungrateful bitch."

A heavy beat blares from the ground, and Grady looks down to where Kimi is holding up her phone, music blasting from the tinny speakers.

"Thanks, bitch." Kimi grins.

With Grady distracted, I pull the essential oils bottle from my pocket, popping the cap and splashing it into his eyes.

"Fuck!" He screams, wiping at his face. Time to put my self-defense class to use with a kick to his kneecap that drops him to the ground. He wails like a baby as Kimi pulls the gun from his grip, and I help her to her feet.

"Are you okay?" I ask.

"I'll feel better when this asshole is dead." Kimi gives me the gun. "But I think you should do the honors."

The weapon feels heavy in my hand as I aim it inches away from Grady's head.

He wipes at his burning eyes. "You're not gonna shoot me, Hannah."

"You said it yourself." I flip the safety off and watch him shudder. "I'm cold-blooded."

"Okay." Grady gulps through the pain. "Prove me right, then." The oil fumes make him cough. "What the fuck is this anyway? Peppermint?"

"Yes." I take a deep breath of the fresh scent. "It clears the heart and mind."

A voice chimes in over my shoulder. "It's also highly flammable."

Tess approaches with a lit torch in hand. She's got a stab wound in her stomach and a bullet in her shoulder.

My knees nearly buckle from relief at the sight. "You're alive."

"I'd really love for that to stop being such a surprise." She hands me the torch.

I stare into the flame, bright and clear. When I turn back to Grady, he's never looked more pathetic.

"Please." He wipes at his teary eyes. "Don't kill me."

"I'm not gonna kill you, Grady. I'm gonna set you free."

"Thank you." Hope creeps into his voice. "Thank you, Hannah. I knew you were—"

"Like a phoenix, rising from the ashes." I thrust the torch into his face, and Grady's whole head bursts into flames. He screams, jumping to his feet and running around like a human matchstick.

Kimi sticks her foot out and trips him. "Oops."

Grady flops and flails in the dirt as the flames consume his whole body. He screams and burns for what feels like forever and not long enough until the twitching finally stops.

Kimi steps between me and Tess, all of us injured and propping each other up as we stare into the human campfire.

"What do we do now?" Tess asks.

"Unless somebody wants to go fishing for his keys..." Kimi motions to the burning corpse. "I think we better start walking."

We trek back through the desert in silence, conserving our energy as the sun rises behind us. Even under the circumstances, it's hard not to appreciate the beautiful pinks and purples streaking across the sky above the mountains.

It's not too long before we come across the body of the mutilated Marine. He was clearly the first victim, but I can only pray he's the last dead body we see today. Now that the sun's out, we can spot his Humvee not too far ahead. I try not to look at the poor man's faceless face as I dig the keys from his pocket.

Kimi quickly takes them from me. "I'm suspending your license for damn near manslaughter."

"Fair," I say. "Sorry about that."

We climb into the military vehicle, and Kimi starts the engine, turning to Tess and me. "I hope you had a restorative retreat."

I stare out the window at the wispy clouds above. "Fucking transcendent."

We rumble out of the desert, away from Avidya and back toward a civilized world that's never felt so distant.

39

IT'S COLD IN THE CEMETERY AS I TREK ACROSS DEAD GRASS to Ben's grave.

Loving Son, it reads. Not *Boyfriend* or *Fiancé* or *Husband*.

I've made no permanent impact on this stone slab.

As I lower myself to sit cross-legged on the frosty earth, the emptiness of the coffin beneath reverberates like an echo chamber.

I practice my own self-guided meditation. Conscious breath, long and deep. I don't need salvia to help me slide into a deep unconscious state. This time, I'm not visualizing a memory but forging something new. Carving a different past.

I'm dragging Ben's body out of that snowy wilderness. All the way out this time, straight to this plot, where an open coffin is waiting.

I place him inside, close the lid, and bury him myself.

When that hard mental labor is finished, I open my eyes. Returning to the present moment to stand on my feet. To give the dead man his due.

"I'm done carrying you."

The engagement ring slides off my finger with ease, and I place it on the cold headstone.

There's a newfound lightness in my step as I walk away.

No longer dragging that weight behind me.

My mantra rings true, but the spirits didn't do this for me.

I release myself.

SCREAM WITH ME

AN AUTHOR'S NOTE

"What's your favorite scary movie?"

No, that's not Ghostface on your landline.

That's me on a dating app.

My girlfriend-to-be had HORROR emblazoned as a top interest on her profile. An instant swipe-right for me. But I knew I'd really hit the Bumble jackpot when she told me that her favorite scary movie was *Scream*. I sent her a photo of me from Halloween, dressed in Stu's bloodstained third-act sweater. She sent one back wearing a Ghostface mask.

It was love at first fright.

Wes Craven's iconic film has been bringing horror lovers together for nearly thirty years now. It breathed fresh life into the slasher subgenre and inspired a whole new generation of fans.

Fans like me.

Every good slasher needs a backstory, and the same holds true of every slasher writer. So gather around the campfire while I tell you mine.

I was only ten years old when I had my first brush with a masked killer. My best friend, Keith, and I rented *Scream* on VHS as soon as it hit the Movie Store shelves in 1997. Our local video store was a staple of my youth, and not a day goes by that I don't daydream about wandering that horror aisle. I was drawn to those creepy box covers but was too scared to actually rent one, until that fateful night.

Keith and I were in the Cub Scouts together, on the precipice of graduating to full-on Boy Scouts. That's why we'd set up a tent in his backyard, aiming to earn a merit badge for our outdoorsy efforts. Watching a horror movie before sleeping in a tent seemed like a good idea at the time. But ten-year-olds rarely have good ideas.

I didn't sleep a wink that night, my eyes fixed open, waiting for a ghostly shadow to appear against the nylon wall and tear a gleaming knife straight through. I was scared, yes, but there was also something thrilling about the anticipation of it all. Something life-affirming beneath the fear engendered by that film.

When the sun finally rose over Keith's backyard, I crawled out of my cocoon transformed. No longer a Cub or even a Boy Scout but rather a burgeoning Blood Scout. I began a new journey, forsaking merit badges in camping and hiking, hungry for horror films with slicing and dicing. I would eventually become the Randy of my friend group, hosting popcorn-fueled screenings and extolling the virtues of my beloved genre. But first, I had to do my homework.

One of the many things that made *Scream* such a perfect gateway horror film was that it provided me with a syllabus. Countless scary movies were referenced by the characters, but I knew I had to start with the patron saints of slasher cinema. I'd seen their iconic faces, heard their mythical names, but had never borne witness to their blood-soaked legacies. Surviving my Ghostface christening meant that I was ready to meet the unholy trinity.

In the name of the Freddy, the Michael, and the Jason Voorhees. Slaymen.

The Movie Store was my cathedral, and I paid homage to these idols by renting every film in their franchises, one tape at a time. Back then, that amounted to seven *Nightmare*s, six *Halloween*s, and a whopping nine *Friday*s. I reveled in each new twist as the mythology grew more ridiculous from one entry to the next. Freddy Krueger had a baby, Michael Myers joined a Celtic cult, and Jason Voorhees took a boat to the big city. Even before their early-aughts forays into reality TV and outer space, these figures captured my imagination the way comic book superheroes did for other kids. They personified eternal questions of the human condition, notions of good and evil, of life and death, all through action-packed serialized stories.

You can keep your Superman. I believe in the boogeyman.

These undying characters would later inspire my debut novel, *Curse of the Reaper*, about an aging slasher actor who gets replaced in his franchise reboot, pushing him to the brink as his mind melds with the violent monster he embodied. Rooting this psychological character study in the world of genre conventions and film sets, I wanted to explore how slashers are more than just lowbrow entertainment for gore hounds. They're existential tragedies. But I also wanted to have fun creating my very own '80s slasher film franchise, including fictional screenplay segments for all nine *Night of the Reaper* films. The Reaper was Freddy, Michael, and Jason all rolled into one referential and reverential homage.

But what separates the *Scream* films from *A Nightmare on Elm Street*, *Halloween*, and *Friday the 13th* is the nature of the killer. We know who's doing all the bloodletting in Springfield, Haddonfield, and Crystal Lake. Woodsboro, on the other hand, is plagued by a different Ghostface every time, an anonymous specter waiting to be unmasked so they can reveal their hideously human motive. We're not dealing with evil personified or a dream demon or some zombie man-child. Ghostface is always someone you know, someone you trust. This whodunit murder mystery angle adds layers of depth beyond the simple hack and slash, centering the "why" amid the gory "how"s. Decoding the puzzle is part of the fun, especially when you're watching along with friends and shouting out suspects along the way.

That magical formula predated *Scream*, starting in Italy with a wave of 1970s films dubbed *giallo*. One can easily see the influence on 1980s American slasher cinema when watching Mario Bava's *A Bay of Blood* (1971), Lucio Fulci's *Don't Torture a Duckling* (1972), and Dario Argento's *Deep Red* (1975). These beautifully photographed slices of cinema often turned the camera into the killer's point of view, pulling viewers through the screen and making us complicit. It's *our* black-gloved hands committing these gruesome executions, some of which were later cribbed shot-for-shot by stateside filmmakers.

I certainly noticed these similarities when my slasher studies grew in later years. By the time I was in high school, I'd exhausted the Movie Store shelves and all the horror they held. But the nascent internet promised me that so many more terrors were waiting out there, far beyond what my suburban New Jersey mom-and-pop shop would ever dare stock. My research soon brought me to a distant mall where a curious man sold foreign genre films from his kiosk. I made many pilgrimages to this peddler of international bloodshed in those pre-Netflix days, expanding my cultural horizons.

At the same time, I was reading up on film theory to contextualize my viewing experiences. *Men, Women, and Chainsaws* by Carol J. Clover found its way into my hands at the perfect time, giving me a feminist appraisal of slasher cinema that helped combat the Catholic guilt. Even though my religious schooling had exposed me to a fourteen-part horror franchise called the Stations of the Cross, I was starting to wonder if there was something wrong with me for enjoying films that featured such suffering. Clover flipped the script by framing the slasher as a parable of survival, centering the final girl as an empowered figure over her oppressor. She showed me how horror films can tackle lofty themes like gender, race, and class, all layered beneath the surface of a bloody good time at the theater. That enlightening book also inspired me to dig into the roots of these cinematic stories, which began on the printed page.

The very namesake of the aforementioned *giallo* (Italian for "yellow") is a nod to a series of 1930s pulp novels with bright-yellow covers, wherein lurid crime yarns pushed the limits of fictional violence. But another important literary precursor to the slasher was Agatha Christie. The mystery genre may claim ownership over this influential titan, but even the title of her 1939 book, *And Then There Were None*, speaks to its classic slasher formula. An assorted cast of characters gets trapped at a remote location where they're murdered one by one until the mysterious killer's identity is finally revealed. Welcome to Camp Christie Lake.

She was also a master of misdirection, a technique that *Scream* would embrace nearly sixty years later. I still remember how one clever scene tricked me during my first viewing. Juvenile Deputy Dewey licks his ice cream cone, discussing the murders with his cigarette-smoking boss. The gruff sheriff tosses his smoldering butt to the ground and stomps it out beneath his black boot.

Gasp! That's the same boot I saw descend in the bathroom stall when Ghostface chased Sidney! I've cracked the case! Sheriff Burke is the killer!

Spoiler alert: Sheriff Burke was not the killer.

I was merely reckoning with my first red herring: an intentional misdirection. Billy and Stu were the ones behind the mask, but the true mastermind was behind the camera. The one wielding not a knife but a pen, guiding me into thinking "Everybody's a suspect!" This unseen magician had been controlling my experience from the opening line through the end credits, laying the tracks for the roller-coaster ride that I never wanted to get off.

They called this evil genius the writer, and I wanted Kevin Williamson's job.

I'd been writing scary stories from an early age, but I shot my first short film on 16mm at a summer filmmaking camp when I was seventeen. *For You* was a silent film set to a Nine Inch Nails song featuring a hooded killer taking vengeance with a lead pipe. When that hood came down in the climactic finale—you guessed it—the killer was not who you thought they were! This film was far from a masterpiece, but I kept at my craft, studying storytelling while writing my way through college and graduate school until I landed in Los Angeles and began my career as a screenwriter.

I cut my teeth writing twisty Lifetime Original Movies with devious villains. The nanny from hell, the sorority president from hell, the online date from hell. These campy thrillers were slasher-adjacent, but I wouldn't go full *Scream* until I started writing novels. I did so, in part, because the Hollywood development process was so fraught with heartache. Whether a project withered on the pre-production vine or made it to the screen in some mutated form, my screenwriting work didn't feel like my truest creative expression. I was eager to write something pure, something for me.

Something for the slasher fans.

I wasn't entirely sure how to tackle this subgenre in novel form, but I knew there were two key elements that made a slasher stand out in any medium. Colorful victims and creative demises. Characters need to feel real, made of flesh and blood; otherwise the killer's just carving through cardboard cutouts. We won't fear for someone's life if we're not invested in them to begin with. To that end, the people who "deserve it" can't be the only ones getting killed. Yes, we all enjoy seeing bullies and creeps get their comeuppance, but we're also way past puritanical punishments for sex, drugs, and rock 'n' roll. *Scream* taught me those tropes while gutting them inside out. When Principal Himbry gets stabbed in his office and cries out in old-man pain, my young-boy brain was rattled to its core. If a paternal protector can't make it out alive, then all bets are off.

But it was Tatum's death scene that affected me the most. Funny and smart and supportive of her bestie, Sidney, she's the kind of character you want to be friends with in real life. True to form, Tatum puts up one hell of a fight. I cheered her on when she slammed a freezer door in Ghostface's ghost face and hurled exploding beer bottles at the killer's crotch. When she tried to escape through the garage doggy door, I thought maybe she'd make it out alive after all.

Until Ghostface pressed the button.

The garage door began to rise, lifting Tatum off the ground, slowly upward toward the metal doorframe. The pulley machine trembled under the weight, defying the laws of physics in the face of unstoppable death.

The kill shot is burned into my retinas forever because slasher films don't look away, don't blink. They make you watch as Tatum's head collides with that metal edge and deflates like a rubber dodgeball. It's an uncanny effect, as silly as it is scary, but that's what makes this singular slaying so utterly unforgettable. It elicits a gasp, a laugh, a scream, all rolled into one visceral moment.

There are plenty of stale slashers who stab and stab before stabbing some more. But the true legends of this subgenre are artists, treating each victim like a fresh canvas, blank and ready for the carnage to come.

This is where I'll pause to address a common question aimed at horror fans.

"What are you, some kind of sadist?!"

On the one hand, all writers are. It's our job to put characters through hell because conflict is the crucible of human existence. Stories show us how to live through it all, but horror teaches us how to dance with death. We often keep this inevitability behind closed doors, do everything in our power not to think about our own mortality. Horror holds up the black mirror and says, "Look. It's coming for us all. So live while you still can." The gory deaths of a slasher tale are the ultimate danse macabre, reinforcing just how fragile our flesh vessels are.

That memento mori mentality was my North Star when I was penning my Christmas slasher duology, *Candy Cain Kills* and *Candy Cain Kills Again*. Leaning into the festive setting allowed my titular slasher to get creative with her two-day slay ride. Starting at a family's cabin on Christmas Eve before slashing through a church on Christmas Day, Candy Cain uses everything from tree ornaments to organ pipes as deadly weapons. My favorite reviews were from non-slasher fans discovering "I think I like slashers?" as the undeniable delights of over-the-top gore won them over. I was especially honored when several readers compared the ornate kill scenes to those in another favorite film franchise. One whose whole thesis can be summed up in four words: You can't cheat death.

This may be a horror hot take, but I would argue that the *Final Destination* films fall neatly into the slasher subgenre. There's always a final girl or boy caught in the path of a relentless killer dispatching their friend group in increasingly gruesome ways. Freddy Krueger is personified by his wisecracks, but the invisible Death has a grim sense of humor too. You can almost hear the gleeful giggle every time the first domino falls in another elaborately staged Rube Goldberg sequence in Death's design. The spectacular gymnastics fatality in *Final Destination 5* was definitely front of mind when I crafted the yoga death in *Breathe In, Bleed Out*. In truth, my entire conception process for this novel was rooted in the kills.

I wanted to write a new slasher but needed to find a fresh angle. Living in Los Angeles for a decade meant that I'd had my fair share of run-ins with wellness culture and spiritualism in various incarnations, from the good to the bad and the ugly. That's when I realized that a wellness retreat offered some unique opportunities for thematically relevant mayhem. Impalement by crystal and immolation by essential oil became the set pieces around which I built my story. The location also spoke to some personal themes that I wanted to reckon with, like the benefits and pitfalls of spiritual self-discovery, especially when it's steeped in cultural appropriation and capitalist greed. Still, a theme is just an empty concept without a protagonist, and central to any proper slasher is the final girl.

Traditionally, these archetypical heroines are morally pure and virginal in contrast to the vulgar violence embodied by the killer. But purity is boring and entirely unrelatable. When Hannah came to life on the page, she was even messier than I had envisioned in my story outline. A ball of self-loathing encased in a prickly shell, she's an imperfect person who's got some growing to do. So did I, through her. It wasn't until I finished writing her story that I realized I was processing the pain of a past relationship just like she was. Searching retroactively for the clues and the clarity as to how and why it all went wrong. Hannah got there a lot faster than I did, but she had a little extra help. Because nothing makes you move quicker than a psychotic killer on your trail.

It was relatively late in the writing process that I discovered the mining history of Joshua Tree. In fact, I had an entirely different placeholder for the killer in this book before Waylon Barlow wandered out of that dark mine and lodged his pickaxe in my brain. I had a blast building this local legend, complete with his own childhood rhyme and haunted stomping ground at Dead Man's Due. Slasher figures cast iconic silhouettes, and the T-shaped weapon plus a big-brimmed hat made for a clear enough outline. Now all I needed was a mask to hide the true villain's identity. Good old Leatherface provided the inspiration there. After all, there's no mask more deceptive than the human face.

So, there you have it. That's how a slasher lover was born and became a slasher writer. Waylon Barlow wasn't my first, and he won't be my last. The tricks and tropes of my beloved subgenre might be malleable, but there's one rule that forever holds true.

Slashers never die.

ACKNOWLEDGMENTS

I want to start by thanking the readers who have been with me from the start. I wish I could name every Bookstagrammer who's shared a thoughtful review of my past books, but it would add too many pages to this manuscript. So if you're reading this and wondering "Is Brian talking about *me*?" please know that yes, I am absolutely talking about *you*. Thanks for sticking with me from rusty chains and candy canes through this dark mine and beyond.

Where would I be without my beloved booksellers and librarians? Those magical humans who pull a book off the shelf, place it in a reader's hand and say, "I think this story is for you." What a gift you are to writers and readers alike.

I've also had the privilege of appearing on some amazing podcasts with brilliant hosts. This is where I *will* attempt to name them all so that you, dear reader, can check out these fantastic outlets for author chats. A million thanks to *Talking Scared, She Wore Black, Books in the Freezer, Thrillers by the Bookclub, Scream Kings, We Bleed Orange and Black, Capes and Tights, Horror in the Margins,*

Sley House Presents, Fearmongers, Killer Mediums, What a Scream, The ARC Party, and *Who's There?*

Thank you to my agent and dream supporter, Dan Milaschewski, for never letting me shortchange myself. I vividly remember the day he called me to say that Poisoned Pen Press wanted to meet about this manuscript. It felt serendipitous, considering I'd recently moved to Arizona, not ten miles from the iconic namesake bookstore. When I first spoke with my soon-to-be editor, Rachel Gilmer, I was overjoyed that she saw and felt everything that I hoped a reader would see and feel about my book. Her notes through the editing process always aligned with making this story more of what it already was, as were the wonderful insights provided by Gretchen Stelter.

I also can't thank the Poisoned Pen marketing team enough. This book had a different title before they conducted their magical brainstorm and came up with *Breathe In, Bleed Out*. I grin like an idiot every time I read it. And don't even get me started on that jaw-dropping cover design by Caitlin Sacks. I can't believe I'm lucky enough to have my name emblazoned on this pulpy pop art masterpiece.

I'm grateful also to Clifford E. Trafzer, whose book *A Chemehuevi Song: The Resilience of a Southern Paiute Tribe* was instrumental in my research. I hope I did justice to the history as well as the present and future of their culture. Any mistakes or misrepresentations were my own unintentional errors.

My local communities in Mesa, Arizona, and at Arizona State University have meant everything to me this past year. Thanks to the friends who cheer me on, the faculty who inspire me, and the students who never cease to impress me. You've all made this hellish desert my happy home. Special shout-out to Katie, who sneakily read this work in progress over my shoulder while I was drafting at Chupacabra Taproom one night. "Scroll down," she said. "I need to know what happens next." That made me feel like maybe I was onto something.

The horror bookshelves are bursting with brilliant talent these days, and I feel incredibly lucky to call so many of the names on those spines my friends. Spending time with the Halloween People at events like StokerCon feeds my dark soul. I love you all dearly.

Mom and Dad, thank you for always supporting my very peculiar career trajectory. It takes a special set of parents to host a neighborhood holiday party in honor of their son's Christmas slasher book release. I promise the *Breathe In, Bleed Out* party will be a lot less heretical.

Thanks as well to my amazing siblings, Steve and Kim. You've always been my loudest cheerleaders, and Uncle Brian will never stop giving your children horror books that they're way too young to be reading.

There's no one I'd rather binge scary movies and Sour Skittles with than you, Jackie. I still can't believe you're real, so please don't turn out to be a red herring.

If you're new to my writing, thank you for taking a chance on this book out of the thousands of others you could've chosen. I hope you enjoyed the ride and that you'll check out my previous work if you did.

I better wrap this up now because there's another killer in the shadows waiting for me to finish their story.

We'll catch you soon, dear reader.

ABOUT THE AUTHOR

Brian McAuley's debut novel, *Curse of the Reaper,* was named one of the Best Horror Books of 2022 by *Esquire*. His holiday slasher novella *Candy Cain Kills* earned praise from *Booklist*, *Library Journal*, and *Kirkus Reviews*, leading to the 2024 sequel, *Candy Cain Kills Again: The Second Slaying*. His short fiction and non-fiction have appeared in *Dark Matter*, *Nightmare*, *Shortwave*, and *Monstrous* magazines. Brian is also a WGA screenwriter who has written everything from family sitcoms (*Fuller House*) to psychological thriller films (*Dismissed*). He teaches as a clinical assistant professor of screenwriting at Arizona State University's Sidney Poitier New American Film School. Connect with him on social media @BrianMcWriter.